For a few moments, the dragon king remained silent, his tail twitching back and forth. Veela wondered at this sudden interest in this elfling known as the Nomad. He had appeared in the city out of nowhere, caused rioting and havoc, and then just as quickly disappeared. No one knew what had become of him.

"It could be. . . ." said Nibenay at last. "It could be the sword called Galdra. If so, its reappearance after all these years is a bad omen. Alone, that would be significant enough, but in the hands of one whose like has never before been seen . . . a preserver who can summon to his aid both the Alliance and the elves, a master of the Way despite his youthful age . . . and then there is his name. The Nomad. The one who always walks alone, and yet is not alone. Everything about him has the air of portent. Curse him. . . ."

TRIBE OF ONE

Simon Hawke

Book One
The Outcast

Book Two
The Seeker

Book Three
The Nomad

The Nomad

Simon Hawke

TRIBE OF ONE TRILOGY
Book Three

THE NOMAD

Cover art by Brom.

Map by Diesel

First Printing: October 1994
Printed in the United States of America
Library of Congress Catalog Card Number: 93-61474

9 8 7 6 5 4 3 2 1

ISBN: 1-56076-702-2

TSR, Inc.   TSR Ltd.
P.O. Box 756   120 Church End, Cherry Hinton
Lake Geneva, WI 53147   Cambridge CB1 3LB
U.S.A.   United Kingdom

FOR BRIAN THOMSEN

Acknowledgments

Special acknowledgments to Rob King, Troy Denning, Robert M. Powers, Sandra West, Jennifer Roberson, Deb Lovell, Bruce and Peggy Wiley, Emily Tuzson, Adele Leone, the crew at Arizona Honda, and my students, who keep me on my toes and teach me as much as I teach them.

PROLOGUE

The heavy, arched wooden door opened by itself with a loud, protracted creaking of its ancient iron hinges. Veela swallowed hard and took a deep breath to steady her nerves. The long climb up the tower steps had winded her, and now the noisome stench that wafted through the doorway made her head spin. Weak-kneed from both exertion and fear, she reached out to lean against the doorjamb, fighting the gorge rising in her throat. The palpable emanations of malevolent power that came from within the room were overwhelming. She had felt them throughout the long climb up the winding stone steps, and it was like swimming against a powerful, oppressive current.

"Enter," said a sepulchral voice from within.

The templar stood unsteadily in the entrance of the gloomy, circular chamber, staring with apprehension at the grotesque figure that loomed before her. It stood at one of the tower windows, looking out over the city as the dark sun sank slowly on the horizon and the shadows lengthened.

"Come closer, so that I may see you," said the dragon.

Veela swallowed nervously. "As you wish, my lord."

1

Hesitantly, she approached the creature as it turned and fixed her with a chilling gaze from its unblinking, yellow eyes.

"Remind me once more," the dragon said. "Which one are you?"

"Veela, my lord," she answered.

"Ah, yes. I remember you now." The remark was delivered flatly, without emotion. Perhaps he really did remember her. And perhaps he would forget again the moment she left his presence.

It was difficult for Veela to believe the frightening creature that stood before her now was once her husband. He was still her husband, but no trace of the man that she had known back then remained. She recalled how honored she had been to be selected as a wife to the Shadow King of Nibenay. Her parents had been very proud. Their daughter was to be a queen, though strictly speaking, Nibenay's many wives were templars, not queens. When they entered into the service of the Shadow King, they were trained for their new role in the society of the city named after its king, rigorously prepared to assume their official duties as Nibenay's factotums and the bearers of his power.

For Veela, it meant leaving the hovel she had shared with her family and moving into the palace, where she would live in unimagined luxury together with the other templars, who were all Nibenay's wives. It meant she would no longer run barefoot on a hard earth floor, but would have her feet and body washed daily by a retinue of servants and would walk in soft hide sandals on exquisite mosaic floors. She would have her dirty hair shaved and would no longer dress in rags, but in robes of flowing white, embroidered with gold and silver, that she could change daily. She would be taught to read and write, and trained how to administer the city's laws, but more important still, she would be trained in sorcery, and would wield the power of the Shadow King.

She had never learned how she was chosen. Nibenay had magic, and it was said he could see everywhere. Perhaps he had seen her in a scrying crystal while she was preparing for bed, and she had caught his fancy. Perhaps one of his other wives had caught a glimpse of her while she was on her errands in the city and had chosen her to join the harem. She was never told, and she had soon learned not to ask. The wives were only told what they were meant to know. "You do not yet know enough to ask questions," she was informed by the senior templars, who had trained her. "And when you know enough, you will have no need to ask."

She was only twelve years old when she came to live in the palace. The marriage ceremony was performed the day after she arrived. She had her hair shaved, was washed and bathed with fragrant oils, then was dressed in a plain white robe. A small gold circlet was placed around her head. Afterward, she was conducted to a large central chamber in the palace, where the king's throne stood. All of the king's wives were present, dressed in their white robes and lining both sides of the throne room. They ranged in age from young and fresh-faced girls to old and wrinkled women.

Veela had felt a sense of mounting excitement and anxiety. She had never seen the Shadow King before . . . nor, as it turned out, was she to see him on her wedding day. The throne remained empty as the senior templar conducted the solemn marriage ceremony. It was brief and incorporated the vows she had to take as a templar of the Shadow King. When it was over, each of the wives came up and kissed her lightly on both cheeks. She was married, and the king had not even been present at his own wedding.

It was five more years before she actually laid eyes on him. In those five years, she had completed her training as a templar. On the night of her official instatement into the templar ranks, the sorcerer-king had sent for her. She was once more bathed and scented with fragrant oils and perfumes, and this time all of the hair on her body was removed. Then she was conducted to the bedchamber of the Shadow King.

She had not known what to expect. She had lived in the palace for five years and never even caught a glimpse of him, nor had she been able to discuss him with any of the other wives. His name was never mentioned, save in official orders. As she was brought into his bedchamber, she found him waiting for her. She stood with downcast eyes for a long while after the attendants left. Finally, she risked raising them. He simply stood there, looking at her.

He was a tall man, standing well over six feet, and gaunt, with deeply sunken features. He was completely bald, and his nose was hooked like that of a predatory bird. His neck and arms seemed unusually long and thin, and his fingers were like talons. His brow was so pronounced that it appeared to be a ridge over his eyes, which were a strange, light golden hue. He had said nothing, but merely held out a clawlike hand toward her. A quick gesture with his skeletal fingers and her robe simply fell away, leaving her naked. Then he beckoned her to the bed.

Whatever she might have expected, it was nothing like what she might have imagined. The room suddenly went dark, so dark she could not even see her hand before her face. She felt him get onto the huge bed and then his naked body seemed to slither on top of her. There were no kisses, no caresses, no tender words exchanged. It was over almost as soon as it had begun. He took her, grunted with satisfaction, though whether it was satisfaction in the act or in the confirmation of her virginity, she could not tell, and then the next thing she knew, the braziers erupted into flame, flooding the room with light, and he was gone. And she did not see him again for ten more years.

Now, it was sixty years since she had first been brought to the palace. She was now among the senior templars, though she was still among the youngest of them. The years had changed her. The power of the Shadow King kept her vital, but her face was lined with age now, and her hands were old and wrinkled. Her flesh sagged, and her skin had become as fine as parchment. But for Nibenay, those years had wrought greater changes still. However, it was not age that had changed him, for the Shadow King was already old when Veela had been born. It was the metamorphosis.

As one of the senior templars who attended to him personally, she saw him more often now than all those years ago. And he was no longer human. He was even taller now, though much of his height came from his long, scaly and reptilian neck. His browridge had become much more pronounced, extending like a bony protrusion out over his eye sockets. His eyes were yellow-gold, with black, vertical pupils, and the lower part of his face had extended into a snout filled with razor-sharp teeth. His feet were dragon's claws, and a long, reptilian tail with a barb on the end of it extended from beneath his robe. His back was humped from protruding shoulder blades, which were slowly sprouting into wings. Though he never alluded to it, Veela knew that he was often in great pain from the slow and excruciating transformation.

It had already begun when she first saw him all those years ago, and it would be many years more before it was completed. The arduous metamorphosis proceeded by slow stages, induced by powerful and complicated spells. For years now, it had occupied all of Nibenay's attention. The people of his kingdom never saw him. He never ventured from his private chambers anymore. There were servants in the palace who had been there all their lives and had never even caught a glimpse of him. Veela was not sure if he ever slept, but each time she came to him, no matter what the hour, he was awake and either making the long and exhausting preparations for the next stage of his metamorphosis or resting from his efforts and battling the pain. What made it all worthwhile for him was the final goal. Once he had fully cast aside the last vestiges of his humanity, he would become the most powerful creature to walk the planet. And for Nibenay, the lust for power was everything. He had time to think of nothing else. . . .

Except for the last few days, when there had arisen a new subject for his interest. And now, it seemed he could think of nothing else.

"The Nomad," he said. "Tell me what you have learned."

"He is an elfling, my lord," she said.

"An *elfling?* What sort of creature is that?"

"The result of a mating between a halfling and an elf," Veela replied.

"What nonsense is this?" said Nibenay. "Halflings and elves are mortal enemies!"

"Nevertheless, my lord, there apparently was such a union. I have personally heard from those who saw him, and they attest that he possesses the characteristics of both races."

"Ill-omened creature," said the Shadow King, turning away from her. "Go on. What more?"

"His name is Sorak, which means 'nomad who travels alone' in the elvish tongue, and hence his appellation. But he does not travel alone. He travels in the company of a villichi priestess."

"Preservers," said Nibenay with disgust, spitting the word out.

"It is also said that he is a master of the Way," said Veela, "though he is scarcely more than a boy. And witnesses attest to this. How else could he have overcome two templars and several squads of half-giants in our city guard?"

"And where did one so young get his training in the Way? How could he have mastered it so quickly?" asked the Shadow King.

"I do not know, my lord," said Veela, "but rumor has it he was trained by the villichi."

"A *male?* In a villichi convent? Preposterous."

"Perhaps, my lord. I have not been able to establish the veracity of this."

"Continue."

"It has been learned that he came to the city to seek out the Veiled Alliance," Veela said.

"More preservers!" said the defiler king. "What has he to do with the Alliance?"

"I do not know, my lord, but they came to help him when he battled our half-giants. There were witnesses to this. And he was assisted by the city's elves, as well."

"Elves?"

"Mostly half-elves, my lord, but it is reported that there were full-blooded elves among them, also," she replied.

"Since when do elves care about anything other than profit for themselves?" asked Nibenay. "The Veiled Alliance coming to assist this Nomad, that I can understand. He was battling the city guard. But why should elves care one way or the other?"

"Once again, my lord, I cannot vouch for the truth of these reports, but it is said that he is regarded by them as some sort of chieftain, perhaps even a king. Many of the city's elves dispute the story, ridiculing it and claiming they would never give allegiance to any would-be elven king. However, elves *did* come to his assistance. That is undeniable. It is said he carries an enchanted sword about which there is some sort of foolish legend . . . the ancient, lost sword of elven kings or some such thing."

"*Galdra!*" said the Shadow King.

Veela frowned. "Why, yes, my lord. That is the name given to the sword in the stories I have heard."

Nibenay stared out the window, as if deep in thought. "It is no mere story," he replied. "At least, not that part of it. Galdra is real enough. The sword exists, though it has been lost for generations. Have you spoken with anyone who claims to have seen this sword?"

"I have, my lord."

"Did they describe it?"

"Yes, my lord. I was told it is made of elven steel, though I have never heard of such a thing, and of an unusual configuration. The blade, as it was described to me, is something of a cross between a falchion and a cutlass, broad and leaf-shaped at the tip, with an ornate hilt wrapped in silver wire."

"And is there a legend inscribed upon the blade?" Nibenay asked anxiously.

"I do not know, my lord."

For a few moments, the dragon king remained silent, his tail twitching back and forth. Veela wondered at this sudden interest in this elfling known as the Nomad. He appeared in the city out of nowhere, caused rioting and havoc, and then just as quickly disappeared. No one knew what had become of him.

"It could be," said Nibenay at last. "It could be the sword called Galdra. If so, its reappearance after all these years is a bad omen. Alone, that would be significant enough, but in the hands of one whose like has never before been seen. . . . a preserver who can summon to his aid both the Alliance and the elves, a master of the Way despite his youthful age . . . and then there is his name. The Nomad. The one who always walks alone, and yet is not alone. Everything about him has the air of portent, curse him."

In spite of herself, Veela could not resist a question. "Portent, my lord?" she said.

"I sensed his presence from the moment he came into the city," said the Shadow King. "Yet, I did not know what it was. I only knew that something . . . someone . . . had impinged on my awareness in a way that had not happened since. . . ." His voice trailed off.

Veela was anxious for him to continue, but she had already overstepped her bounds. Nibenay seemed not to notice. She had never seen him like this before.

"What does a nomad do, Veela?" Nibenay asked finally.

"Why . . ." She was not sure how to respond. Should she take the question literally? "I suppose he . . . wanders, my lord."

"Yes," said the Shadow King, drawing the word out into a sibilant hiss. "He *wanders*. Yes, indeed."

Veela was at a loss to understand what he meant. Who was this Nomad that Nibenay, who had long since ceased to have any concerns about what went on in his city, was so preoccupied with? What was his significance that he should so trouble a sorcerer-king, before whose power every living creature quaked?

"Have you learned nothing else?" asked Nibenay.

"No, my lord. I have told you all I have been able to discover. And as I have said before, I cannot vouch for the veracity of some of the things I have been told."

Nibenay nodded. "You have done well," he said, giving her an unprecedented compliment. "There is more I need to know, however."

"I shall make further inquiries at once, my lord," said Veela.

"No," he said. "He has left the city. I can no longer sense his presence. I doubt there is much more you can discover now."

"As you wish, my lord," she said, bowing her head.

She waited to be dismissed, but the order was not immediately forthcoming. Instead, the Shadow King issued another command.

"Bring me Valsavis."

Veela's eyes grew wide at the mention of the name. It was a name she had not heard spoken in years, a name that those few who still knew it rarely dared to speak aloud.

"It has been many years, my lord," she said, uneasily. "He may no longer be alive."

"Valsavis lives," said Nibenay, stating it as a fact not to be disputed. "Bring him to me."

"As you command, my lord," said Veela, bowing as

she backed out of the chamber. The heavy, carved wooden door closed behind her of its own accord.

★ ★ ★ ★ ★

The light carriage lurched up the rutted trail leading through the foothills of the Barrier Mountains. Seated in the shade of its canopy, Veela watched the trail carefully as the driver urged the kank forward up the slope. It had been many years since she had been here last, many years since she had even left the city, and she was concerned that she might not remember the way. Yet, even after all this time, here and there, details of the trail looked familiar. She had recalled the wide, sweeping bend in the trail as it circled around a large rock outcropping and ran parallel to the slope for a short distance before it circled around again and continued on an incline through the canyon.

About midway through the canyon, she recalled, there should be a path leading off to the left, into the trees. She remembered that it was difficult to spot, and so she kept a careful watch for it. Nevertheless, she missed it, and the carriage had to turn around— no easy feat on such a narrow trail. She had to get out while the driver backed the kank up, slowly pushing the small carriage off the trail and up the slope, then forward slightly. Swearing to himself, he repeated the process twice more before he could turn the rig around. Veela got back in, and this time they proceeded at an even slower pace as she carefully scanned the slope for the path. She almost missed it again.

"Stop!" she called out to the driver.

As the carriage stopped, she got out and walked

back several yards. Yes, there it was, almost impossible to see, it was so heavily overgrown. Merely a narrow footpath, scarcely more than a run left by an animal on its habitual daily trek. There was no possibility of proceeding any other way than on foot.

"Wait here till I return," she told the driver, and started up the path. She used the power bestowed upon her by the Shadow King to clear the way as she walked up the slope. The underbrush that had overgrown the path withered and died before her as she went.

The path followed a serpentine course up the steep slope, bending to the left, then to the right, then to the left again through the trees and around rock outcroppings as it wound its way up to the summit of the hill. After a while, she passed the tree line and emerged between two boulders into a clear area near the summit, covered only by rocks and scrub brush, short mountain grass and wildflowers. She had reached the summit of the foothills, and the mountains beyond loomed above her. The path continued up the steep incline for a short distance and then gradually leveled off as it curved around some rocks.

As she passed the boulders, she glanced down and saw the lower slopes of the foothills, one of the very few places on Athas, aside from the forest ridge of the Ringing Mountains, where green and growing things could still be found. In the crescent-shaped valley below was the city of Nibenay, and in the distance to the southwest lay the city of Gulg. And all around, as far as the eye could see, was barren desert. Directly to the south, stretching out like a gleaming ocean of crystal, was the Great Ivory Plain, a vast, wide sea of salt. It was a spectacular view, and for a moment, she simply stood there, catching her breath and taking it all in. Then, in the distance, she heard the unmistakable sound of wood being chopped.

She continued on, entering the not-quite-level clearing at the top. Before her was a small cabin made entirely of rough-hewn logs. Behind it was a smaller building, a shed for storage, and some animal pens. The cabin was otherwise completely isolated. Some smoke curled up from the stone chimney.

As Veela came closer, following the path that led around to the front of the cabin, she could smell the pleasant aroma of burning pagafa wood. There was a small covered porch attached to the cabin, with some crudely built wood furniture, but no sign of the wood chopper. The chopping sounds had ceased. In front of the porch, she saw a large pagafa stump with an axe embedded in it, and beside the stump, a pile of freshly chopped firewood. She looked around. There was no sign of anyone. She was about to climb the four wooden steps to the porch when a deep, gravelly voice suddenly spoke behind her.

"I thought I smelled templar."

She whirled around. The man standing directly behind her, no more than four feet away, had suddenly appeared as if out of nowhere, moving silent as a ghost. He was tall and massively built, with a full head of long gray hair that fell down past his shoulders.

He had a thick gray beard, and his face was lined with age and well seasoned by the weather. He had been a very handsome man, and was handsome still, for all his years and fearsome aspect. He had once had a well-shaped nose, but it had been broken several times. He still had all his teeth, and his eyes belied his age, sparkling with alertness. They were a startling shade of azure blue. An old scar made by a knife or sword came up out his beard, crossed his left cheekbone and disappeared beneath his hair.

He wore a sleeveless hide tunic fastened by a thick belt with several daggers at his waist, studded wristlets, and hide breeches tucked into high, laced moccasins. His shoulders were broad and powerful, and his chest was huge, rippling with muscle, tapering in a V-shape to his narrow waist. His forearms were scarred and corded with dense muscle, and his upper arms were thicker around than Veela's thighs. His bearing was erect and loose, and he conveyed an impression of immense physical power.

"Greetings, Valsavis," she said.

"Veela," he said, in his rough voice. "It has been a long, long time. You have grown old."

She smiled at his insolence. He always was direct. "And so have you," she said. "Perhaps too old," she added, lifting her chin to gaze challengingly into his eyes.

"For what?" he asked.

"For that which you had once done best."

"If the Shadow King believed that, he would not have sent you," said Valsavis simply, reaching for his axe. He picked up a piece of pagafa wood and placed it on the stump. He raised the axe and split it with one powerful blow.

Veela marveled at his insolence. He had turned his back upon a templar and gone back to work! "You have not changed," she said. "You are still the same insufferable barbarian you always were."

He continued splitting wood at a leisurely pace. "If that offends you, you know the way back," he said.

She smiled despite herself. Most men would have trembled at being addressed by a templar of the Shadow King. This one spoke to her as if she were no more than a serving wench. She *should* have been offended, gravely so, and yet was not. It had always been that way with him. She had never quite understood why.

"His Majesty King Nibenay wishes to see you," she said.

"I had deduced as much," Valsavis said. "I did not think you came all this way merely for a social call." He continued chopping wood.

"He wishes to see you at once," Veela added emphatically.

Valsavis kept on splitting wood. "Is he in immanent danger of death?"

Veela looked surprised, "Why, no. Of course not. The Shadow King shall live forever."

"Then what is another day?" Valsavis asked.

Veela felt the color rising to her cheeks. "I may be tolerant of your insolence, Valsavis, for the fact that it amuses me, but the Shadow King has no such forgiving traits!"

Valsavis stuck his axe back in the stump and turned around slowly, stretching his bulging muscles. "Nibenay has not required my services in years," he said. "And for all those years, I have remained forgotten by His Majesty the Shadow King. Now, suddenly, he is impatient for my presence. Clearly, he has need for a service only I am able to perform. I have waited years for him to find me useful once again. Now let him wait."

Veela's jaw dropped open with disbelief. "No one defies the Shadow King!" she said with shock. "No one!"

"Then let him strike me down," Valsavis said. He made a dismissive motion with one hand before she could respond. "Oh, I know he could, and easily, with no more effort than it would take for him to blink one of his evil yellow eyes. But he shall not, because he needs me. And it must be a task of some importance, else he would not have sent you, rather than some lowly messenger, as he had done in years gone by. I was preparing supper. Will you share it with me?"

She gaped at him as he turned without awaiting a reply, picked up an armload of wood, ascended the porch steps, and went into the cabin. Not knowing what else to do, she followed him.

After a hearty supper of roasted kirre steaks, together with wild mountain rice seasoned with herbs, they sat down on wood benches by the fireplace to enjoy some hot, spiced tea brewed from a mixture of wild herbs. It was a blend Valsavis had concocted, and it was delicious.

"You may have missed your calling," Veela said as she took another sip. "You could have been a master cook. Dinner was superb."

"I master everything I attempt," Valsavis said simply. "There is no point in doing anything by halfway measures."

"So do it with a master's skill, or do not do it at all?" she asked. "Is that why you have never had a woman?"

"I have had many women," replied Valsavis.

"But no wife."

"I have no use for a wife," Valsavis said with a shrug. "I occasionally have use for a woman. I had wondered when you would finally ask me about that."

Veela stared at him. "Finally?" she said.

"You often used to wonder about it many years ago," Valsavis said, speaking as calmly as if he were discussing the weather. "I see you wonder still, though you no longer seem to entertain the notion of bedding me to find out for yourself."

Veela's eyebrows shot up with surprise. "I? Bed *you?* Why . . . you insufferable . . . *arrogant . . .*"

"You can deny it all you wish, but it is true, nevertheless," Valsavis said. "You've asked the question with your body and your eyes more times than I could count. Do not forget, Veela, that I am a hunter, and a hunter always takes care to learn the nature of his prey. That is why I have always studied people. Just as a beast will reveal things about itself from the trail that it leaves, so do people reveal much more than they realize by the motions of their bodies, by attitude and gesture. As a young woman, you had entertained the fantasy on numerous occasions. Doubtless because the Shadow King is, at best, an inattentive and infrequent lover. His passions do not flow in the direction of the flesh. But yours . . . well, perhaps when you were young. . . ." He shrugged.

Veela stared at him open-mouthed, and then, to her own surprise, she chuckled. "It is true," she admitted. "I had often wondered what it would be like to be your lover. I never quite knew why. You always were, and still are, such an ugly brute."

"It was precisely for that reason you felt attracted to me," said Valsavis. "Women are strange creatures. They claim to be repelled by brutish men, and yet they are attracted to their power. And the stronger a woman is, the more she is drawn to men who are stronger still."

"Why should a weak man interest a strong woman?" Veela asked.

"A weak man may have many other virtues," said Valsavis. "If he is weak in body and spirit, he may yet be kind and gentle and devoted. But a strong woman will always be able to control him. It is the man whom she cannot control that she is drawn to, for he represents a challenge, and the stimulation of unpredictability."

"And what sort of woman are *you* drawn to?" Veela asked.

"One who is capable of gaining mastery over the one thing most women never do learn to control," he said.

"And that is?"

"Herself," Valsavis said.

"You are an interesting man, Valsavis. There is more to you than meets the eye," she said.

"There is more to everyone than meets the eye," he replied. "The trick is learning how to look. Now then, tell me what Nibenay wants of me."

"I do not know," she said.

"Yes, you do," he said. "Tell me."

Veela relented. "There is an elfling . . ." she began.

"An elfling?" Valsavis raised his eyebrows.

"Part elf, part halfling," she replied. "He goes by the name Sorak, and he is called the Nomad. . . ."

Valsavis listened intently as she spoke, telling him all that she had told the king, and what the king had said in response. When she was finished, Valsavis sat in silence for a moment, digesting what he had heard, then suddenly, he got up.

"We shall leave at once," he said.

"What . . . *now?* But it will be dark soon!"

"The kank drawing your carriage does not need the light of day to see," he said. "And your driver will be thankful not to have to spend the night waiting on the trail."

"How did you know I came with a carriage and a driver?" she asked.

"I think it most unlikely you would have come all this way on foot," he said. "And a senior templar of the Shadow King would never drive her own carriage."

She grimaced. "Of course," she said. "But you said the king could wait another day, and you gave no thought to the comfort of my driver earlier."

"Nor do I now. I merely said he would be thankful."

"Then why the sudden desire to leave now?" she asked.

"Because the elfling interests me," he said. "And it has been a long time since I have had a worthy challenge."

"Perhaps," she said. "But it has also been a long time since you have had any challenge at all. And you are not as young as you once were."

Valsavis moved, and suddenly two daggers thunked into the bench to either side of her, so close they pinned her robe to the wood. He had thrown them with such speed, one with each hand, that she had not even had time to react. She stared down at the daggers flanking her and cleared her throat slightly. "On the other hand, there is something to be said for the experience of age."

ONE

The door to the dragon king's chamber swung open with an ominous creaking sound, and as Valsavis stepped through, he said, "Your hinges need oiling."

The Shadow King turned toward him slowly, regarding him with a steady gaze. Valsavis returned it unflinchingly. He had aged, thought Nibenay, but he looked as fit as ever, and he still moved with the lithe tread of a cat. He also still possessed the same annoying insolence. Even the Shadow King's own templars trembled before Nibenay and found it difficult to meet his gaze. Not so Valsavis. There was an irritating absence of deference in his manner, and a complete absence of fear.

"I sent for you—" the dragon king said, then paused, breathing heavily, as he felt a rush of incandescent agony sweep through him. The pain was particularly bad this morning. "Come closer."

Valsavis approached him without hesitation, stepping into the shaft of sunlight coming through the tower window.

"You have grown much older, Valsavis."

"And you have grown much uglier, my lord."

20

The Shadow King hissed with anger, and his tail twitched. "Do not try my patience, Valsavis! I know that you do not fear death. But there are worse fates that can befall a man."

"And I am confident you know them all, my lord," Valsavis replied casually, leaving the Shadow King to wonder if he had intended any double meaning. "Veela said you needed me."

"I do not need," the Shadow King replied with irritation. "But there is a matter I desire to have resolved. It concerns a wanderer from the Ringing Mountains."

"Sorak the elfling, yes—and his villichi whore," Valsavis said. "I know of them." Before coming to the palace, he had first stopped at several taverns frequented by known informers, and with the knowledge he already had from Veela, it was not difficult to piece together most of the story and separate the probable from the improbable. "Apparently, they came through Tyr, across the barrens and the Barrier Mountains, to cause some trouble for a suitor of one of your brood. I gather it was fatal for the suitor, and the girl in question has gone over to the Veiled Alliance."

"Your sources are accurate, as ever," said the Shadow King, "but it is not some slip of a rebellious daughter that concerns me now. It is the elven myth."

"About his being some fated king of all the elves?" Valsavis asked with amusement. "It is said he bears the sword of ancient elven kings—Galdra, I believe it's called. A wandering stranger and a fabled sword. What better fodder for a minstrel? He slays a few of your slow-witted giants and drunken bards make him the hero of the moment. Surely you do not give credence to such nonsense?"

"It is far from nonsense," Nibenay replied. "Galdra exists, but it seems you have heard the bastardized version of the myth. The bearer of Galdra is not the King of Elves, according to the prophecy, but the *Crown* of Elves. So if the legend is true, then he is not a king, but a king-maker."

"Shall I kill him for you, then?"

"No," Nibenay replied firmly. "Not yet. First, find for me the king that this Nomad would make. The crown shall lead you to the king."

Valsavis frowned. "Why should you be concerned about an elven king? The elves are tribal; they don't even desire a king."

"The Crown of Elves, according to the legend, will not merely empower an elven king, but a great mage, a ruler who shall bring all of Athas under his thrall," said Nibenay.

"Another sorcerer-king?" Valsavis asked.

"Worse," Nibenay replied with a sibilant hiss. "So find this king for me, and the crown shall be your prize, to dispose of as you will."

Valsavis raised his eyebrow at the thought that any coming ruler could be worse than a sorcerer-king, but he kept his peace. Instead, he addressed himself to more immediate concerns. "So I trail this elfling for you, find and kill the king that he would make, and for my trouble, you offer me nothing but the elfling and his woman, to dispose of as I wish? Who would ransom such a pair? Even on the slave markets, they would bring a paltry reward in return for all my effort."

"You would bargain with *me?*" the dragon king said, lashing his tail back and forth angrily.

"No, my lord, I would never stoop to bargain. My fee for such a task would be ten thousand gold pieces."

"*What?* You must be mad!" said Nibenay, more astonished than angered at his temerity.

"It is a price you could easily afford," Valsavis said. "Such a sum means nothing to you, and a comfortable old age for me. With such an incentive, I would approach my task with zeal and vigor. Without it, I would face my old age and infirmity alone and destitute." He shrugged. "I might as well refuse and be killed now than die so mean a death."

In spite of himself, the dragon king chuckled. The mercenary's arrogance amused him, and it had been a long time since he had felt amused. "Very well. You will have your ten thousand in gold. And I will even throw in one of my young wives to care for you in your dotage. Is that incentive enough for you?"

"Will I have my choice from among your harem?" Valsavis asked.

"As you please," the dragon king replied. "They mean nothing to me anymore."

"Very well, then. Consider it done," Valsavis said, turning to leave.

"Wait," said the Shadow King. "I have not yet dismissed you."

"There is something more, my lord?"

"Take this," said Nibenay, holding out a ring to him with his clawed fingers. It was made of gold and carved in the shape of a closed eye. "Through this, I shall monitor your progress. And if you should need my aid, you may reach me through this ring."

Valsavis took the ring and put it on. "Will that be all, my lord?"

"Yes. You may go now."

The hulking mercenary turned to leave.

"Do not fail me, Valsavis," said the Shadow King.

Valsavis paused and glanced back over his shoulder. "I never fail, my lord."

* * * * *

"Sorak, stop! Please! I must rest," said Ryana.

"We shall stop to rest at dawn," he said, walking on.

"I don't have your elfling constitution," she replied, wearily. "I'm merely human, and though I'm villichi, there is nevertheless a limit to my endurance."

"Very well," he said, relenting. "We shall stop. But only for a little while; then we must press on."

She gratefully sank to her knees and unslung her waterskin to take a drink.

"Be sparing with that water," he said when he saw her take several large swallows. "There is no way of telling when we may find more."

She looked at him, puzzled. "Why should we fear running out of water," she asked, "when we can scoop out a depression and employ a druid spell to bring it from the ground?"

"You must, indeed, be tired," Sorak replied. "Have you forgotten the surface we are walking on? It is all salt. And salty water will not quench your thirst; it will merely make it worse."

"Oh," she said with a wry grimace. "Of course. How thoughtless of me." With an air of regret, she slung the waterskin back over her shoulder. She looked out into the distance ahead of them, where the dark shapes of the Mekillot Mountains were silhouetted against the night sky. "They seem no closer than the day before," she said.

"We should reach them in another three or four days, at most," said Sorak. "That is, if we do not stop for frequent rests."

She took a deep breath and expelled it in a long and weary sigh as she got back to her feet. "You have made your point," she said. "I am ready to go on."

"It should be dawn in another hour or so," said Sorak, looking at the sky. "Then we will stop to sleep."

"And roast," she said as they started walking once again. "Even at night, this salt is still warm beneath my feet. I can feel it through my moccasins. It soaks up the day's heat like a rock placed into a fire. I do not think that I shall ever again season my vegetables with salt!"

They were five days out on their journey across the Great Ivory Plain. They traveled only at night, for in the daytime, the searing dark sun of Athas made the plain a furnace of unbearable heat. Its rays, reflecting off the salt crystals, were blinding. During the day, they rested, stretched out on the salt and covered by their cloaks. They had little to fear from the predatory creatures that roamed the wastes of the Athasian desert, for even the hardiest forms of desert life knew better than to venture out upon the Great Ivory Plain. Nothing grew here, nothing lived. For as far as they could see, from the Barrier Mountains to the north to the Mekillot Mountains to the south, and from the Estuary of the Forked Tongue to the West and the vast Sea of Silt to the East, there was nothing but a level plain of salt crystals, gleaming with a ghostly luminescence in the moonlight.

Perhaps, thought Sorak, he was pushing her too hard. Crossing the Great Ivory Plain was far from a simple task. For most ordinary humans, it could easily mean death, but Ryana was villichi, strong and well trained in the arts of survival. She was far from an ordinary human female. On the other hand, he was not human at all, and possessed the greater strength and powers of endurance of both his races. It was unfair to expect her to keep the pace he set. Still, it was a dangerous journey, and he was anxious to have the crossing over with. However, there were other dangers still awaiting them when they finally reached the mountains.

The marauders of Nibenay had their base camp somewhere near the mountains, and Sorak knew they had no cause to love him. He had foiled their plot to ambush a merchant caravan from Tyr, and had brought down one of their leaders. If they encountered the marauders, things would not go well for them.

In order to reach their destination, the village of Salt View, they had to cross the mountains—in itself no easy task. And once they reached the village, they would have other thorny problems to resolve. The Sage had sent them there to find a druid named the Silent One, who was to guide them to the city of Bodach, where they were to seek an ancient artifact known as the Breastplate of Argentum. However, they did not even know what this mysterious druid looked like. For that matter, they did not know what the Breastplate of Argentum looked like, either, and Bodach was the worst place in the world to search for anything.

Legend had it there was a great treasure to be found in Bodach, but few adventurers who went in search of it ever managed to return. Located at the tip of a peninsula extending into one of the great inland silt basins, Bodach was a city of the undead. Formerly a mighty domain of the ancients, its once-magnificent towers could be seen from a great distance, and it covered many square miles of the peninsula. Finding one relic in a large city that had fallen into ruin would be, in itself, a daunting task; but once the sun went down, thousands of undead crept from their lairs and prowled the ancient city streets. As a result, very few were tempted to seek out Bodach's riches. The greatest treasure in the world was of no use to one who never lived to spend it.

Sorak cared nothing for treasure. What he sought, no amount of riches could buy, and that was the truth. Ever since he was a child, he had wanted to know who his parents were and what had become of them. Were they still alive? How did it come about that a halfling had mated with an elf? Had they met and somehow, against all odds, fallen in love? Or was it that his mother had been raped by an invader, making him a hated offspring, cast out because she had not wanted him? Perhaps it had not been her choice to cast him out. Had she loved him and tried to protect him, only to have his true nature discovered by the other members of her tribe, who had refused to accept him in their midst? That seemed to be the most likely possibility, since he had been about five or six years old when he was left out on the desert. In that case, what had become of his mother? Had she remained with her tribe, or was she, too, cast out? Or worse. He knew that he would never find true peace within himself until he had the answers to those questions, which had plagued him all his life.

Beyond that, he now had another purpose. Even if he did succeed in discovering the truth about himself, he would still forever remain an outsider. He was not human, nor had he ever met, among the other races of Athas, anyone even remotely like himself. Perhaps he was the only elfling. Where was there a place for him? If he wished, he could return to the villichi convent in the Ringing Mountains, where he had been raised. They would always accept him there, yet he was not truly one of them and never could be. And somehow, he believed his destiny lay elsewhere. He had sworn to follow the Path of the Preserver and the Way of the Druid. Could there be any higher calling for him than to enter into the service of the one man who stood alone against the power of the sorcerer-kings?

The Sage was testing him. Perhaps the wizard who had once been called the Wanderer required these items they were collecting to aid him in his metamorphosis into an avangion. On the other hand, perhaps it was merely a test of their mettle and resolve to see if they were truly worthy and capable of serving him. Sorak did not know, but there was only one way to find out, and that was to see the quest through to its end. He had to find the Sage. He had resolved that nothing would deter him from it.

For a long time, they walked in silence, conserving their energy for the long trek across the salt plain.

Finally, the golden light of dawn began to show on the horizon. Soon, the Great Ivory Plain would burn with incandescent heat as the rays of the dark sun beat down upon it mercilessly. They stopped, their footsteps crunching on the salt, and lay down close to one another, wrapping themselves in their cloaks, tenting them to provide some shade against the searing sunlight. Almost immediately, Ryana fell asleep from sheer exhaustion.

Sorak, too, was tired, but he had no need of sleep—at least, not in the same way that most people understood what sleep was. He could duck under and allow one of his other personalities to come forth, and while he "slept," the Ranger or perhaps the Watcher could take over, standing guard. He sensed the restlessness of all the others in his tribe, the Tribe of One of which he was but a part. He knew that they were hungry. He tried not to think about that.

Sorak was, himself, a vegetarian, as were all villichi. That was the way he had been raised back at the convent. However, elves and halflings were both flesh-eating races, and halflings frequently ate human flesh. He had no need to worry that there was any danger to Ryana from any of his other personalities. They had long ago learned how to coexist.

Often while Sorak "slept," the Ranger would emerge and go out hunting. He would make his kill, and the others would enjoy the flesh they craved, while Sorak would awaken with no memory of the experience. He knew about it, of course, but it was something they did not discuss between them, one of the compromises they had made so they could coexist within one body. And the others understood, though they did not share in the emotion, that Sorak loved Ryana. It was a love, however, that never could be consummated, for at least three of Sorak's personalities were female and could not bear such contact.

Well, possibly Kivara could, he thought, simply out of curiosity. Kivara was a willful creature of the senses, and any sort of stimulation fascinated her. She was a child in many ways, and utterly amoral. However, the Guardian and the Watcher could not countenance such a relationship, and so Sorak was left with loving Ryana the only way he could—spiritually and chastely.

He knew that she returned that love, for she had broken her vows for him and left the convent, following his trail because she could not bear to be separated

from him. She knew the love she had for him was
something she could never physically express, and she
knew why. She had accepted it, though Sorak realized
she nursed the hope that somehow, someday, it would
come to pass. He longed for it himself, but had
resigned himself to the inevitable inequities of his fate.

He wondered what the future held in store for
them. Perhaps the Sage knew, but if so, then he had
given them no clues. Life on Athas could be harsh,
and there were many who were far less fortunate than
he. There were those condemned to live out their
lives in slavery, laboring for others or fighting for the
entertainment of aristocrats and merchants in the
bloody arenas of the city-states. And then there were
those who lived in abject poverty and squalor in the
warrens of the cities, many of them beggars with no
roofs over their heads and no idea where their next
meal would be coming from. They lived in terror of
starvation or eviction, or of having their throats cut
over a few measly ceramics or a crust of bread. Some
were crippled, many were diseased, and even more
never survived their childhood. Sorak knew his lot in
life was much more fortunate than theirs.

Perhaps he never could be normal. He had no idea
what that really meant, save in the abstract sense. He
could not remember ever being any other way. He
was not only born abnormal, an elfling who was possibly the only being of his kind, but his childhood
ordeal in the desert had left him with at least a dozen
different personalities all trapped within one body.
Yet, despite that, he was *free*. Free to make of his life
what he chose. Free to breathe the night air of the
desert, free to go wherever the wind at his back took
him, free to undertake a quest that would determine
the meaning of his life. Whatever challenges he would

encounter on the way, he would meet on his own terms, and either prevail or die in the attempt, but at least he would die free. His lambent gaze swept the desolate, silvery, salt plain, where he and Ryana were the only living beings, and he thought, indeed, I *am* fortunate.

And with that thought, he ducked under and allowed the Watcher to the fore. Alert and silent as ever, she sat very still, her gaze sweeping the desolate waste around them, keeping watch as the first, faint light of dawn slowly crept over the shadow of the distant mountains.

As she sat, scanning the horizon and the silvery salt plain, the Watcher never for a moment wavered in her concentration on her surroundings. Her mind did not wander, and she was not plagued with the sort of distracting thoughts that came to ordinary people when they found themselves alone, in the still hours of the night. She was not given to contemplating what had happened in the past, or what might happen in the future. She did not entertain any hopes or fears, or suffer from any emotional concerns. The Watcher remained always completely and perfectly in the present and, as a result, nothing escaped her notice.

While Sorak could dwell upon self-doubts or the uncertainty of the task ahead, the Watcher observed every detail: the tiniest insect crawling on the ground; the smallest bird winging its way overhead; the wind blowing minute particles of salt across the plain, creating a barely perceptible blur immediately above the ground; the faint shifting of light as dawn began to break. No detail of her surroundings escaped her notice. Her senses sharp, alert, and tuned to the slightest sound or motion, she would become one with the world around her and detect the faintest disturbance in its fabric.

She was, therefore, astonished when she turned and saw the woman standing there, not more than fifteen or twenty feet away.

Taken aback, the Watcher did not respond at once, the way she usually did, by awakening the Guardian. She stared, unaccustomedly enraptured at the incongruous sight of a beautiful young woman who had suddenly appeared out of nowhere. The plain was level and open in all directions. In the moonlight cast by Ral and Guthay, anyone approaching would have been visible for miles, and yet this woman was suddenly, inexplicably just *there*.

"Help me, please . . ." she said in a soft and plaintive voice.

Belatedly, the Watcher woke the Guardian. She had no explanation for the sudden appearance of this woman. She *should* have seen her coming, yet she had not. That anyone could have come up on her so quietly alarmed her. That it could happen in a place where the visibility was clear for miles around was simply beyond belief.

As the Guardian awoke and came to the fore of Sorak's consciousness, she gazed out through his eyes and scrutinized the stranger. She looked young, no more than twenty years old, and her hair was long and black and lustrous. Her skin was pale and flawless, her legs lean and exquisitely shaped, her waist narrow and encircled by a thin girdle of beads. Her arms were slender and her breasts were full and upturned, supported by a thin leather halter. The young woman had sandals on her well-shaped, graceful feet, and she wore barely enough for modesty—a brief, diagonally cut wraparound that scarcely came down to her upper thighs, with nothing but a cloak to protect her from the desert chill. She had the aspect of a slave girl, but it didn't look as if she had ever performed any sort of demanding physical labor.

"Please . . ." she said. "Please, I beg you, can you help me?"

"Who are you?" asked the Guardian. "Where did you come from?"

"I am Teela," said the girl. "I was taken from a slave caravan by the marauders, but I escaped them and have been wandering this forsaken plain for days. I am so tired, and I thirst. Can't you please help me?"

She stood in a seductive pose, calculated to display her lush body to its best advantage, completely oblivious of the fact that it was a female she was addressing. What she saw was Sorak, not the Guardian, and it was clear she was appealing to his male instincts.

The Guardian immediately became suspicious. The effect such a beautiful and apparently vulnerable young woman would have had on a male was indisputable, but the Guardian was immune to her obvious charms, and her protective instincts were aroused, instincts that were protective not of the vulnerable-seeming girl, but of the Tribe.

"You do not look as if you have been traveling on foot for days," she said with Sorak's voice.

"Perhaps only a day or two, I do not know. I have lost all track of time. I am at my wit's end. I have been lost, and I could not find any trail. It is a miracle I have encountered you. Surely you will not turn away a young girl in distress? I would do anything to show my gratitude." She paused, significantly. "Anything," she said again, in a low voice. She started to come closer.

"Stay where you are," the Guardian said.

The young girl kept coming forward, placing one

foot directly in front of the other, so that her hips would sway provocatively. "I have been alone so long," she said, "and I had lost all hope. I was sure that I would die out here in this terrible place. And now, providence has sent a handsome, strong protector. . . ."

"Stop!" the Guardian said. "Do not come any closer."

Ryana stirred slightly.

The young woman kept on coming. She was only about ten feet away now. She held out her arms, spreading her cloak wide in the process and revealing her lovely figure. "I know you will not turn me away," she said in a breathy voice that was full of promise. "Your companion is sound asleep, and if we are quiet, we need not disturb her. . . ."

"*Ranger!*" said the Guardian, speaking internally and slipping back, allowing the Ranger to the fore. Immediately, Sorak's posture changed. He stood up straighter, shoulders back, and his body tensed, though outwardly he looked relaxed. As the young woman kept on coming, the Ranger's hand swept down to the knife sheathed at his belt. He quickly drew the blade and, in one smooth motion, hurled it at the advancing woman.

It passed right through her.

With an angry hiss, the young woman lunged at him suddenly, and as she did so, her form blurred and became indistinct. The Ranger adroitly side-stepped as she leapt, and she fell onto the ground.

When she got back up, she was no longer a beautiful young woman. The illusion of the scanty clothing that she wore had disappeared, and the warm, pale tone of her flesh had gone a milky white with shimmering highlights. She no longer had long thick black hair, but a shifting mane of salt crystals, and her facial features had disappeared. Two indentations marked where her eyes had been, a slight ridge where there should have been a nose, and a gaping, lipless travesty of a mouth that opened wide, with a sifting dribble of salt crystals, like sands running through an hourglass.

Sorak awoke and beheld the sand bride, a creature he had only read about before. Like the blasted landscape of the planet, the creature was a result of unchecked defiler magic. A powerful defiler spell that drained the life energy from everything in its vicinity could, at times, open a rift to the negative material plane, and a creature like the sand bride could slip through. No one knew exactly what they were, but trapped on a plane of existence alien to them, they assumed their shape from the soil around them, usually sand, but in this case, the creature had assembled its corporeal self from the salt crystals of the Great Ivory Plain. Its illusion shattered, it was now on the attack.

Ryana awoke at the half howling, half hissing inhuman sounds it made, and she rolled quickly to her feet, drawing her sword.

"Stay back!" shouted Sorak. He knew that ordinary weapons would not harm the creature. They would pass right through the shifting salt crystals, like knives stabbing into sand. Galdra, however, was no ordinary weapon. As the creature lunged at him once more, Sorak leapt to one side, rolled, and drew Galdra from its scabbard as he came back up.

Ryana kept her distance, crouching warily. The creature stood between them, trying to decide on its next attack. It was not in the least intimidated by their blades. Suddenly, it melted into the salt surface of the plain in a cascade of crystals.

"What happened?" asked Ryana.

"Stand by me, quickly!" Sorak said.

As Ryana moved to comply, the creature suddenly rose up out of the ground behind her.

"Behind you!" Sorak cried.

Ryana spun around, slashing out with her blade. It passed right through the creature's neck, but the stroke that would have decapitated any other being had absolutely no effect. The blade simply passed through the shifting salt crystals, which reformed right behind it. As the creature stretched its arms out toward Ryana, seeking to seize her and drain her life energy, Sorak leapt forward, bringing Galdra down in a sweeping arc. The enchanted blade of elven steel whistled through the air and sliced off one of the creature's arms.

The connection to the body severed, the arm simply burst apart into a spray of gleaming salt crystals that pattered to the ground. In both pain and astonishment, the creature howled out an unearthly sound. Sorak swung his blade once more, but this time, the creature danced back out of its reach, fearful now that it knew this was no ordinary sword. Once more, it melted into the ground with a sound like sand being spilled.

Ryana stood back-to-back with Sorak, and they started circling cautiously, maintaining contact, watching warily all around them. With a sudden rush of sound, the creature sprang up once again, reforming at their feet, trying to separate them. Ryana was thrown forward and fell sprawling, but Sorak twisted, pivoting around, and brought Galdra in close to his body, slashing in a horizontal arc as he turned. The blade passed right through the creature's torso, severing it, and salt erupted in a spray, engulfing him as the creature wailed its death agony. Like tiny rain-drops, the salt crystals pattered to the ground, and the creature's howl died away upon the wind. Once more, the morning was still.

Ryana exhaled heavily and sheathed her sword. "All I wanted was a little sleep," she said. "Was that too much to ask?"

Sorak grinned at her. "I'm sorry if I woke you," he replied. "I tried to be quiet."

Ryana gazed out at the dark sun, just now rising malevolently from behind the mountains. Already, the salt beneath their feet was growing warmer. "I don't think I could sleep now, anyway," she said. "We might as well move on. All I want is to be quit of this forsaken place."

"It will be a hard journey in the daylight," Sorak said.

"No harder than getting killed while you're asleep," she replied. She shouldered her pack with a sigh. "Let's go."

"As you wish," said Sorak, picking up his pack and staff. He gazed longingly toward the mountains, but at the same time, wondered what new dangers would await them there.

* * * * *

Valsavis stood by a large rock outcropping on a slope just outside the city, overlooking the Great Ivory Plain. He examined the ground around him, noting the subtle signs most others would have missed. Yes, they had made camp here, there was no doubt about it. They had not built a fire, which would have given away their location this close to the city. And that, in itself, was as clear an indication of

who had stopped to rest here as if they had chiseled
their names into the rock behind them. They had
carefully tried to avoid leaving any evidence of their
presence, and most trackers would probably have
failed to find this spot where they had stopped to rest.
However, Valsavis was no ordinary tracker.

He knew that they had left the city. The Shadow
King had told him that much. What Nibenay had not
known was how they left, or which direction they had
taken. Had he wanted to, Nibenay could easily have
discovered that for himself through the agency of a
spell, but Valsavis had known better than to suggest
that. He knew that Nibenay was miserly with expend-
ing any power that was not directly related to his
ongoing metamorphosis.

The old bastard had grown truly ugly and
detestable, Valsavis thought. He could not fathom
how his templar wives could even stand to look at
him, much less perform their wifely duties, not that
Nibenay concerned himself any longer with matters
of the flesh. As a rule, sorcerers rarely indulged in
such ephemeral and energy-sapping pleasures.
Nonetheless, Valsavis would never understand what
would make a man want to transform himself into a
monstrosity. Power, obviously, but still . . . For Valsavis, it would have been much too high a price to
pay. But then again, he reminded himself, he was not
a sorcerer-king and had never had any such lofty
ambitions.

In fact, ambition had always been conspicuously
absent from his life. He had little, but what he had was
more than sufficient. He lived an isolated existence in
the foothills of the Barrier Mountains because he did
not much care for the company of people. He knew
them entirely too well. He had studied them a great

deal, and the more he had learned about their nature, the less he wanted to do with them. He lived quietly and simply, not requiring anybody's company except his own. The woods of the Barrier Mountains held a plentitude of game; the sky was clear and the air untainted by the pestiferous odors of the city. No one disturbed his solitude. No one except—on certain rare occasions—the Shadow King, Nibenay.

It had been many years since Nibenay had required any service from him. In his youth, Valsavis had been a soldier, a mercenary who had traveled the world and hired on with whomever needed fighting men and could afford to pay. At one time or another, he had served in the armies of almost every city-state on Athas, and on numerous occasions, he had been employed by most of the large merchant houses as a caravan guard. One did not become rich by serving as a mercenary, but Valsavis did not require riches. He had always managed to survive. That seemed enough. The turning point in his life came when he had served as a captain in the army of the Shadow King, many years ago.

In those days, Nibenay still had not withdrawn from the political affairs of his city, as he had done once he had achieved significant progression in his dragon metamorphosis. Now, he left the government of his domain largely to his templars, but back then, he had taken a much more active role. A time had come when one of the city's most influential aristocrats had tried to make a bid for power, with the bold aim of unseating the Shadow King and supplanting him upon the throne. Using the riches of his family, he had left the city and established his headquarters in Gulg, where he had forged a powerful alliance with the oba, Sorcerer-Queen Lalali-Puy. Word had reached the Shadow King that this aristocrat was starting to recruit an army, with an aim toward marching on the city of the Shadow King. It was then that Nibenay had turned to a young captain in his guard.

Valsavis never did discover why or how the Shadow King had chosen him. Perhaps he had learned something of his history and reputation. Perhaps he had seen something in him that made him realize the young captain of the guard possessed untapped potential. Perhaps he had used some form of divination. Valsavis never knew. He only knew that the Shadow King had chosen him for a special and highly dangerous task, one that he would have to perform alone. He had been sent to Gulg, to infiltrate the army being raised by the rebel aristocrat and then assassinate him.

It had not proved difficult at all. His target had been so confident of the loyalty of his well-paid troops and so intent on proving himself an unpretentious commander who mingled with his men that he had taken almost no security precautions. Valsavis had carried off the assignment successfully, in far less time than he expected, and then made good his escape in the confusion that ensued. The Shadow King was pleased. He soon had other, similar services for Valsavis to perform.

In time, Valsavis was relieved of all his other duties. He became the Shadow King's personal assassin, stalking his enemies and eliminating them, wherever they were to be found. His reputation grew, and people learned to fear his name. No one had ever escaped him. No matter where they tried to flee, he had always tracked them down. He was very, very good at what he did.

The years passed, and as the Shadow King became more and more withdrawn, obsessively preoccupied with his spells of metamorphosis, Valsavis was forgotten. The time came when he was no longer summoned to the palace to be sent out upon some deadly errand. No longer did he track the most elusive game afoot. The city guard had no further use for his abilities. Indeed, its commanders feared him. Valsavis did not really mind. He had no wish to reduce himself to being a mere guardsman once again, and serving as an ordinary mercenary no longer held much interest for him. He had long since left the city to reside in his isolated cabin in the foothills, and it was there he had remained, avoiding the company of his fellow creatures, living the life of a recluse. And now, after all these years, the Shadow King had once more sent for him.

How long had it been? Twenty years? Thirty? More? Valsavis had lost count. He thought the Shadow King had forgotten all about him. The elfling had to be someone very special, indeed, to distract Nibenay from the one pursuit that occupied his every waking moment. Valsavis had questioned Veela extensively about the elfling, and then he had conducted his own brief investigation. It had taken less time and proven easier than he expected. After all those years, his usual sources had either disappeared or died, but just the mention of his name had been enough to quickly lead him to those who had the answers he sought. Even after all this time, he thought, they still recalled Valsavis. And feared him. Nibenay himself had provided further information, but there was still much about his quarry Valsavis did not know. No matter. Before long, he would learn. There was no better way to learn about a man—or an elfling, for that matter—than by stalking him.

He glanced at the strange, gold ring that Nibenay had given him and recalled the Shadow King's ominous parting words. *"Do not fail me, Valsavis."*

Valsavis had no intention of failing, but not because he feared the Shadow King. He was afraid of nothing; he did not fear death, in any of its forms. He had always known that sooner or later, one way or another, death was simply inevitable. It was preferable to postpone it for as long as possible, but when the time came, he would meet it with equanimity. There were, of course, worse things than death, as the Shadow King had pointedly reminded him, and Valsavis knew that Nibenay could visit any number of unpleasant fates on him if he should fail. But that was not what drove him. What drove him was the thrill of the chase, the intricacies of it, the challenge of the pursuit and final outcome.

Valsavis had seen fear in men's faces more times than he could count. It had always fascinated him, because he had never felt it himself. He could not say why. It was as if some essential part of him were missing. He had never truly been capable of strong emotions. He had enjoyed the lustful embrace of many women, but he had never felt love for any of them. What they had given him was ephemeral physical pleasure and, on occasion, some mental stimulation, but nothing more. He had never felt hate or joy or sadness. He knew that he completely lacked emotions most men took for granted. He was capable of a wry, sardonic humor, but only because it was something he had learned, not developed naturally. He could laugh, but that, too, was a learned response. He did not really enjoy the sound of it.

What he enjoyed—to the extent that he was capable of enjoying anything—was engendering strong emotional responses in others. He was always fascinated by the effect he had on women, the way they looked at him, were drawn to him, the sounds they made during lovemaking. He wondered what they *felt* at such times. He was also intrigued by the effect he had on men, the way they looked at him with apprehension when he passed, their gazes of envy and respect and fear. But most of all, he sought the stimulation of the responses he engendered in his quarry.

Whenever possible, he had avoided striking without warning, because he *wanted* them to know that he was on their trail. He wanted to see the effect it would have on them. He often played with them, the way a mountain cat played with its prey, just to see what reactions they would have. And, just prior the kill, he always tried to look into their eyes, so he could see their realization of their fate and watch how they responded to it. Some gave way to abject terror; some broke down and begged and pleaded with him; some gazed at him with hate, defiant to the end; and some simply accepted death with resignation. He had seen every possible response, but different as they were, there was one thing they all had in common. For a brief instant, as they died, he had always seen a glimmer in their eyes that mixed puzzlement and horror as they realized that *he* felt nothing, that their deaths meant absolutely nothing to him. It was an agonized look, and he always wondered how they felt in that brief instant.

He stood and looked out across the Great Ivory Plain. That was the way they had gone. He wondered why. It was no easy journey, not even for someone mounted on a kank, as he was. The elfling and the priestess had both gone on foot. However, he knew that they were trained in the Way of the Druid and

the Path of the Preserver. As a result, they would be
far more prepared than most to undertake so arduous
an expedition. Doubtless, they would travel by night
and rest during the day. He would do the same, but
mounted, he would make much better time. He tried
to estimate how much of a head start they had on
him. Four days, maybe five. No more than six. It
would not prove very difficult for him to make up the
distance.

They appeared to be heading toward the Mekillot
Mountains. What did they hope to find there? Did
they hope to find a haven with the marauders? Perhaps enlist their aid? Maybe, thought Valsavis, but
that seemed doubtful. The marauders had no sympathy for preservers. They had no sympathy for anyone.
They cared only for ill-gotten gains, and they would
just as soon kill anyone who tried to hire them and
take the money from his corpse. The elfling was no
fool, by all accounts, and he would doubtless know
that. Chances were they would steer clear of the
marauders, if they could.

What else could they be seeking in that direction?
There were no settlements in the Mekillot Mountains; there was only the small village of Salt View
that lay beyond them, a haven for runaway slaves
ruled by an aging former gladiator by the name of
Xaynon. Until Xaynon came, the villagers had survived, after a fashion, by hunting in the mountains
and raiding caravans bound for Gulg and Nibenay.
However, as raiders, they had to compete with the
marauders, who claimed exclusive raiding rights on
caravans in the vicinity. This had resulted in raids by
the ex-slaves on the marauders, who would reciprocate by attacking the village of Salt View, and eventually, both factions realized that they were spending

more time attacking one another than attacking caravans.

Xaynon had come up with a unique solution. As a former gladiator, he had witnessed many theatrical productions staged in the arena, and he decided to organize the villagers into traveling troupes of players who would go out to meet the caravans and, rather than attacking them, perform for them, instead. Needless to say, they charged for the entertainment they provided, and when they left, they reported back to the marauders—for a fee, of course—the disposition of the caravans, the goods they carried, and the strength of the accompanying guard. The marauders would then raid the caravan, the players would receive part of the booty, and they would then perform for the marauders as they celebrated their success together.

It was a venture that benefitted both parties, and Salt View had become a rowdy, boisterous little village of itinerant players, acrobats, jugglers and musicians, with the occasional visiting bard thrown in for good measure. The marauders now often came as welcome visitors instead of raiders. And travelers, in search of stimulation with an edge of danger, often made a detour to the village of Salt View, where they could indulge in gaming to their heart's content, attend elaborate theatrical productions, drink their fill, and take their pick of willing wenches. Usually, they would depart without so much as a ceramic in their purses. And yet that never seemed to stop the flow of eager new arrivals.

Salt View had to be their destination, then. Was it possible this king they sought to raise was residing in Salt View, so close to Nibenay? Valsavis frowned. He disliked the thought of the game ending so quickly.

But surely, he thought, if there were a powerful wizard in the village of Salt View, the Shadow King would have been made aware of it. The people of Salt View would sell their own mothers for a profit. No, thought Valsavis, it seemed unlikely. What then?

There was, apparently, some connection between the elfling and the Veiled Alliance. Was there a chapter of the Veiled Alliance in Salt View? If so, he had never heard any mention of it. The members of the Veiled Alliance were all preservers in active opposition to defilers, and there were no defilers in Salt View. Magic-users were unwelcome there, whether preservers or defilers. So the probability was that the elfling and the priestess were seeking someone or something else. Valsavis could not imagine who or what that could be.

It was a puzzle. Valsavis was intrigued by puzzles, especially when they were posed by those he stalked. He mounted his kank as the dark sun began to set on the horizon. He checked his waterskins to make certain they were full. It was going to be a long, hard journey, but he was sure to find something of interest at its end. An elfling Master of the Way with a priceless magic sword, assuming it really was the legendary blade called Galdra. A beautiful, young villichi priestess well schooled in the arts of combat and survival. And a mysterious wizard king to be, powerful enough to excite the caution of Nibenay himself.

Yes, worthy adversaries, all.

Valsavis urged the kank forward, down the slope to the Great Ivory Plain. And so the chase begins, he thought with satisfaction.

TWO

Sorak knew the marauders had their base on the western slopes of the Mekillot Mountains. Those foothills were near the caravan route from Altaruk to Gulg so, to give the marauders a wide berth, he headed on a diagonal, southeasterly course, rather than going straight south. It added at least another day to their journey across the Great Ivory Plain, which was not an attractive proposition, but on the other hand, it reduced their chances of encountering marauder scouts.

It also brought them closer to the village of Salt View, which was located just beyond the mountains, near the eastern tip of the range. According to *The Wanderer's Journal,* there was a pass roughly at the middle of the range, which was the normal route that one would take to reach Salt View, but Sorak intended to give that a wide berth, as well. It would be a logical place for the marauders to post lookouts. What better place to ambush unwary travelers than in a desolate mountain pass?

They reached the northern slopes of the foothills just before daybreak on the seventh day of their journey. According to the rough map in *The Wanderer's*

Journal, the distance across the Great Ivory Plain
from Nibenay to the mountains was approximately
forty or fifty miles. The actual distance they had traveled had been easily twice that. In his days as the
Wanderer, thought Sorak, the Sage was obviously not
a very accurate cartographer. Either that, or errors
had crept in over the years as the journal had been
copied numerous times for distribution. Sorak hoped
the former was the case, for if errors had crept into
the journal, then he had no way of knowing how far
he could trust its contents. It was an unsettling
notion, especially since the journal was supposed to
contain clues that would guide them on their quest.

They had been as sparing with their water as possible, but they had still run out. For Sorak, with his
elfling powers of endurance, going without water was
not as much a hardship as for Ryana, whose human
constitution had greater need of it, especially on the
Great Ivory Plain. It was much cooler traveling at
night, but when they stopped to rest during the day,
the heat was so intense that moisture had to be
replaced. Ryana's lips were parched and cracked, and
it had been all she could do to put one foot before the
other. Sorak had offered to carry her, but she refused
to burden him. Exhausted and at the utter limit of
her resources, she still had her stubborn pride.

As soon as they had reached the foothills, they
stopped to rest, and Sorak dug a shallow depression in
the ground. He used a druid spell to draw water up out
of the sandy soil. Ryana could have done it, but she
lacked the strength. It took a while for the liquid to
percolate up through the soil, because the water table
was far below the surface. Once it did, he watched to
make sure that Ryana took only small sips.

She crouched on hands and knees to drink, then

sat up and sighed, wearily and gratefully. "I never thought that dirty water could taste this good," she said. "It was still a little salty, though."

"We should be able to find better water once we get up into the mountains," Sorak said.

"I think I could sleep for at least a week," Ryana said, stretching out on her back and shading her eyes with her arm.

"Do not fall asleep yet," Sorak told her. "We are still out in the open here. I will feel safer once we find some cover."

She groaned. "Can't we rest here for just a little while?"

"Of course," he said, relenting. "But we must be moving on soon. We will make camp among those rocks up there, where we should find both shade and shelter."

She looked in the direction that he indicated and sighed once more. "Sometimes I wish I were an elf," she said.

Sorak smiled. "Elves are carnivorous, remember. And they have great, big, pointed ears."

"Well, an elfling, then," she said. "Then I could be like you, resist my flesh-eating impulses, and have ears with only little points."

"On you, they would look most attractive," Sorak said.

"That's right, flatter me when I'm weak and have no strength to respond," she said.

"It *is* safer that way," he replied.

"Ouch," she said. "It hurts to smile. My face is so dried out it may crack."

"I will find some cactus and pulp it so that you may spread it on your skin."

"Ohhh, that would feel wonderful. Now if only we

could find a small stream that I could wash in!"

"I shall do my best," said Sorak.

"You remember that stream that ran down from the spring by the convent?" she said.

He smiled. "Yes, I remember. We all used to bathe there every day, after our weapons training sessions."

"I remember the bracing, cold water of the pool, and the way the stream ran down over the rocks below," she said. "I can almost feel it now. I took it all for granted. The stream, the forest, the cool and refreshing mountain breezes. . . . I had never truly realized how dry and desolate our world is."

"You miss the Ringing Mountains, don't you?" he said.

"I shall always think of them as home," she replied. And then she added, quickly, "But I am not sorry I came."

Sorak remained silent.

"Do you wish I had remained there?" she asked softly after a moment.

Sorak did not reply at once, and she felt a sharp pang of anxiety. Finally, he said, "A part of me does, I suppose. And I am not referring to any of the tribe. I mean that part of me wishes you could have been spared all this."

"I made the choice to follow you of my own free will," she said.

"Yes, I know. And I cannot begin to tell you how glad I am to have you with me. But I also cannot help thinking sometimes of the life you could have led had it not been for me."

"Had it not been for you, I do not think I would have had much of a life," she replied, gazing at him earnestly.

"And I cannot imagine my life without you," he said.

"But if the Elder Al'Kali had never brought me to the convent, we never would have met. You would have grown up among the sisters, and by this time, doubtless you would have replaced Tamura as weapons and combat trainer. You would have had the love and respect of all your fellow sisters, and you would have continued to live in that verdant valley high in your beloved Ringing Mountains, a peaceful oasis of green tranquility in a parched and dying world. Instead, you met me and fell in love, a love I share with all my heart, but never can reciprocate the way love is meant to be, because of who and what I am. And when I consider all that you have gone through for my sake, and what still lies ahead . . ." He sighed and looked away. "It all seems monstrously unfair."

She moved closer to him and took his hand in hers. "I am not complaining," she said. "Without you, I never would have had a friend my own age back at the convent. And without you, I never would have truly known what it means to love someone. I would have grown up like all the other sisters, having little use for men and thinking even less of them. And chances are that if I ever had a man, I would have done it in the same way as the older sisters who go out on their pilgrimages and use the opportunity to indulge their curiosity about the pleasures of the flesh. It would have meant nothing to me, and I would most likely have reacted the same way they all did, wondering why people made so much of it if that was all there was to love. But now, I know that they are wrong, and there is so much more. I may wonder sometimes what it feels like to couple with a male, but since I have never done it, I do not really know what I am missing. In truth, I do not require a male to make me feel whole as a woman."

"I often wonder if I shall ever feel complete as a male without having made love to a female," Sorak said. "And not just any female," he added, looking at her. "Only one would do."

"I know," she said, squeezing his hand gently. "But Mistress Varanna told me once that love can be all the more intense for being chaste."

Sorak looked surprised. "Varanna said that?"

Ryana smiled. "Varanna is wise in the ways of the world, as well as the ways of the spirit."

"Yes, I suppose she is," Sorak replied. "It is just that I find it difficult to imagine her speaking of such things."

"We had a long talk about you just before I left the convent," said Ryana. "I had already made up my mind to leave and follow you. I did not think she suspected it, but now I am certain she knew. I thought I was being so clever, sneaking out at night the way I did. She knew, though, and she could have stopped me but didn't."

"I am certain she would take you back," said Sorak.

"Yes, I think she would," Ryana replied, "but though I miss the sisters and the Ringing Mountains, I really have no desire to return."

"Because of me?"

"Yes, but there is much more to it than you and me. What we are doing is important, Sorak, much more important than anything I could have done back at the convent. The villichi are preservers, first and foremost, followers of the Druid Way. We are taught from childhood to dedicate ourselves to saving our world, and we all dream that, one day, Athas will be green again. Perhaps that is a dream that shall never come to pass, but at least we can work to prevent the world from being despoiled further by defiler magic. The Sage represents our one true hope for that. The avangion is the only power that can stand against the dragon sorcerers. We must help the Sage achieve that metamorphosis. For a true preserver, there can be no higher calling."

"True," said Sorak, "but it also means that we will be in active opposition to the sorcerer-kings and every defiler on the planet. And you know that they shall stop at nothing to prevent the Sage from achieving his goal. That means they shall stop at nothing to prevent us from helping him. I often think I should have undertaken this alone, the way I started out. What right have I to expose you to such risks?"

"What makes you think it was your decision?" she asked. "No one ever said the Path of the Preserver was an easy one. It is not enough merely to talk about the path as an ideal. To be a true preserver, one must also walk it."

"Yes," said Sorak. "And speaking of walking . . ."

"So soon?" Ryana said.

"Only a little farther," he replied, "and then we can make camp."

Wearily, she got to her feet. "Well, I came this far. I suppose I can walk a little farther. But I am going to sleep like the dead when we make camp."

"I see no reason why we cannot call a halt and rest for one whole day once we reach the shelter of those rocks up there," he said. "No one is chasing us." He looked out across the Great Ivory Plain. "Who in his right mind would follow us across all that?"

* * * * *

Valsavis stopped and dismounted from his kank. He opened up his feed bag and set it down before the beast, pouring a little water in it to give the giant insect some moisture. Kanks were well adapted for travel in the desert, but the Great Ivory Plain offered them nothing in the way of forage, not even a cactus to chew on, and he had been driving the beast hard. As the beetle fed, Valsavis carefully examined it to see how it was holding up. The kank was tired, but he had not pushed it past its limits. So long as his supplies held out, he would have no difficulty maintaining this pace.

His mount seen to, Valsavis next examined the trail. Most trackers would have found no trail at all to follow, but Valsavis did. It was far more difficult to detect a trail on the hard salt than on the sandy desert, but here and there, he could see the faintest sign of a disturbance in the salt where his quarry had stopped to rest briefly or paused to shift their packs. Another day and the wind would have obliterated even those faint signs.

One of them was growing much more tired than the other. He guessed it would have to be the priestess. The elfling had a stronger constitution. Here and there, he could see a sign of where her foot had dragged as she had walked. They had altered their course slightly, from south to southeast. Valsavis looked up at the mountains, now no more than a day's ride distant. The elfling and the priestess appeared to be headed on a diagonal course toward the northeastern tip of the range. It would have been easier for them to head straight south and take the pass through the Mekillots to the village of Salt View, but they had chosen a more prudent course.

It made sense, Valsavis thought. His analysis had proved correct. They were giving the marauders a wide berth and aiming to cross the mountains to reach Salt View rather than going through the pass. Smart, thought Valsavis. There was still a possibility they might encounter a small raiding or hunting party of marauders, but they had reduced those chances dramatically by choosing their present course, even though it meant that it would take longer for them to reach the mountains. They would arrive tired, or at least the priestess would, and they would probably stop to rest, perhaps for a full day, before they proceeded on their journey. That would give him time to close the distance between them.

However, he did not wish to reveal himself just yet. He wanted to get close enough to observe them without being observed, himself. He did not wish to force a confrontation. When the time came, he would allow them to discover they were being followed. And then the game would become more interesting.

His left hand suddenly began to tingle. He held it up before his face, gazing at the ring the Shadow King had given him before he left. It was a very old ring, made of solid gold, a commodity so rare on Athas that most people had never even seen it. It was much more than a gift, however, magnificent though it was. The face of the large ring was round and raised, molded into the shape of a human eye that was closed. As his hand began to tingle and he raised it up to see the ring, the golden eyelid opened, revealing the staring, yellow eye of Nibenay, the Shadow King.

"*Have you picked up the trail of the elfling and the priestess?*" asked the Shadow King's voice within his mind.

"I am within a day's ride of them, my lord," Valsavis answered aloud. "They have crossed the Great Ivory Plain and should just now be reaching the

northeastern foothills of the Mekillots. They are
clearly bound for the village of Salt View, though
what they hope to find there, I cannot say."

"*Salt View . . .*" the dragon king said. The golden
eye blinked once. "*There is a preserver living in Salt
View, a druid known only as the Silent One.*"

"I had not thought that preservers would find a
welcome in Salt View, my lord," Valsavis replied.

"*Under ordinary circumstances, they would not,*" the
dragon king replied. "*But the Silent One is no ordinary
preserver. The Silent One has been to Bodach and survived to tell the tale—except that the experience stole the
Silent One's voice, and so the tale of what the druid found
there has never yet been told. There are those who believe
the Silent One knows the secret of Bodach's treasure, and
hope to see it written down. Many have tried to find this
reclusive druid, but there are also those who venerate the
Silent One for surviving the ordeal, and grant the old
druid their protection.*"

"Then you believe the elfling seeks this Silent One,
my lord?" Valsavis asked.

"*The city of the undead lies to the southeast of Salt
View, across the inland silt basins,*" said the Shadow
King as the golden eye blinked once more. "*If they
seek the Silent One, doubtless it is because they seek a
guide to Bodach.*"

"They seek the legendary treasure, then?" Valsavis
said.

"*It is no mere legend,*" said the Shadow King. "*The
treasure horde of Bodach is real enough. But hidden
somewhere among that fabulous horde is a treasure greater
still—the Breastplate of Argentum.*"

"I have never heard of it, my lord," Valsavis said.

"*Nor have most people,*" said the Shadow King. "*It is
a relic of the ancients, made of finely linked silver chain*

mail and imbued with powerful preserver magic."

"What is the nature of the talisman, my lord?"

"I must admit I do not know," the Shadow King replied. *"It is warded against spell detection by defilers, nor shall it serve them. But it must not be allowed to fall into the elfling's hands. It would arm him while he wore it, and its magic would empower this king that he would make. You must find the Breastplate of Argentum and destroy it."*

"But . . . how would I know it, my lord?" Valsavis asked. "A breastplate of silver chain mail would be very rare, of course, but among the treasure of the ancients, there could easily be any number of such items. Can you not tell me anything that would distinguish it?"

"It is said to gleam with a peculiar light," the Shadow King replied. *"More than that, I cannot tell you."*

"I will find it if I can, my lord."

"If you do not find it, see that the elfling does not, either," said the Shadow King. *"And if he finds it before you do, then he must not be allowed to keep it."*

"If he finds the breastplate first, my lord, do you wish him to be killed?" Valsavis asked.

"No," the Shadow King replied. *"He must lead us to the king that he would crown. If he finds the breastplate first, then you must devise some method whereby you can take it from him. How you manage that is no concern of mine. But the elfling must not die until he leads us to the one he serves. Remember that, Valsavis. That is your primary objective. The uncrowned king must be found and eliminated, at all costs."*

The golden eyelid closed, and the tingling sensation went away. Valsavis lowered his arm back to his side. He had wanted an interesting challenge. Well, he was certainly going to get his wish. He was stalking an apparently clever, resourceful and dangerous victim, and the trick was not to kill him until he had served his purpose in leading him to his master. Added to that, he had to find an ancient magic talisman before the elfling did, and to do that, he would have to search for it in Bodach, a city teeming with undead, while at the same time maintaining observation of the elfling and the priestess. And if the elfling managed to find the Breastplate of Argentum first, then he had somehow to devise a way of wresting it away from him—without killing the elfling. Last, but by no means least of all, he had to trail the elfling and the priestess to this uncrowned king and execute him, which would be no easy task. The elfling's master was undoubtedly a powerful preserver if he was feared even by the Shadow King, and Valsavis had never before tried to kill a wizard.

For years now, he had thought his days of stalking the most dangerous game of all were far behind him. Now, the greatest challenge of his life beckoned.

Valsavis remounted the kank and set off on the trail. He took in a deep breath, filling his lungs with the hot, dry, desert air, and exhaled heavily, with satisfaction. He almost felt young again.

★   ★   ★   ★   ★

Sorak and Ryana had made camp once they reached the shelter of the rock formations on the steep slope of the northeastern foothills. It had not been a very difficult climb, but it had been a time-consuming one, especially since Ryana was so tired; it was late in the afternoon before they stopped. They had chosen a spot where several large rock outcroppings formed a sort of miniature fortress with a patch of ground inside that afforded some shelter from the wind. At the same time, the ring of rocks would serve to mask their fire from any observers who might happen to be in the vicinity. The wind sweeping across the slopes would quickly dissipate the smoke, and the flames would be hidden by the stone.

They gathered some wood and scrub brush for the fire, and Ryana spread her cloak out on the ground to lie beside the warming flames. The location seemed secure enough, but no place on Athas was ever totally secure, so Sorak cautioned Ryana to stay alert while he went foraging to find her something to eat. At the same time, he would allow the Ranger to go hunting for the tribe.

As he ducked under and let the Ranger take the fore, Sorak retired to some much-needed sleep. The Ranger, fully rested, emerged to take over the body and go hunting. The tribe had discovered that their body did not really need to sleep so long as they, themselves, did. It was the mind that grew tired, more so than the body, which needed rest and nourishment much more than sleep for recuperation. Before long, the Ranger picked up the scent of a kirre. It was a male in rut, spraying to mark its territory. The scent made its trail that much easier to follow.

With his long and loping strides, the Ranger moved quickly through the wooded foothills, following the beast's trail effortlessly. It was headed up into the higher elevations, having probably come down to hunt for food. Now, its instincts drove it to seek a female of its species, and it was ranging wide, moving up and back, scouring the countryside. At times like these, the Ranger was not only at his best, doing what his personality was ideally suited for, but also at his happiest. He reveled in the hunt. It was a primal pleasure, stalking dangerous elusive prey for food, testing his knowledge and his instincts, and at the same time, it brought him intimately into contact with the land in a way that was almost a spiritual communion.

To track a man was one thing, but to track an animal was entirely another. A man, unless he was unusually gifted with a knowledge of the land and well practiced in treading on it lightly, left a trail that was far easier to follow. He walked heavily and often clumsily by contrast to the beasts, and where his footsteps did not leave easy tracks to follow, his movement through the underbrush snapped twigs, dislodged small stones and bent down desert grass.

An animal moved lightly, leaving but the faintest trail by comparison. However, the Ranger knew the track of every beast that roamed the Athasian wilderness, and he could read a trail so effectively that he could even tell what movements the animal had made.

Here, the kirre had stopped for a few moments, sniffing the air tentatively, shifting its weight slightly as it turned, then took a few more steps and sniffed again. There, it had paused to investigate a jankx's burrow, scratching at the entrance lightly to remove some of the brush the smaller beast had used to camouflage its home, and then sniffing once or twice to see if it was hiding inside.

As he followed the kirre's trail, the Ranger came to know the beast from the way it moved and acted. It was full grown and healthy, a powerful, young adult male that had recently shed the velvety covering of several inches of new growth on its curving, swept-back horns. From time to time, it still paused to scrape against an agafari tree, leaving telltale scratches on its trunk. It was inquisitive, a fact demonstrated by its frequent pauses to investigate the abandoned lair of a smaller animal or the spoor of a rasclinn that had passed not long ago.

Before long, the quarry was in sight, and the Ranger crept up stealthily from downwind of the beast. It was moving slowly, sniffing the air as if it sensed his presence. The Ranger reached down to his belt for the hunting knife Sorak carried in his sheath. Any other hunter would have used a bow and shot from as great a distance as he could, for safety, to allow time for a second shot in case the first one missed. But the Ranger, while an archer of great skill, eschewed such an advantage. There was no purity in such a kill.

He moved in slowly, with agonizing care, placing his feet so as not to make the slightest sound. He kept track of the wind, making sure it did not shift and give away his position.

There it was, upon a nearby outcrop, crouched on its eight powerful legs. Already, the kirre was tense and agitated, its psionic senses alerting it that there was something wrong. It was prepared to spring in any direction at the slightest warning as it raised its twin-horned head to sniff the air. It was a magnificent looking beast, a great, brown- and gray-striped cat fully eight feet in length and weighing several hundred pounds. Its barbed tail twitched back and forth nervously.

Then, suddenly, the wind shifted, and with a low growl, the cat turned directly toward the Ranger, gathering its legs beneath it for a leap. There was no time to attack now; the beast was already bounding into the air, taking the initiative, launching itself at the Ranger with a roar, its four front legs extended, claws poised to rake and shred.

The Ranger timed it perfectly. He rolled beneath the beast as it hurtled toward him, came up fast as it landed, and leapt onto its back before it could turn to face him. He locked his legs around the great cat's torso and seized one of its horns with his left hand, ignoring the painful lashing of its barbed tail as he bent its head back to expose its throat. The kirre threw itself down, trying to dislodge him, but the Ranger held firm, gritting his teeth with the effort of forcing back its head against the pull of the cat's powerful neck muscles. The knife flashed, and the cat gave a gurgling cry as its blood spilled out onto the ground. Still holding on, the Ranger plunged the knife into the creature's heart, ending its agony. It shuddered once, then lay still.

The Ranger relaxed and disengaged himself from the dead beast, getting back to his feet and standing over it. He crouched beside the body and stroked its flank, then placed his hand upon the creature's massive head and softly said, "Thank you for your life, my friend. May your strength become ours."

After the Ranger made his kill and the tribe had fed, he gathered some wild berries and kory seeds, as well as some pulpy, succulent leaves from the lotus mint, which grew in abundance on the slopes. He filled his pouch so that there would be a plentiful supply for Ryana to take with them when they set out in the morning. With any luck, they might a find a small mountain stream where they could stop and refresh themselves and fill their waterskins. It was a clear, cool night, and the Ranger always felt better in the mountains than on the desert tablelands, so he allowed Lyric to come forth and join him so that he could enjoy a song.

As they made their way back to the camp, Lyric

sang a song in elvish, a ballad Sorak no longer remembered but had once heard his mother sing. The Ranger walked along at a steady pace, enjoying the feeling of the breeze blowing through his hair and the lilting voice of Lyric issuing from between his lips. As they approached the campsite, they could see the soft glow of the fire reflected on the rock walls of the outcropping. The Ranger smiled, thinking how Ryana would enjoy the meal he had gathered for her. As they rounded the far side of the rock outcropping, the Ranger suddenly heard something hissing toward them through the air. Lyric's voice fell silent as the arrow struck them in the back, and they fell to the ground, both of them spinning away into the darkness.

* * * * *

Sorak came to his senses not knowing what had happened. He was lying stretched out on his stomach, with his own cloak covering him. It was early morning. The campfire was burning brightly, and he could smell the aroma of roasting flesh. He opened his eyes and saw a man seated cross-legged by the fire, cooking some meat on a spit. He sat up instantly, and gasped as he felt a sharp pain shoot through his shoulder.

"Easy, friend," said the man seated by the fire. "Move slowly, else you will undo all of my good work."

Sorak looked at shoulder. His tunic had been removed, and his shoulder crudely but effectively bandaged. Some kanna leaves had been pressed together underneath the bandage to make a poultice.

"You did this?" asked Sorak.

"I applied the poultice and the bandage," the man replied. "I did not inflict the wound, however."

"Who did?"

"You do not know?"

Sorak shook his head. "No, I remember nothing." Suddenly, he looked around. "*Ryana!* Where is she?"

"I saw no one save you when I arrived," the stranger said. "But there was a party of men here not long before. If your companion was here alone, it seems they have made off with her."

"Then I must go after them at once," said Sorak. He tried to get to his feet, but winced at the pain in his shoulder when he moved. A wave of dizziness came over him.

"I do not think you would be of much use to your companion in your present condition," said the stranger. "We will see to your friend presently. For now, you need your strength." He held up a piece of uncooked meat, spitted on a dagger. "Elves eat their flesh raw, do they not?"

Despite himself, Sorak started salivating at the sight of the meat. He knew the tribe had fed earlier, but he did not know how long he had been unconscious, and the wound had made him weak. Druid vows be damned, he thought to himself as he accepted the meat from the stranger. Ryana needs me, and I need my strength to heal. "Thank you," he said to the big stranger.

"You are small for an elf," the stranger said. "Are you part human?"

"Part halfling," Sorak said.

The stranger raised his eyebrows in surprise. "Indeed? And how did such a curious thing occur?"

"I do not know," said Sorak. "I did not know my parents."

"Ah," the stranger said, nodding with understanding. "The ways of Athas can be harsh."

As he ate, Sorak looked the man over. He was a large and powerful-looking man, very muscular, with a fighter's build, but he was no longer young. His features betrayed his age, but his body belied it. He had long gray hair that hung down past his shoulders and a thick gray beard. He was dressed in a sleeveless hide tunic that displayed his mighty arms, hide breeches, high moccasins with fringe at the tops, and studded wristlets. He wore an iron sword and several daggers in his belt, and given the extreme rarity of any kind of metal on Athas, it was clear testimony to his prowess as a fighting man. Some very rich and grateful aristocratic patron had bestowed the weapons on him, and he was skilled enough to keep them and not let a better fighter take them away. Sorak immediately thought of his own sword and clapped his hand to his side. It was not there.

"Your blade is safe enough," the stranger said with a smile, noting his alarmed reaction. "It is in its scabbard, lying with your tunic, there."

Sorak looked where the stranger pointed and saw that Galdra was, indeed, safely lying by his side, not three feet away, atop his tunic. "A lot of men would have been tempted to take it for themselves," he said.

The stranger merely shrugged. "I did not care for the shape of it," he said simply. "A handsome weapon, to be sure, but not suited to my style of fighting. I suppose I could have sold it. No doubt, it would have fetched a great deal of money, but then I would have had the worry of wondering what to spend it on. Too much money can only bring trouble to a man."

"What is your name, stranger?" Sorak asked.

"I am called Valsavis."

"I am in your debt, Valsavis. My name is Sorak."

Valsavis merely grunted.

Sorak felt his strength returning to him as he finished the raw meat. It was z'tal flesh, and it tasted exceedingly good. "I must heal myself, Valsavis, so that I can go after the men who took my friend."

"So? You are adept at healing? You are a druid, then?"

"What of it if I am?"

Valsavis shrugged. "I have had occasion to be healed by druids in the past. I bear them no ill will."

Sorak closed his eyes and allowed the Guardian to come to the fore. Under her breath, she spoke the words of a healing spell and concentrated her energies, drawing some additional power from the earth, but not enough to harm any growing thing. Sorak felt his strength returning as the wound began to heal.

Moments later, it was done, and the Guardian withdrew. Sorak stood, removed the bandage and the poultice, and went over to get his tunic and sword.

"That was uncommonly quick," Valsavis said, watching him with interest.

"I have a gift for healing," Sorak replied as he buckled on his sword.

"And apparently a gift for recovering from the effort it requires," Valsavis said. "I have seen druids perform healing spells before. It nearly always leaves them drained, and they require hours of rest."

"I have no time for that," said Sorak. "I thank you for your kindness, Valsavis, but I must go help my friend."

"Alone?" Valsavis said. "And on foot?"

"I have no mount," said Sorak.

"I do," Valsavis said. "My kank is staked just behind these rocks."

Sorak stared at him. "Are you offering to help?"

Valsavis shrugged. "I have nothing better to do."

"You owe me nothing," Sorak said. "Rather, it is I who owe a debt to you. Those men who took my friend were probably a party of marauders. They will be heading for their camp. We will be greatly outnumbered."

"If they reach their camp," Valsavis said.

Sorak examined the trail leading from the rocks. "There are six or seven of them, at least," he said.

"Nine," said Valsavis.

Sorak glanced at him with interest. "Nine, then. And we are only two."

"Without me, you would be only one."

"Why would you risk your life for me?" asked Sorak. "I have no money, and cannot pay you."

"I did not ask for payment."

"Why, then?" Sorak asked, puzzled.

Valsavis shrugged again. "Why not? It has been a long and uneventful journey. And I am no longer of an age where I can afford to remain idle very long. I need to keep my hand in, or all of the good jobs will go to younger men."

"And what if we should fail?" Sorak asked.

"I had never thought that I would live this long," Valsavis replied flatly. "And the thought of dying in bed does not appeal to me. It lacks flamboyance."

Sorak smiled. "Somehow, I had never thought of death as flamboyant."

"Death itself is merely death," Valsavis said. "It's how one lives, up to the final moment, that matters."

"Well then, let us see if we can introduce some marauders to their final moment," Sorak said.

"*That* was not spoken like a druid healer," said Valsavis, raising an eyebrow at him.

"As you said, the ways of Athas can be harsh," Sorak replied. "Even a healer must learn how to adapt." He clapped his hand to his sword.

"Indeed," Valsavis said, getting to his feet. He kicked some dirt onto the fire to put it out. "I estimate they have perhaps three or four hours' start. And they are mounted."

"Then there is no time to waste," said Sorak.

"We shall catch them, never fear," Valsavis said.

"You seem very confident," said Sorak.

"I always catch my quarry," said Valsavis.

THREE

The trail was not difficult to follow. Nine riders, mounted on overburdened kanks, could not move without marking their passage. They seemed to be in no hurry. And why not? thought Sorak. They think I'm dead. They hadn't even paused to check his body. He had been down on the ground, unmoving, with an arrow in his back, and they had Ryana to occupy all their attention. A chill went through Sorak as he considered what they might have done to her.

She would never have gone quietly, and under normal circumstances, the marauders would have had a fight on their hands that would have proved much more than they had bargained for. But Ryana had been utterly exhausted from their long trek across the plain. If she had fallen asleep, they might have taken her easily.

Sorak tried not to think about what they might do to her. She was no ordinary woman. She was not only very beautiful, she was also a villichi priestess. However, it was possible her captors might not have realized that. Ryana did not look like most villichi. Her coloring was different, and though she was tall for a woman, she lacked the exaggerated length of neck and limb that characterized villichi females. Her proportions were closer to the human norm. If Ryana was smart—and she was—she would not reveal herself, but would bide her time while she regained her strength so that she could pick her opportunity. But if they had harmed so much as one hair on her head . . .

For the most part, Sorak and Valsavis rode in silence, save for the occasional exchange regarding signs that the marauders left behind. Sorak's respect for the muscular old warrior was growing rapidly. The mercenary was a superb tracker. Nothing missed his alert gaze. At an age when most warriors would have long since retired, with a woman to take care of them in their declining years, Valsavis was still at the peak of his powers. Sorak wondered what sort of life the man had led, where he had come from, and where he was bound. The tribe wondered about him, too, and in a way that made them feel profoundly uneasy.

"*I do not trust this man, Sorak,*" said the Guardian. "*Be careful.*"

"*Can you not see what is in his mind?*" asked Sorak mentally.

The Guardian did not reply at once. After a moment, she said, "*No, I cannot.*"

Her reply surprised him. "*You cannot probe his thoughts?*"

"*I have tried, but it is of no avail. I simply cannot penetrate his defenses.*"

"*Is he warded against telepaths?*" asked Sorak.

"*I cannot tell,*" the Guardian replied, "*but if he is, the wards are powerful and subtle. There are some individuals who cannot be probed, whose minds are shielded by their own self-contained defenses. Such individuals are strong in spirit, emotionally powerful, and rarely reveal themselves.*"

They do not trust easily, and they are often dangerous to trust. Their essence remains locked away deep within themselves. They are often loners who do not feel the lack of love or warm companionship. They often do not feel much of anything at all."

"This man felt compassion," Sorak said. "He stopped to give aid to a wounded stranger, and he is going with us to Ryana's rescue with no thought of any gain."

"No thought of payment in money, perhaps," the Guardian replied, "but you do not yet know that he does not think of gain."

"You think he wants something from me?"

"Few people act unselfishly," the Guardian said. "Most do not undertake risks without some thought of benefit to themselves. I do not like this Valsavis, and the rest of tribe senses an aura of danger about him."

"I will remain on my guard, then," Sorak said. "But Ryana's safety is foremost in my mind."

"As it is in ours," the Guardian assured. "We all know what she means to you. And most of us have come to care for her, in our own way. But this man has appeared very conveniently, and in a very timely manner. Where did he come from? What was he doing traveling alone in so remote an area?"

"Perhaps, as we were, he was bound for the village of Salt View," said Sorak. "It seems a logical destination. And he chose a roundabout course, as we did, to avoid marauders."

"If that is so, then why does he pursue them with you now, when there is no personal stake in it for him?"

"It is possible that he was earnest in his explanation," Sorak said. "Perhaps he craves adventure. He is a fighter, and obviously, he has been a mercenary. Such men are often different."

"That may be so," the Guardian countered, "but all

my instincts say this man is not what he appears to be."

"If he means to play us false," said Sorak, *"then he will discover that I am much more than I appear to be, as well."*

"Do not allow your confidence to blind you, Sorak," said the Guardian. *"Remember, though we are strong, we are not invulnerable. We took an arrow in the back that could easily have killed us, and not even the Watcher saw it coming."*

"I have not forgotten," Sorak said. *"From now on, I will watch my back more carefully."*

"See that you do not leave Valsavis there," she said.

"I will remember," Sorak said.

The terrain they traversed was difficult, but Sorak was sure they were moving faster than the marauders. He rode behind Valsavis on his kank, watching the trail ahead, noticing that the old mercenary was picking up every detail of the spoor. By late afternoon, they were approaching the pass midway through the mountain range.

"They will doubtless stop to camp soon," said Valsavis.

"In the canyon?" Sorak asked.

"Perhaps," Valsavis replied, "but I would not if I were in their place. I would seek higher ground, the better to avoid surprises."

"You think they suspect we may be on their trail?"

"I doubt it," said Valsavis. "They are traveling at an easy pace. They most likely think they left you dead back there, and they can know nothing about me. Unless we are very clumsy, we will have the advantage of surprise."

"I am very much looking forward to surprising them," said Sorak grimly.

"We shall have to move quickly," said Valsavis.

"They will not hesitate to use your friend as a hostage. Meanwhile, you need to consider what you want to do if that should come to pass."

"They must not be allowed to reach their camp," said Sorak. "Once we make our move, we must commit ourselves. There can be no retreat."

"And what of your companion?"

"I know that she would not wish me to hesitate on her account," said Sorak.

"Suppose they put a knife to her throat when we attack? What then?" Valsavis asked.

"Then I will try to save her if I can," Sorak replied. "But she would not wish me to surrender or withdraw. And they would find that killing her may not prove as easy as they think."

"She sounds like an unusual woman," said Valsavis.

"She is villichi."

"Indeed?" said Valsavis. "I met a villichi priestess once . . . a long, long time ago. And if she was a typical example of their order, then I am surprised your friend allowed herself to be taken without a struggle."

"She was exhausted from our journey," Sorak said, "and no doubt she fell asleep. If she had not been taken by surprise, she would have left bodies littering the ground."

Valsavis did not fail to note the elfling's vehemence. "She is more to you than just a traveling companion, is she not?"

"She is my friend," Sorak replied in a tone that did not invite further questions.

Valsavis chose not to press the issue. He had already learned what he wanted to know. The elfling cared about the priestess. And more than merely as a friend. That was good to know, he thought. It could come in very useful.

They reached the canyon by late afternoon and could tell by the trail that the marauders were not far ahead. They scouted the canyon carefully from the ridge before venturing down the slope. The marauders had descended to the canyon floor, near the entrance where the foothills sloped up to meet the mountains. Sorak thought it ironic that they had taken an extra day in their trek across the plain just to avoid the canyon pass, and now he had doubled back to it.

He cursed himself for leaving Ryana alone. He had not expected to encounter marauders so far from their camp, but he should have realized how tired she was and that it would be impossible for her not to fall asleep. How much trouble would it have been to let her sleep awhile and recover some strength before he allowed the Ranger to go hunting? He blamed himself for this, and if anything happened to Ryana, he did not know how he would be able to go on.

Toward evening, they finally caught up with the marauders. They had made camp on a trail winding through the lower foothills, one they had obviously used many times before. The clearing showed signs of having been used as a campsite before. Sorak saw that it was not a raiding party, but a hunting party. Sorak observed several of the kanks bearing the beasts they had slain. He and Valsavis had smelled the smoke of the marauders' campfire long before they saw them. The marauders were taking no trouble to conceal their presence. This was their territory, and they were confident in the security of numbers.

Valsavis had been exactly right. There were nine of them. They had not even taken the trouble to post guards. They were all grouped together around the campfire, laughing boisterously and cooking their supper. Passing around a wineskin, they seemed well pleased with themselves.

And why shouldn't they be, thought Sorak as he and Valsavis watched the marauders from the shelter of some bushes. They had not only enjoyed a successful hunt, but had stumbled upon an unexpected prize, as well.

Ryana sat nearby, leaning back against a boulder. Her hands were tied behind her, and her arms were bound tightly to her sides by a rope around her chest. Her feet were tied, as well, at the ankles and the knees. She could barely move at all, and the position she was in had to be excruciatingly uncomfortable. Sorak could not tell if she was hurt or not. She was not moving.

"We are going to have to get in closer," he said, softly.

"Not yet," Valsavis said, putting a restraining hand on his chest. "Your priestess is safe, for the moment. The marauders will not harm her. She will fetch a high price at a slave auction, and the bidders do not like damaged goods. Let these carrion eat and drink their fill. A man does not move as quickly when his belly is full."

Sorak nodded in agreement. "Your advice is sound," he said. "They will be more vulnerable after they have bedded down for the night."

"Especially if they continue to drink like that," Valsavis said. "This may be a great deal easier than we had thought. Pity."

"Pity?" Sorak said with surprise.

Valsavis shrugged. "There is no challenge in slitting the throats of sleeping drunks."

"I am not interested in challenge, but in Ryana's safety," Sorak replied.

"Yes, I can see that," said Valsavis. "But I have been curious about something. Villichi priestesses possess psionic powers that their training hones to a fine edge. I wonder, why has she not used them to free herself?"

Sorak shook his head. "I do not know. Perhaps she bides her time, as we do, and waits for the best opportunity."

"She does not look like a villichi," said Valsavis. "I would not have taken her for one. Doubtless, the marauders have not either, else they would have been more careful with her." He paused a moment, then, as if it were no more than a casual question that had just occurred to him, he asked, "What is the nature of her gifts?"

"Mind over matter," Sorak replied. "It is called telekinesis. It is the most common ability with which villichi are born."

Valsavis noted that for future reference. "Then she can use her power to free herself from her bonds," he said. "That will help us when the time comes to make our move. Let us hope that she does not make her move first, and prematurely."

"She is clever," Sorak said. "She will choose her time."

"Why does she travel with you?" asked Valsavis. "In my experience, villichi priestesses do not much care for the company of males, regardless of their race. Nor are they generally in need of their protection."

"Ryana is my friend," said Sorak, as if that explained everything. He suddenly became aware that Valsavis was asking a great many questions, and volunteering little information about himself. "It was fortunate for us you came along when you did. How did it happen that you were traveling in such an isolated area?"

"I was on my way to the village of Salt View," Valsavis said, "as I assume you must have been."

"Why do you assume that?"

Valsavis shrugged. "Where else would you be going? Save for the marauder camp, it is the only settlement for many miles around."

"Most travelers would have taken the canyon pass," said Sorak.

"Where a man traveling alone may easily be ambushed," said Valsavis. "You and I are not so different. We are both able trackers, and we are both wise in the ways of the desert. We evidently had the same idea. Crossing the mountains at the eastern tip of the range would have brought us to the other side directly above Salt View, and taken us farthest from the marauder camp, where we would have been certain to encounter large and well-armed raiding parties. Logic and prudence chose our way for us."

"Then you came across the Ivory Plain?" said Sorak.

"Of course," Valsavis said. "How else can one reach the Mekillots? The Ivory Plain bounds them on all sides."

"So it does," said Sorak. "You came from Nibenay, then?"

"From Gulg, where the caravan route ends."

"What brings you to Salt View?"

Valsavis shrugged again. "Amusement and diversion," he replied. "Gulg does not offer much in the way of night life. The oba is too austere a ruler for such things. I had heard the gaming clubs of Salt View have much to offer in the way of entertainment, and their theater is said to be among the best."

"Somehow, you do not seem to be the sort to be attracted by the theater," Sorak said.

"Well, in truth, I care little for the theater itself," Valsavis admitted, "but wherever one finds theatrical troupes, one also finds actresses and dancing girls."

"Ah," said Sorak, nodding. "I see."

"And what of yourself?" Valsavis asked. "Salt View seems like an unusual destination for a druid and a villichi priestess. Besides, I have heard that they are not very fond of preservers there."

"There would be little purpose in preaching to the converted," Sorak said.

"So then you are on a pilgrimage?"

"Salt View is an isolated village," Sorak said. "If they are not fond of preservers, it is doubtless because they have had little if any contact with them. People are always suspicious and wary of that which they do not understand."

"I seem to recall having heard somewhere that there is at least one preserver already in Salt View," Valsavis said. "An old druid called the Quiet One. Or perhaps it was the Silent One, I do not quite recall."

"The Silent One?" said Sorak, keeping his facial expression carefully neutral. "A curious name."

"Then you have not heard it before?"

Sorak shrugged. "A druid who is silent does not do much to advance the preserver cause. How could he preach the Path and teach others how to follow it?"

"I suppose that's true," Valsavis replied. "I had not really thought of it that way."

"And what of your sympathies?" asked Sorak. "Where do they lie?"

"I do not concern myself overmuch with the struggle between preservers and defilers," said Valsavis. "I am just a soldier. I fail to see where it has anything to do with me."

"It has very much to do with you," said Sorak, "as

it will determine the fate of the world you live in."

"Perhaps," Valsavis said dismissively, "but then there are many things that can determine a man's fate, and most of them are things over which he has little control, if any. Political struggles concern me only insofar as whether one side or the other will employ me. As for the larger questions, there is not much a man like me can do to influence their outcome, so I pay them little heed."

"If everyone believed that way, then there would be no hope for the world," said Sorak. "I have found that there is much one man can do if he truly sets his mind to it."

"Well, in that case, I shall leave the saving of the world to young idealists such as yourself," Valsavis said wryly. "I am much too old and set in my ways to change. I shall help you save your priestess, Sorak. You may consider that my contribution to the larger struggle, if you wish."

"Forgive me," Sorak said. "I meant no offense. I have no right to tell you how to live your life, and I did not mean to sound ungrateful. I owe you much."

"You owe me nothing," said Valsavis. "Each man does what he does for his own reasons."

"*And he has not told you the truth about his,*" the Guardian reminded Sorak.

Sorak chose not to press the issue. All that mattered now was Ryana's safety. They spent the remainder of their wait in silence, watching the marauders bed down for the night. They took their time about it, however. As darkness fell, they remained gathered around their campfire, joking and drinking. Someone pulled out some dice and they played for a while. An argument broke out, and two of the marauders came to blows while the others watched and shouted their encouragement. They didn't seem to care who won, just so that it would be an entertaining fight. Sorak thought it might be a good time to make their move, but Valsavis anticipated him, grasping him by the arm even before he had suggested it and saying, "No, not yet. Wait. Soon."

Sorak's patience was starting to wear thin. He was not sure how much longer he could wait. Eventually, several of the marauders retired to their bedrolls. The others remained awake, talking and drinking for a while, but soon they, too, went to sleep, leaving two of their number standing watch. As the others slept, the two who remained awake stayed by the campfire, rolling dice and talking quietly. After a while, their gaming became more animated.

"I suspect that they have just increased the stakes to something rather more interesting than money," said Valsavis.

For a moment, Sorak did not know what he meant, but then he saw the two marauders casting covetous glances at Ryana. He tensed and clapped his hand to his sword hilt.

"Softly, my friend, softly," said Valsavis.

"Surely, you do not intend for us to simply sit by idly and wait while those two misbegotten—"

"Keep your voice down," said Valsavis. "It carries easily on the night wind. Their lust for your priestess friend works in our favor. Clearly, they do not suspect she is villichi. Consider, if they wish to have their way with her, they will first have to loosen her bonds. And I would be very much surprised if a priestess who can control matter with her mind has not already thought of doing that herself. Remember, she does not know that we are here. Only two of them remain awake now. If she plans escape, now would be the perfect time. I will wager that she makes her move when they do."

A moment later, one of the marauders rolled and turned away, swearing softly in disgust. The other looked extremely pleased. He clapped his comrade on the shoulder, and Sorak's excellent hearing picked up his words.

"Never fear, Tarl. You can have her when I'm finished. You can hold her down for me, and then I shall hold her down for you. But we must be sure to keep her quiet, else we shall wake the others."

They got up and started moving toward Ryana.

"Now," said Valsavis softly.

They started to move in.

The marauders reached Ryana and stood there, looking down at her for a moment. She appeared to be asleep. One of them crouched over her and started to untie her legs. The other kept glancing nervously from Ryana to his sleeping companions. Sorak and Valsavis moved in closer, making not the slightest sound.

The first marauder finished untying her legs and started to unwind the rope. The second one reached down to grasp her by the shoulders, so that he could move her away from the rock she was leaning against and lower her to the ground. However, the moment he took hold of her, Ryana made her move. The knife he wore suddenly leapt free of its scabbard on his belt and plunged itself to the hilt into his throat, directly into the larynx.

The man jerked up and back, making horrible, choking, rasping noises as the blood spurted from between his lips. His hands went up to the knife; he staggered several steps, and fell. His companion glanced up suddenly, not having seen what happened, and for a moment, was completely disoriented. He saw his friend staggering, with a knife sticking in his throat, and thinking that someone had thrown it, he glanced around quickly with alarm and saw Sorak and Valsavis entering the clearing. He was about to cry out a warning to the others, but suddenly felt Ryana's legs scissoring around his throat as his own obsidian knife floated free of its scabbard.

He made a grab for it, and then a struggle ensued as he fought the power of Ryana's mind, trying to keep the knife from plunging into him. Ryana was weakened from her ordeal, however. She could not both maintain the pressure with her legs and fight his efforts against her control of the knife. Her legs' grip loosened, and the marauder managed to cry out.

The others came awake. The ones who had drunk the most were slower to respond, but a couple of them roused themselves at once, and the first thing they saw was Sorak and Valsavis quickly moving toward them. They instantly added their voices to the alarm as they lunged for their weapons.

Valsavis drew two daggers, one with each hand, and threw them with lightning speed. Each found its target, and two marauders fell dead with the blades in their hearts. Another lunged at Sorak with an obsidian sword, but as he brought it down in a vicious stroke, Sorak parried with Galdra, and the marauder's obsidian blade shattered into fragments. Before the astonished man could react, Sorak ran him through. By now, all of the marauders were awake and grabbing for their weapons.

Ryana suddenly released her hold on the marauder she was wrestling with, and he fell to the ground. In that moment, she used her will to force the obsidian knife into his chest. He cried out as it penetrated and twisted. Ryana immediately began struggling free of her bonds, which she had already loosened with her mind while the marauders had been gaming for her.

Two of the marauders went for Valsavis, while the remaining two approached Sorak. Valsavis disposed of his two antagonists with unbelievable speed, executing a circular parry and disarming one man, then, in one motion, pirouetting aside from the second man's lunge and making a sweeping stroke with his sword, cleanly decapitating the marauder. The man he had disarmed turned to run for his weapon, but Valsavis seized him by the hair, jerked him back, and plunged his sword through his back and out his chest. As he shoved the corpse off his blade, he turned to see how Sorak was faring.

One marauder had already fallen, his blade shattered on Sorak's sword. Galdra had made short work of him. The second, having seen what happened to the first two, backed away fearfully, reaching for his dagger. He drew it and hurled it at Sorak. Instinctively, Sorak ducked under and allowed the Guardian to the fore. The knife suddenly stopped in midair, frozen about a foot away from his chest.

The marauder gaped in astonishment, and then his amazement turned to horror as the knife slowly turned end over end and then shot toward him like an angry hornet. With a cry, he leapt aside, barely in time. As the knife passed him, he scrambled to his feet, only to see the blade describe an arc in the air and come back at him once again. Panic took him, and he broke, screaming as he turned to run. The blade plunged into his back before he took three steps, and he fell, sprawling, to the dirt. Valsavis had watched it all with great interest.

As Valsavis went to retrieve his daggers and wipe

them on the bodies of the slain marauders, Sorak ran to Ryana and helped her to her feet. She was weak from having had her circulation cut off by her bonds, but she stood, unsteadily, staring at him with joy and relief.

"Sorak!" she said. "I thought you were dead!"

"Only wounded," he replied. "Forgive me. I never should have left you all alone."

"It was my fault," she said. "You warned me not to fall asleep. . . ." She glanced at Valsavis, who stood by, gazing at them as he sheathed his daggers. "Who is that man?"

Sorak turned toward him. "A friend," he said.

"*Perhaps,*" the Guardian cautioned him internally. "*And then again, perhaps not.*"

"His name is Valsavis," Sorak said aloud. "He found me and tended to my wound. And now I am doubly indebted to him."

"Then I am indebted to him also," said Ryana. "Thank you, Valsavis. How may we repay you?"

Valsavis shrugged. "It was nothing," he said. "Merely an amusing diversion on an otherwise dull and uneventful journey."

Ryana frowned. "Amusing?" she said in a puzzled tone.

"One finds one's amusement where one can," Valsavis replied. "And replenishment of one's supplies, as well. It seems that these marauders have not only provided us with fresh game and a warm fire, but also a string of kanks well laden with supplies. They will not only make the remainder of our journey easier, but will no doubt find ready purchasers in Salt View. All told, I would say that this has been a rather profitable venture."

"I suppose one could look at it that way," said

Ryana, gazing at him strangely.

Valsavis shrugged. "How else should a mercenary look at it?"

"I do not know," Ryana said. "But you fight very well, even for a mercenary."

"I have had some experience."

"No doubt," she said. "You are bound for Salt View, then?"

"Where else is there to go in this forsaken wilderness?" Valsavis replied.

"Since we are bound for the same destination, then it makes sense for us to travel together," Sorak said. "And when we reach Salt View, you will have the liberty of selling the goods of these marauders and keeping all the profits for yourself. It is, after all, the very least that we can do to repay you for your service."

"I appreciate the offer," said Valsavis, "however, keeping at least two of the kanks for yourselves would make your journey easier when you choose to leave Salt View. And Salt View is not the sort of place where one can get by without money. Allow me to propose a somewhat more equitable distribution. With your permission, I will undertake to dispose of the marauders' goods when we reach Salt View. I have some experience in such things, and can negotiate the best price. Then we may distribute the profits equally, in thirds."

"There is no need for that," said Sorak. "Why not half to you and half to us? It will be more than sufficient for our needs."

"Very well, agreed," Valsavis said.

Ryana shook her head. "Killing these men was necessary," she said, "and they deserved it richly, but it still seems wrong for us to profit by their deaths."

"I appreciate the sentiment, but would it seem

right simply to leave all this behind?" Valsavis asked. "That would be rather wasteful, and not very practical."

"I must agree," said Sorak. "And it would not be the first time that I have profited by the deaths of such as these. The world profits from their absence."

"A most unpreserverlike sentiment," Valsavis said with a smile, "but I heartily concur. And now that we have settled that, I suggest we remove these bodies to a suitable distance, so that we are not plagued by flies and carrion beasts. Then I, for one, intend to enjoy some of that wine these departed souls have been so kind as to provide us with. I have worked up a mighty thirst."

Later that night, after they had disposed of the marauders' bodies by tossing them into a nearby ravine, Ryana sat with Sorak by the fire, and Valsavis slept nearby in his bedroll, having emptied an entire skinful of wine. The marauders had brought some food with them among their supplies, some bread as well as a mixture of dried fruits and nuts and seeds that Ryana was able to eat without breaking her druidic vows. She had regained some of her strength, though the ordeal of the journey and her captivity had clearly taken a lot out of her.

"What do you make of him?" she asked Sorak very softly, so that only he could hear. Valsavis appeared to be asleep, but she did not want him to overhear in case he was still awake.

"I am not yet entirely sure," said Sorak. "He seems a most peculiar man, but he did come to my aid, and yours."

"Does the Guardian tell you nothing of him?" asked Ryana with surprise.

"She does not trust him," Sorak replied. "She is

unable to probe his thoughts, and so cautions me to be wary of him."

Ryana frowned. "The Guardian cannot detect anything about him?"

Sorak shook his head. "No, nothing."

"Is he warded?"

"The Guardian does not know," he replied. "She says that if he is protected by a magical ward, then it is both strong and subtle enough to escape detection. But she also says that there are some people who are immune to psionic probes."

"Yes, that is true," Ryana said. "But such people are often very dangerous." She glanced at Valsavis, stretched out on the ground nearby. "And he has already proven that."

"He fought with us, not against us," Sorak reminded her.

"Yes, he did," she said, "but he appeared from out of nowhere, and at a most convenient time. Where did he come from?"

"Gulg, I think he said."

"He said," Ryana repeated. "But how can we know for certain? He may have followed us from Nibenay."

"I suppose it is possible," Sorak admitted. "He is one of the finest trackers I have ever seen. It is conceivable that he could have followed our trail. But if the Shadow King wanted us pursued, why would he not send a well-armed force instead of just one man?"

"Perhaps because he does not intend to capture us," Ryana said. "He could want to have us lead him to the Sage. And what better way for his agent to keep track of us than to take advantage of this opportunity and join us on our journey?"

Sorak pursed his lips, thoughtfully. "All this is merely supposition," he said.

"Perhaps," Ryana replied. "But he is a highly skilled and experienced fighter. The best and the quickest I have ever seen, despite his age. And a fine tracker, as you said. He also carries iron weapons. That makes him no ordinary mercenary. And did you note the ring he wears on his left hand? It looks like gold."

Sorak nodded. "Yes, I saw," he said. "But then it is also possible that he had served some rich aristocrat who gifted him with the weapons and the ring."

"The Guardian has cautioned you about him," said Ryana, "and everything about him raises questions. Yet you seem to want to trust him. Why?"

"I do not wish to think ill of a man merely because he is extraordinary," Sorak replied.

"As you are," said Ryana with sudden insight. "Sorak, we cannot afford to be trusting. We have powerful enemies. Enemies who would stop at nothing to find the Sage and destroy him."

"Valsavis will accompany us to Salt View," said Sorak. "That is not very far from here. If what he told me was the truth, our paths will diverge once we depart Salt View for Bodach."

"Suppose he discovers that is where we are bound and decides to follow us. What then?"

"Then we would have ample reason to suspect his motives."

"Suspect?" Ryana said.

Sorak shrugged. "It would not necessarily be proof that he is an agent of the Shadow King. He is an adventurer who seems to regard danger as a mild amusement. If he learns that we are bound for Bodach, he might be tempted to join us and search for the legendary treasure. And I am not so sure we should refuse him if he makes the offer. A fighter of his skill would be a welcome asset in the city of the undead."

"We will have more than enough to worry about in Bodach without having him around," she said.

"If he hopes to have us lead him to the Sage, then I think we can at least trust him to help us live long enough to find him," Sorak said.

Ryana nodded. "Good point," she said. "But what happens after we leave Bodach?"

Sorak smiled. "Finding the Breastplate of Argentum and leaving Bodach alive will prove challenge enough for now," he said. "There will be time to decide what to do about Valsavis afterward. And now you'd better get some sleep. You'll need your strength. I will keep watch."

She glanced at Valsavis again and shook her head. "If he is an agent of the Shadow King, then he sleeps very comfortably in our presence."

"What would he have to fear?" asked Sorak wryly. "He knows we are preservers and would not kill him while he slept, merely on suspicion."

Ryana grimaced. "Somehow, I doubt that he would hesitate to do that very thing should our roles have been reversed. Or do you disagree?"

"No," Sorak said, nodding in agreement, "I do not think he would have any problem with that at all."

"That knowledge isn't exactly going to help me sleep any easier," she said.

"I will keep a wary eye on him," said Sorak. "And we shall see what he does once we reach Salt View."

"I would not be disappointed if he chose to remain there, despite the dangers we will face in Bodach," Ryana said.

"If he is truly an agent of the Shadow King," said Sorak, "then I would much rather have him with us, where we can watch him, rather than have him on our trail, where we cannot. At least one thing is for certain. If he is in the service of the Shadow King, then he has tracked us all the way from Nibenay, across the Great Ivory Plain. We shall not be able to shake him off our trail."

"Which means that we may have to kill him," said Ryana.

Sorak stared at Valsavis for a long moment as he lay stretched out on his bedroll, with his back to them. "I fear that we shall have no choice, in that event," he said at last. "And from what I've seen, that will be no easy task."

"He would be no match for the Shade," Ryana said.

"I am not so sure," said Sorak. "But even if our suspicions prove correct, we cannot kill a man if he has done nothing to warrant it. That would be cold-blooded murder."

Ryana nodded. "Yes, I know. So what are we going to do?"

Sorak shook his head. "I do not know," he said. "At least, not yet. But I will dwell upon it carefully."

"You think he knows we suspect him?"

"Perhaps," said Sorak. "He may, after all, simply be a wandering mercenary in search of adventure, just as he claims. On the other hand, he knows about the Silent One. He told me as much. He is either innocent of any guile, or else he is enjoying playing a game with us, the way a mountain cat toys with its prey before the kill. The question is, how long will he toy with us before he makes his move?"

Ryana stretched out on her bedroll. "An unpleasant question to ponder as I try to sleep," she said wearily.

"Good night, little sister," Sorak said. "Sleep well."

"Good night, my love," she said softly.

Soon, she was asleep. But Sorak remained awake for a long time, staring at the flames and wondering about their new companion. Eventually, he ducked under and slept while the Watcher came to the fore and looked out through his eyes.

All night long, she sat silently by the fire, alert to everything around her, to the slightest sound and the faintest scent on the night breeze. And not once did her sharp gaze leave Valsavis.

FOUR

The village of Salt View lay remote and isolated at the foot of the southern slope of the Mekillot Mountains. Far to the north, across the Great Ivory Plain, the caravan route from the northern territories ended at the city of Nibenay. To the west, across the mountains and the Great Ivory Plain, the caravan route from Altaruk skirted the westernmost boundary of the salt plain and arced to the northeast, where it ended at the city of Gulg. To the east and south, there was nothing but a desolate wasteland stretching out for miles. Farther south, the salt plain gave way to large, inland silt basins that were dotted by sandy and deserted islands. At the southernmost end of the silt basins, a peninsula extended from the narrow band of land that separated the basins from the Sea of Silt, and at the tip of that peninsula, far removed from civilization, lay the ruins of Bodach, the city of the undead.

No one stopped in Salt View on the way to anywhere, because Salt View was about as out of the way as it was possible to get. Salt View possessed no strategic importance of any kind, so the wars of Athas never touched it. Salt View possessed no natural resources to speak of, so there was no competition for them, unlike the rivalry of Gulg and Nibenay over the agafari forests of the Barrier Mountains. In short, Salt View had nothing whatsoever to recommend it to anyone, except the one commodity that humans and demihumans alike had always gone out of their way for—a wild and rollicking, freewheeling atmosphere of nonstop entertainment and cheap thrills.

The village had been founded by runaway slaves as nothing more than a dirty little settlement of ramshackle huts and adobe buildings, but it had come a long way since then. It was not a large village, but its one main street was packed with theaters and gaming houses, hotels and eating establishments and taverns, bawdy houses and fighting rings, none of which ever closed. Over the years, other buildings had sprung up around the main street, mostly residences for the villagers, but also little shops that sold everything imaginable, from weapons to magic talismans. One could buy a vial of deadly poison or a love philter, or something as innocent and decorative as an earthen pot or sculpture. Almost anything could be had in Salt View—for a price.

The most common way to reach Salt View was from the city of Gulg. There was no established caravan route running across the Great Ivory Plain, but periodically, small parties or caravans were organized by enterprising individuals who, for a fee, would take travelers across the plain and through the Mekillot Pass to Salt View. These small, informal caravans offered no significant temptation to the marauders, since they freighted no significant amount of trade goods, but to avoid being ambushed for the money carried by the travelers, they paid a tribute to the bandits, which was reflected in the fee they charged their patrons.

Another way to reach Salt View was from North
Ledopolus, the dwarven village to the southwest, on
the northern bank of the Estuary of the Forked
Tongue. Small caravans made regular trips to Salt
View from North Ledopolus, following a northeast-
erly course along the southern boundary of the Great
Ivory Plain, where it met the sandy desert south of
the inland silt basins. Circling around the basins,
these small caravans would bypass the marauder
camp by many miles and follow a course parallel to
the Mekillot Range, then straight north across a short
stretch of the Ivory Plain.

The wise traveler paid for a round trip in advance,
for it was not at all uncommon for travelers to arrive
in Salt View with full purses and then be forced to
leave with empty ones. At least, those who had paid
their return passage in advance *could* leave. Those
who could not were stuck with some unenviable
choices. They could either work their way back as
indentured servants to their guides, who took full
advantage of the situation to get their money's worth
from these unfortunates, or else, if the guides were
not in need of servants—and they had no shortage of
applicants—they were forced to remain behind in
Salt View and seek some form of employment. Most
of the good jobs, however, were already held down by
the permanent residents, or else by those who had
become permanent residents over time because they
could not afford to leave and had managed, slowly
and painstakingly, to improve their lots. What
remained were dirty, menial jobs, or dangerous ones,
such as fighting in the rings or hiring on to help keep
order in a tavern. And such jobs often had very high
mortality rates, especially in a freewheeling place like

Salt View.

In this way, the population of Salt View had slowly grown over the years. Some came for the diversions and were, themselves, diverted. Others were slaves who had escaped their bondage and had found a welcome in a town that was predisposed to accept them. Still others were criminals who sought refuge from the authorities, but finding sanctuary in Salt View was a two-edged sword; it was one of the first places where bounty hunters would look. There were also entertainers of one stripe or another, who had tired of the competition for patrons in the cities or sought the freedom of expression in Salt View, where there were no sorcerer-kings or templars to offend.

Frequently, there were more people in Salt View than the hotels and inns could easily accommodate, and so transient camps had sprung up on the outskirts of the village. They provided cheap if not comfortable or sanitary housing, and they were generally full. It was always possible to squeeze another body or two into a tent. Order was kept in the camps, after a fashion, by mercenary guards hired by the campmasters, frequently among those who found themselves with empty purses and no way to get back home. And these jobs, too, often had high mortality rates.

Salt View was a wide-open town, but not a very forgiving one to those who could not pay their way. Xaynon had decreed that beggars would not be tolerated in Salt View, as they were a blight upon the village. When their numbers had grown so great that they had practically choked the streets, Xaynon had instituted the Law of Vagrancy, one of the few laws that was formally enforced in Salt View. If a beggar was caught upon the streets of the town, he was given a choice. Either accept a free waterskin and start walking out into the desert, or else find a job—any job—within twenty-four hours. If he then failed to do so, he would be put to work in the indentured labor force, performing whatever tasks the village council deemed required. This could entail being assigned to the sanitation detail, to keep the village streets clean and attractive, or working on construction details to build and maintain buildings. As a result, Salt View was always clean, and refuse was always picked up. Its buildings, while not large and opulent, were kept in good repair and regularly plastered and whitewashed. The brickyards never had a shortage of laborers, and the streets were all neatly paved with the dark, red, sunbaked bricks that they turned out. There were even gardens along the main street that were regularly tended and watered by workers hauling barrels from the springs on the slopes north of the town.

A vagrant would thus remain constructively employed by the village, provided with a tent to sleep in and two square meals a day, until such time as he managed to secure employment. And he was generously given some time at the end of every work day to look for it. If he was fortunate enough to find a job and save up enough money to buy passage back home, he would usually depart, never to return. And that suited the village council very well. They welcomed tourists, but they could do without those who were financially irresponsible and became a burden on the community.

Slowly, in this manner, the village grew a little larger every year. It was still known as a village, but it was more properly a small town. Someday, Xaynon hoped to see Salt View become a city—perhaps named after himself, which was only fitting consider-

ing his visionary leadership. He did not know if he
would ever live to see that, though chances were
excellent that he would, for the growth increased significantly every year. But he wanted to guide its
course and leave it as his legacy. And, indeed, it
would be quite a legacy for a former slave who had
become a gladiator, fought in the arena, gained his
freedom, and guided the development of a dirty little
mudhole of a village into a handsome and well-
organized oasis of entertainment in the desert.

Sorak, Ryana, and Valsavis passed through the
gates of Salt View and onto the main street, which
ran the entire length of the town. From inside the
gates, it was quite a view, even more attractive than
the town had looked as seen from the slopes of the
foothills.

Before them stretched a wide street paved with
clean red brick and lined by freshly whitewashed
adobe buildings two or three stories in height. Each
building was flat-roofed, and each had a covered
walkway in front of it, supported by columns and
roofed with rounded, overlapping, red ceramic tiles.
Each arched entryway was decorated with a border of
glazed tiles in various patterns and colors, as were the
windows. Most of the buildings on the main street
had covered balconies where people could sit outside,
shaded from the sun. Along the street and in the center of it were raised, square planters constructed of
plastered adobe brick and holding spreading agafari
or pagafa trees, beneath which were planted various
desert succulents, wildflowers, and cacti. All around
these planters, merchants had set up covered booths
with colorful cloth awnings. Here, one could buy
food and drink, clothing, jewelry, and various others
items.

The main street was crowded with pedestrians. It was not very long, and one could walk from one end to the other in thirty minutes or so, but there were various side streets and alleys leading off it on both sides, to where the other buildings of the town were tightly clustered together. Salt View was growing outward, with side streets radiating from the center like spokes from a wheel.

"Why, it's beautiful!" Ryana said as she looked all around. "I had imagined an ordinary little village, much like any other, but this is like an aristocrat's estate!"

"People come to Salt View and leave their money behind," Valsavis said. "Xaynon puts it to good use. Most travelers arriving in Salt View for the first time have the same impression as you. But first impressions can often be deceptive."

"How so?" asked Sorak.

"As the priestess said, during the day, Salt View resembles some wealthy aristocrat's estate, well kept and inviting, but when night falls, its character changes dramatically, as you will soon see for yourselves. I would advise you to keep an eye to your purse, and a hand near your sword."

"That is a good philosophy to follow no matter where one finds himself," said Sorak.

"Then practice it here especially," Valsavis said. "And be wary of temptation. You will find every sort imaginable here. Salt View will welcome you with open arms so long as you have plenty of money to spend. But when you have spent it all, or lost it, you will not find the place so friendly."

"We have no money now," said Sorak.

"That situation will be shortly remedied," Valsavis said. "We will sell these kanks at the nearest stables, and as they are soldiers, they will be sure to fetch a decent price. Then we will dispose of the arms that our marauder friends have so thoughtfully provided us with, as well as their supplies and the game they were taking back to their camp. I imagine that should fill our purses well enough to see us comfortably through the next few days, if we do not spend profligately."

"You said that there are gaming houses here?" said Sorak.

Valsavis snorted. "Every other building on this main street is a tavern or a gaming house," he said. "And you can be sure that every tavern has at least a game or two. But I thought you came here to preach the preserver cause and not to game."

"One does not win many converts by preaching to a multitude these days," said Sorak. "Especially in a place such as this, where appetites are bound to be jaded and people can be easily distracted. I prefer to influence individuals, so that I can speak to them one on one and see their eyes."

"And you hope to do this in a gaming house?" Valsavis said. "Good luck."

"There are more ways than one to win people to your cause," said Sorak. "And sometimes it helps to win some money, first. People always listen attentively to winners."

"Suit yourself," Valsavis said. "I came here for the entertainment, and it should prove very entertaining to watch you at the tables. Just remember this: I do not make loans."

"I promise not to ask," said Sorak. "Besides, I am not entirely inexperienced at gaming. I once worked in a gaming house in Tyr."

"Indeed?" Valsavis said as they led their string of kanks to the stables by the walls around the town. "I once lived in Tyr and served in its city guard. Which house did you work in?"

"The Crystal Spider."

"Hmm," Valsavis said. "I do not know it. It must have been opened after I had left the city. Of course, that was a long time ago."

They sold their kanks, and Valsavis negotiated a good price. The stablekeeper was intimidated by his manner and appearance and did not attempt to cheat them. The haggling was extraordinarily brief. Next, they disposed of the remainder of the marauders' goods in the same fashion and divided up the proceeds. By the time they had completed their transactions, it was late afternoon.

"Well, we had best see about getting lodgings for the night," Valsavis said. "I do not know about you, but I prefer to spend the night in comfort after the long and dusty journey. However, in this town, there are different degrees of comfort. Of course, it all depends on how much you are willing to spend."

"How much do you intend to spend?" asked Sorak.

"Enough to have a soft bed, a warm bath, and a beautiful woman with strong and skillful hands to ease the soreness in my aching, tired, old muscles," said Valsavis.

"Then we shall have the same," said Sorak.

"Except for the beautiful woman with the strong and skillful hands," said Ryana, looking at him archly.

"But I already have one," Sorak replied, raising his eyebrows as he glanced at her.

They walked down the main street until Valsavis found a place that struck his fancy. It was an establishment called the Oasis, and as they entered through the archway, they came into a well-tended garden of raked sand, desert plants, and wildflowers, with a paved path running through it and up to the double, intricately carved front doors. A doorman admitted them, and they came into a spacious tiled lobby with a high ceiling of oiled cactus ribs and heavy wooden beams. A small pool was in the center of the floor, surrounded by plants set in a sand garden designed to create the illusion of a miniature oasis in the desert. An open gallery ran around the lobby on the second story, leading to rooms in either wing of the building, and there were corridors leading off to the left and right from the lobby itself.

They took two rooms. Valsavis took the most expensive one they had, while Sorak and Ryana settled for one that was slightly cheaper. Theirs was on the first floor; Valsavis had his room up on the second. If he was bothered by this separation, which would render it difficult for him to keep an eye on them, he did not show it.

"I, for one, am going to enjoy a long bath and a massage," he said. "And then I will see about my dinner. What plans do you two have?"

"I thought we would rest after our journey," Sorak said.

"And a bath sounds wonderful," Ryana added.

"Would you care to join me for dinner?" asked Valsavis. "And afterward, perhaps, we can tour some of the gaming houses."

"Why not?" said Sorak. "What time should we meet?"

"There is no reason to hurry," said Valsavis. "Take your time. Salt View never closes. Why not meet in the lobby at sundown?"

"Sundown, then," said Sorak.

They went their separate ways to their rooms. Sorak and Ryana's room was floored with red ceramic

tile and had a large, arched window looking out onto
the garden. There were two big, comfortable beds
with ornate headboards carved from agafari wood
and cushioned furniture fashioned by master craftsmen from pagafa wood inlaid with contrasting agafari
pieces. A woven rug was on the floor, and there were
braziers and oil lamps for light. The ceiling was
planked, with wooden beams running across it. It was
a room fit for an aristocrat. The baths were located
on the ground floor, in the rear of the building. After
leaving their cloaks and packs in their room, they
went down to bathe, taking their weapons with them.
Neither Sorak nor Ryana were about to leave them
unattended.

The cavernous baths were heated by fires stoked
beneath the floor, and it felt wonderful to soak in
them as the steam rose from the water. On a desert
planet, where water was so scarce and precious, this
was an unimagined luxury and one of the main reasons why the rooms here were so expensive. It was
the first time since they had left the grotto in the
Stony Barrens that they had a chance to wash the dirt
of their journey away. They did not see Valsavis, but
there were private chambers located at the far end of
the baths, through several small archways, where
those clients who had paid for the best rooms could
enjoy a superior class of service, with beautiful, naked
young attendants to scrub their backs and wash their
hair and perform any other services that they might
have in mind, for certain additional fees, of course.

"Mmm," Ryana sighed with contentment as she lay
back on the tiled step in water up to her neck. "I
could get used to this."

"I much prefer to bathe in the bracing, cold waters
of a desert spring or mountain stream," said Sorak

with a grimace. "It is unnatural to bathe in heated water."

"Perhaps," Ryana said, "but it feels *soooo* good!"

Sorak snorted. "All this water," he said, "delivered here by aqueducts and heated by fires underneath the floor . . . Even in the largest cities, most people have to wash from buckets they must draw from public wells and carry back to their homes." He shook his head. "I feel like some pampered and decadent aristocrat. And I must say, I do not at all care for the feeling."

"Relax and enjoy it, Sorak," said Ryana. "We are paying dearly for the privilege. And after the way those misbegotten, flea-bitten marauders treated me, I enjoy thinking that the sale of their goods and belongings paid for all of this."

"We did not come here to luxuriate in hot baths and quarters fit for a templar," Sorak said. "We came to find the Silent One."

"There will be time enough for that," Ryana said.

"With Valsavis tagging along with us?" Sorak said.

"What difference does it make?" she asked. "He has no reason to prevent us from finding the Silent One. If he is merely a mercenary here to enjoy himself, as he claims, then he should not care what we do, one way or the other. But if he is an agent of the Shadow King, then it would be in his best interest that we find the druid, because, as you have pointed out yourself, he will want to follow us so that we may lead him to the Sage."

"I will be very curious to see what he does when he discovers that we are bound for Bodach," Sorak said.

Ryana shrugged. "If he offers to come with us, then we will have all the more reason to suspect his motives."

"Yes, but it will still not prove them conclusively," Sorak said. "He might simply be tempted by the treasure of the ancient city."

"As you said before," Ryana replied, "there is nothing we can do about Valsavis for the moment. And we may be suspecting him unjustly. We shall simply have to wait and see what he will do."

"Yes, but I do not like not knowing," Sorak said.

"Nor do I," Ryana replied, "but worrying about it will change nothing. Try to relax and enjoy yourself. We will not have such an opportunity again anytime soon, if ever."

She leaned back into the water and sighed deeply with serene contentment. But Sorak kept staring at the archways in the rear, wondering what Valsavis really had on his mind.

* * * * *

Valsavis lay stretched out, naked on his stomach, upon thick towels laid on a wooden table while two beautiful young women worked on his muscular back and legs. They were skilled in their trade, and it felt good to have their strong fingers deeply probing his muscles, easing the soreness and the tension. He knew that he was in superb condition for a man of his age—for a man of any age, for that matter—but he was still not immune to the effects of time. He was no longer as flexible as he once was, and his muscles now developed lumps of tension far more frequently than they had when he was younger.

I am getting too old for this trade, he thought. Too old for chasing across the desert, too old for sleeping on the hard ground, and too tired for playing at intrigue. He had not expected to fall in with the elfling and the priestess as he had. His initial plan had been to follow them, at a distance, and then, to add some spice to the chase, allow them to discover that he was on their trail, so he could watch what they would try to do to shake him. However, a much more interesting opportunity had presented itself, and he had been quick to take advantage of it.

When he had first found the elfling lying on the ground with a crossbow bolt in his back, he had feared that he was dead. There had been no sign of the priestess, and it had not been difficult to guess what must have happened. A quick examination of the ground in the vicinity had immediately confirmed his guess. The two preservers had been ambushed, and the priestess had been taken. It might have ended there and then, but luckily, the elfling wasn't dead. And when he realized that, Valsavis had quickly changed his plans.

Why not join them? Help the elfling trail the ambushers and rescue the priestess. That would place them in his debt and make it easier for them to trust him. He frowned thoughtfully as one of the girls started working on his massive arms while the other one massaged his feet. He may have succeeded in joining them, but he was not so sure that he had won their trust.

That night, when they had slept in the slain marauders' camp, they had remained awake for a long time by the fire, talking softly. He could feel them staring at him. He had strained to hear what they were saying, but their voices were too low. Even so, he had studied people too long and too well not to pick up certain indications in their manner.

He felt reasonably sure now that they suspected him. To his knowledge, he had done nothing to give

himself away, but he was aware of it when the elfling
had tried to probe his thoughts. It had felt, at first,
like someone tugging very slightly at a string within
his mind. He had still been a young man when he discovered that he was immune to psionic probes. Not
even the Shadow King could do it, and he had tried,
unsuccessfully, on a number of occasions. Of course,
when Nibenay had tried it, he had been none too
gentle, and the dragon king was strong. Valsavis well
recalled how the experience had left his head throb-
bing for hours afterward. Perhaps it was one of the
reasons Nibenay employed him. Even a master psionicist could not read his thoughts. Valsavis had no idea
why this was so, but he was grateful for it. He did not
like the idea of anyone being able to know what he
was thinking. That sort of thing gave enemies an
enormous advantage.

Still, he had not expected such an effort from the
elfling, and it had surprised him. The Shadow King
had warned him that the elfling was a master of the
Way, but that had not worried Valsavis overmuch. He
had dealt with such people before. They were often
formidable, but not invulnerable. And besting them
was always a fascinating challenge.

However, when the elfling had first tried to probe
his thoughts, Valsavis had expected that it would feel
no different from the times when others had tried to
do the same. He had been wrong.

The first attempt had felt like the familiar, faint tugging at an imaginary string within his mind. He had
carefully avoided displaying any reaction, because he
did not want the elfling to know he was aware of it. But
the second tug had been much stronger, as strong as
when Nibenay had tried it, and Nibenay was a
sorcerer-king. That had surprised Valsavis, and it had

been difficult to keep that surprise from showing. There had then followed several more attempts, each one stronger than the one preceding it, until it felt almost as if someone were trying to pull his brain out through his skull. And for the first time in his life, Valsavis had not known if he could resist.

He had no idea of the nature of his apparent immunity, and so there was no way he could control it. It was not something he did consciously. It was simply the way he was. But he had never before encountered anything like the elfling's attempts to batter down his natural mental defenses. It had taken a supreme effort of will to avoid displaying a physical reaction. It had *hurt*. He had been in agony for most of the next day. Only now had the pain fully abated.

The elfling's will was incredibly strong, far stronger than he had given him credit for, stronger than he could have imagined. Not even the Shadow King had tried to probe him with such force. It was astonishing. Small wonder Nibenay feared him, and had brought his best assassin out of retirement to deal with him. The probes had failed, however, and Valsavis did not think the elfling would try again. And that was fortunate, for he had no wish to repeat the experience. It had been difficult to get through the day without revealing his discomfort. He had taken staff blows to the head that had hurt less. It was most unsettling.

The repeated probes had also meant that the elfling did not trust him. One did not try to smash his way into another's mind if he felt trust. The question was, exactly what did the elfling suspect? Was he suspicious merely because he had encountered a stranger in the wilderness who had offered aid for no apparent reason? It was certainly not illogical for Sorak to

suspect he might have hidden motives. But did he
suspect exactly what those motives were?

Valsavis had to admit that possibility. The elfling
was no fool. Neither, for that matter, was the priestess. The elfling had noted how good a tracker he was.
Perhaps that had been a mistake, Valsavis thought.
He should have allowed the elfling to track down the
marauders, but he had revealed the extent of his ability when he had told him how many marauders there
had been. That had been foolish. It had been showing off. He should have resisted the temptation, but it
had simply slipped out. Now the elfling knew he was
an experienced tracker, and that meant Sorak realized he would certainly have been capable of tracking
them from Nibenay, across the Ivory Plain.

He may have diverted some suspicion by telling
him he came from Gulg, but then Sorak could easily
assume that he was lying. No, they suspected,
thought Valsavis. He was certain of it. Yet, in a way,
that only made the game more interesting. Especially
because it placed him completely in control of the situation.

They suspect, he thought, but they do not *know*.
And, unlike him, they would not act on mere suspicion. If he suspected that someone he was traveling
with might be an enemy, Valsavis would have no
compunction about slitting his throat while he slept,
just to be on the safe side. Sorak and Ryana, on the
other hand, were avowed preservers, followers of the
Druid Way, and that meant they had scruples. They
subscribed to a morality that he was not encumbered
with, a morality that gave him a marked advantage.

It would be fascinating to play out the game and
watch them watching him, waiting to see if he made
some slip and gave himself away. Only he would

make no such slip. He would watch them squirm in their uncertainty, and he would sleep soundly in their presence, knowing that he could safely turn his back on them because they were preservers and would not attempt to harm him without demonstrable and justifiable cause. Even now, they were probably wondering about him, discussing him, trying to decide what they would do if he chose not to remain in Salt View, but offered to go with them when they moved on to Bodach.

He had already decided what he would do about that. He would stick to them with the tenacity of a spider cactus, following them everywhere they went while they were in Salt View, merely professing concern for their safety as his fellow travelers. They would not protest, because to do so would mean explaining why they did not want him around, and they were still uncertain of him, uncertain enough to think that he might just be exactly what he claimed to be. And when they left for Bodach, he would go along with them, claiming that it would be insanity for them to refuse his help in such a place, and that they owed him at least that much for having come to their aid. He would insist that they owed him a chance at the legendary treasure, a chance at one last, glorious adventure for an old man who would soon retire to live out the twilight of his years in solitude, with nothing but his memories.

They might not believe him, but they would have no way of being certain that he was *not* telling them the truth. They might still refuse him, but he did not think they would. They would certainly need all the help that they could get in the city of the undead, whether he was an agent of the Shadow King or not. And they would doubtless realize that there was no

way they could prevent him from following them . . .
short of killing him, of course, and their preserver
sense of morality would not allow for that.

He smiled. Yes, he thought, this was going to be
enjoyable. It would be a fitting cap to his career.
When this was over, the Shadow King would show
his gratitude and reward him richly. His greatest
enemy would be eliminated, and Nibenay would even
be generous enough to ask him to name his prize
among the templar harem. He might even be generous enough to offer him a further bonus, and if he did
not offer, Valsavis would not hesitate to ask.

He already knew what he would ask for. He would
ask for a spell from the dragon king to bring his youth
back. He already had a great deal of money hidden
away, money he had earned in the service of the
Shadow King, money he never had any reason to
spend because he had lived simply and quietly. It was
money that he had painstakingly set aside for his old
age, when he became infirm and could no longer care
for himself. On the other hand, with his youth back,
he could use that money to buy himself a very different sort of life. He could come back to Salt View and
settle down, perhaps purchase an inn or build a gaming house, which would, over the years, produce
more than ample funds to see him through his second
old age. And meanwhile, he could enjoy himself and
do anything he chose to do. It was a pleasant fantasy,
and one that was by no means out of reach.

The two girls were finishing their rubdown. Their
touches were become lighter and softer, more like
caresses. They were trying to place him in a mood of
receptivity for further services of a more intimate
nature. And, he thought, why not? It had been a long
time since he had sported with a woman, much less

with two at the same time. The elfling and the priestess would keep. They had already agreed to meet with him for dinner and an evening's entertainment on the town. Besides, he had taken care to bribe the clerk to inform him if they tried to go anywhere without him. He sighed deeply and turned over onto his back. The two girls smiled at him and began to stroke his chest, slowly working their way down. And then his hand began to tingle.

"Leave me," he said, at once.

They started to protest, but he insisted. "Leave me, I said. I want a few moments to be alone and rest. I will call you when I need you."

Reassured that they were not being summarily dismissed, the two girls left, and Valsavis brought his hand up before his face. The eye on his ring opened.

"*What progress have you made?*" the Shadow King inquired.

"Much," Valsavis replied. "I have joined the elfling and priestess as a traveling companion. They were set upon by marauders, and I had the opportunity to come to their aid. We are now in Salt View together, and in an hour's time, we shall be sitting down to dinner."

"*And they suspect nothing?*" asked the Shadow King. "*They have no idea who you really are?*"

"They may suspect, but they do not know for sure," Valsavis replied. "And that only makes things more interesting."

"*Have they attempted to contact the Silent One?*" asked Nibenay.

"Not yet," Valsavis said, "but I have no doubt that will try to do so soon. Perhaps even tonight."

"*You must not let them slip away,*" said Nibenay. "*You must not lose them, Valsavis.*"

"I will not lose them, my lord. You may count on that. In fact, I intend to accompany them to Bodach."

"*What? You mean travel* with *them?*"

"Why not? Everyone has heard of Bodach's legendary treasure. Why shouldn't that tempt a mercenary like myself, who has no other immediate prospects?"

"*Take care. You are playing a dangerous game, Valsavis,*" said the Shadow King.

"I find dangerous games amusing, my lord."

"*Do not be insolent with me, Valsavis! I did not send you out to be amused, but to follow the elfling to his master.*"

"I am doing just that, my lord. And you must admit that it is easier by far to follow someone you are traveling with."

"*See that you do not become overconfident, Valsavis. The elfling is far more dangerous than you may realize. He is not someone to be trifled with or underestimated.*"

"I have already discovered that, my lord."

"*Remember the Breastplate of Argentum,*" said the Shadow King. "*It must not be allowed to fall into his hands.*"

"I have not forgotten that, my lord. Rest assured, if he should find it before I do, he shall not keep it long. I have never failed you before, have I?"

"*There is a first time for everything,*" Nibenay replied. "*See to it that this is not* your *first time, Valsavis. If it is, then I promise you that you shall not survive it.*"

The golden eyelid closed.

"Ho, girls!" Valsavis called out.

The two girls came running back into the small, private room, wearing nothing but their smiles.

"I am ready for you now," Valsavis said.

FIVE

The dining room of the Oasis served a sumptuous repast. After a hearty dinner of braised z'tal and wild mountain rice for Valsavis and stir-fried seasoned vegetables with kanna sauce for Sorak and Ryana, they went out to tour the main street of Salt View. The sun had already gone down and the main street was brightly lit by torches and braziers. Shadows danced upon the neatly whitewashed buildings lining both sides of the street, and the number of vendors had grown, many of them setting up new booths in the center of the street, or else simply spreading out their goods on blankets laid upon the ground.

The character of the town had, indeed, changed, as Valsavis had predicted. There were many more people on the street now, drawn out by the cool night air; scantily clad human and half-elf females strolled up and down the street provocatively, boldly propositioning passers-by. Barkers stood by the entrances to the bawdy houses, seeking to entice people inside with lurid descriptions of the thrills that awaited them within. Strolling groups of players wandered up and down the street, stopping every now and then to give a small performance, a brief scene followed by a

pitch to see the rest of the production at the theater
down the street. There were acrobats and jugglers
and musicians who performed for coins tossed into
their hats or on their cloaks, which they had spread
out on the ground before them. Valsavis explained
that the village council did not object to street per-
formers, as they plied a vocation and added color and
atmosphere to the town by their presence, whereas
beggars merely clogged the walkways and the alleys
and provided nothing but pathetic whining.

As they walked along, Sorak slipped slightly to the
background and allowed the Guardian to the fore, so
that she could gently probe the minds of passers-by
and find out if anyone knew anything about the Silent
One. However, no one seemed to be thinking about
the mysterious druid, and the Guardian soon
despaired of looking into jaded, shallow minds that
were filled only with a hungry desperation for sensual
stimulation and depravity.

Before long, they came to a gaming house with a
carved wooden sign outside identifying it as the
Desert Palace. It was a neat, attractive building, but it
hardly looked palatial. It was a structure of sunbaked
and plastered, whitewashed adobe brick, as were all
the buildings on the main street of Salt View, built in
a long, rectangular shape. It had a small, paved
courtyard in front of it, which one entered through an
archway with a gate of cactus ribs and agafari wood.
The small courtyard led to a covered portal that
shaded the front doors.

They went inside and came into a large, cavernous
chamber. The entire first floor of the Desert Palace
was one large open room. There was a partial second
floor, open in the center, making a gallery running
around on all four sides from which people could

look down on the action at the tables below. The rooms up on the second floor were probably private rooms and offices for the management. Sorak noted that there were several elf archers stationed up on the gallery, armed with small, powerful crossbows. They walked slowly back and forth along the gallery, keeping a careful watch on the crowd below. Undoubtedly, they were fine marksmen, but Sorak made a mental note to keep an eye on them in case any trouble erupted on the gaming floor. He did not wish to be near such an outbreak and accidentally wind up with another arrow in his back. Even for a superior bowman, it would be difficult to shoot accurately under such crowded conditions. On the other hand, knowing that probably had a pacifying effect upon the clientele.

Light was provided by candles set in sconces mounted upon large, wooden wheels suspended from the beamed ceiling. There were also oil lamps and braziers adding illumination. A dimly lit gaming house, Sorak recalled from his days at the Crystal Spider, only made it easier for the patrons to attempt cheating. And, along with the archers on the upper gallery, there were also well-armed, burly guards stationed at various points throughout the main hall, making sure none of the customers got out of line.

They wandered through the gaming hall toward the long bar at the rear. This, too, was clever planning, Sorak thought. Many such establishments built their bars along the side, which afforded them more room to squeeze people in, but here, if one was thirsty, one first had to walk past all the tables to get to the bar, and that made it easier for patrons to be drawn into a game, especially since attractive human and half-elf serving wenches constantly moved among the tables with their trays, bringing drinks to those at the tables.

And the tables seemed to offer every conceivable sort of game. There were roulette wheels and dice tables, round tables where patrons played cards against one another—with an attendant to make sure the house took a percentage of each pot—and U-shaped tables where people played against a dealer. There were even several tables where a game was played that Sorak had never seen before. They stopped on their way through to watch one of these curious new games.

The first thing that they noticed was that no cards were used, nor were there any playing pieces. There were no wheels or boards, and the players were in teams. Instead of a dealer, there was a sort of gamemaster who directed the play. Each player assumed a character at the beginning of the game and rolled dice to determine the character's abilities. The gamemaster then presented them with an imaginary scenario through which they had to play, as teams, supporting one another with their respective skills. One character might be a thief, another might be a druid, still another a fighter or an adept, and so forth. And the game that they had stopped to watch just happened to be called, ironically, "The Lost Treasure of Bodach."

The players had already chosen their characters and rolled to determine their strengths and abilities. They had already completed the preliminary rounds, and now the climax of the game was about to begin.

"You have just entered the lost city of Bodach," said the gamemaster to the players. He proceeded to set the stage for them. "It has been a long and dusty journey on a hot, sweltering day, and you are all exhausted. You long to rest, but you cannot, because you know that in another hour's time, the sun will go down, and then the undead will creep forth from their lairs, where they molder throughout the day. Therefore, your first priority must be to find a place to hide, a shelter that is defensible, where you may spend the night in safety—inasmuch as one can ever be safe in the city of the undead, of course. If you succeed in finding such a shelter, then perhaps the undead will not find you. On the other hand," he paused dramatically ". . . perhaps they shall. There is no predicting what may happen in the city of doomed souls. But for now, remember that you have but one hour before the sun goes down. Consider what you choose to do next very carefully."

Sorak and Ryana noticed that they were not the only ones who had stopped to watch and listen. A number of other people were standing around, observing the play with fascination. It was, in a way, much like watching a small, informal theatrical production of an improvisational nature. The players had to improvise, because they had no idea what the gamemaster would present them with next. He was the only one who had a script. And the players had to improvise in character, just like actors on a stage.

"As you stand inside the ancient city gates," the gamemaster continued, "you see a narrow street stretching out before you, leading to a plaza with a large fountain that has been dry for countless generations. All around are ancient buildings, crumbling into ruin. Sand blows across the streets, piling up into small dunes against the ruined building walls. As you approach the plaza, you see that it is littered with bones, the skeletons of adventurers just like yourselves who came to Bodach in search of the lost treasure and found, instead, their deaths. As you

approach still closer, you see that many of these
bones are broken, snapped open so that the marrow
could have been sucked out, and many of these bones
also bear the marks of chewing."

The players glanced at one another uneasily. The
gamemaster had a deep, mellifluous and dramatic
voice, and he knew how to use it to its best effect.
They could all see in their minds' eyes the image that
he was constructing for them, and his presentation
had them all caught up in the illusion he was spinning
out.

"Beyond the ancient bones," he continued, "on the
opposite side of the fountain, three streets radiate
outward from the plaza. One of these streets leads
straight north and affords a clear and unobstructed
view. One leads to the northwest, but it curves off
sharply to the left after thirty or forty yards, so that
you cannot see what lies beyond this curve. And the
third street leads to the northeast. However, there is a
pile of rubble from a collapsed building in the center
of it, almost completely blocking the street. You cannot see what lies beyond this pile of rubble, but you
can see that it does not block the street entirely.
There is a very narrow passage to the right, just
barely wide enough to allow one individual to pass
through at a time. You must now choose which way
you will go."

The players huddled briefly in conference. One of
them was in favor of taking the street in the middle, the
one that led straight north and afforded them an unobstructed field of view. The others did not trust that
choice, and they argued in character. They thought it
was too easy and too tempting. The gamemaster
seemed to want them to go that way. It could be a trap.
Three of the players wanted to take the street to the

left, the one that curved around. The fifth player argued in favor of the street to the right, the one that was almost completely blocked by the pile of rubble. His arguments were persuasive. It was clearly the most ominous choice, he said. They could not see what lay beyond the rubble, and only one of them could squeeze through the narrow opening at a time. There was every reason not to choose that path, the fifth player said, because it not only hid what lay beyond from view, but it also exposed them to the greatest danger, since they could only go through one at a time. The gamemaster had purposely designed the scenario in such a way as to make that the least attractive choice for them, the fifth player insisted, which was precisely why it was the choice that they should make. The fifth player convinced the others, and they all elected to take the street to the right, past the pile of rubble from the partially collapsed building.

"Very well," the gamemaster said, revealing absolutely nothing by his tone. "You proceed and come to the pile of rubble. Only one of you can get around it at a time. Even if you turn sideways, two cannot squeeze through together. So now, you must decide who will go first."

Without hesitation, the other four players agreed that the fifth player, the one who had argued for the choice, should go through first. Suddenly, the fifth player seemed to find this choice much less attractive than he had moments earlier.

"And so it is decided that the thief goes first," the gamemaster said, referring to the character of the fifth player. He gazed directly at the fifth player, once again, revealing nothing in either his manner or his tone. "Your wager, Thief?"

The gambling element entered the game with each

new dramatic situation that the players were presented. Before they rolled the dice to see how the scenario would progress, depending on their characters' strengths and abilities, they would first wager on the outcome. It was a game in which the players were pitted against the house, represented by the gamemaster. And even though the gamemaster knew what was coming up next, he had to work from a prepared script, and he could not control the roll of the dice that determined a character's strengths and abilities, and the outcome of any given confrontation.

The fifth player swallowed nervously. "I will wager three ceramics," he said, cautiously.

The gamemaster raised his eyebrows. "Is that all? You had argued so insistently for your choice, and yet now, suddenly you do not seem very confident."

"Very well, then, curse you! Five ceramics!" said the thief.

The gamemaster smiled faintly. "Make your roll."

The thief rolled, and the gamemaster noted the score. It was a low score, and the fifth player licked his lips nervously. "Very well, who goes next?" the gamemaster said. The other players would all complete their rolls before the gamemaster revealed the outcome, based on their scores and their strength and ability rolls at the beginning of the game.

One at a time, the other players wagered and then rolled. Each time, the gamemaster noted down the score to balance off against the strengths and abilities rolled earlier. When they had all finished, the gamemaster consulted the scores that he had written down, taking his time about it to allow the tension to build among the players, and many of the onlookers, as well.

"You have walked into a trap," he said at last.

The thief swore in disgust.

"The undead are often stupid," the gamemaster continued, "but unfortunately, some of them can be quite clever. They had dug a pit in the space where you passed through, and then covered it with a woven mat of reeds that would support a thin layer of dirt, but not a person's weight. At the bottom of that pit, they had placed long, sharpened wooden stakes. The thief went first, and he scored low, so he fell through and was impaled. The undead will feast upon his corpse tonight. Player Number Five has died, and the game is now over for him, unless he wishes to pay a new character fee, roll to determine strength and abilities, and then continue."

"*Bah!*" said the fifth player, pushing his chair back from the table. "I have had enough of this! You tricked us into that trap!"

"The choice was yours," the gamemaster pointed out, "and you had even argued for it. You should have listened instead to your fellow players. Better luck next time."

"Next time I will find a better game!" the fifth player said, then left the table angrily.

The gamemaster was unperturbed at this display, and continued smoothly. "The dwarf fighter went next," he said. "However, his roll was high, as are his strength and ability scores, and therefore, he managed to avoid the pit by leaping over it as the thief fell through. Player Number Four, you have passed through successfully and won your wager. You are now richer to the tune of ten ceramics. My congratulations."

Player Number Four collected his winnings with a pleased expression on his face.

"Player Number Three, the merchant," the gamemaster continued, "rolled only a four, and unfortunately, it was not enough to compensate for her low dexterity score at the beginning of the game. She was, therefore, unable to avoid the pit, and so also fell inside and was impaled. Player Number Three has died and lost her wager, and now has the option of paying a new character fee, rolling for strength and ability, and continuing in the game, or else leaving the table."

Player Number Three chose to leave the table, sighing and shaking her head sadly at the outcome.

"Player Number Two, the cleric," said the gamemaster. "You rolled high, and your skill rolls were also high, so you also managed to avoid the pit by leaping over it. You have survived and won your wager. Congratulations."

Player One, the templar, had also passed through successfully, won her wager, and would continue in the game. That completed the round of the diverging streets scenario.

"There is now room at the table for two more players," the gamemaster announced to those who had gathered around to watch. "Would anyone care to try their luck on the quest for 'The Lost Treasure of Bodach?'"

"An interesting game," Valsavis said. "I have never played this one before. I think I will try my luck and see what happens."

The gamemaster waved him to a chair.

"I will play, as well," said Sorak, taking the other empty chair. Ryana stood behind him and watched.

Before the game proceeded, Sorak and Valsavis chose their characters and rolled the dice for their strength and ability scores. Valsavis, not surprisingly, chose to be a fighter, and his character was a mercenary. Sorak followed his example of playing close to home and chose to be a druid. Valsavis rolled high on strength and only average on ability. Sorak rolled high on ability and average on strength.

"Very well," the gamemaster said, when they were done. "Let us now proceed. You are all past the pit, though Players One, Two, and Four have accumulated more experience points, which will count toward their winnings if they successfully complete the quest. Player Number Three, the mercenary, and Player Number Five, the druid, have no experience points as yet. We shall continue.

"The street before you is one that twists and turns in serpentine fashion through the ancient, ruined buildings. Perhaps the treasure may be found in one of them, perhaps not. But daylight is quickly running out, and the shadows are lengthening. You must find a place of refuge, for before long, the streets of Bodach will be crowded with undead, searching to satisfy their lust for living flesh. As you gaze at your surroundings, you see that none of the buildings in your immediate vicinity look especially secure.

"However, farther down the street, around a bend, you see an old stone tavern. The walls look thick, and the door, which is still in place, appears stout. The windows are all heavily barred. The structure appears to offer a safe haven for the night. So, now you must decide. Do you proceed toward it?"

The players all quickly agreed that they would.

"Very well," the gamemaster continued. "You have reached the stone tavern, but as you stand upon its threshold, you can now see farther down the twisting street, and at another bend, you see a walled enclosure that surrounds what was once the home of an aristocrat. The walls are high and thick, and the gate is made of iron, once common in the ancient world, now rare. Beyond this gate, visible through its thick and heavy bars, you see a courtyard, and past this courtyard, you see the house itself. It is set back from the street, and has three stories, surmounted by a tower at each wing. The house is built of stone, and appears to be more or less intact. Its front door is thick agafari wood, banded with iron. This house seems to present a safe haven, as well. Do you choose to go inside the stone tavern, with the barred windows and the stout front door, or do you proceed to the towered house of the aristocrat, surrounded by the thickly walled enclosure? Only one will afford safe shelter for the night, but which? You must decide."

The players discussed their options.

"I say we choose the aristocrat's house, with the iron gate and the walled enclosure," said the dwarf fighter. "Clearly, it is the more secure."

"I disagree," said the templar. "The walled house clearly appears to be more secure, but that is an obvious temptation. The stone tavern seems secure, as well."

"Yes, but remember what happened to the thief," the cleric pointedly reminded them. "He attempted to second guess the gamemaster and died for it. We must not proceed in such a manner. I say we must deal with the city of Bodach on its own terms, and not with what we think the gamemaster may have in store."

"What do *you* think, druid?" asked Valsavis, turning to Sorak with an amused smile.

Sorak slipped back and allowed the Guardian to come forth and gently probe the mind of the gamemaster. He was, indeed, very clever. The first encounter had been purposely designed to tempt the players with an apparently easy choice, so that they would think the more difficult choice was the right one. But the gamemaster had anticipated that in his script, and had outwitted them. In fact, the only safe choice would have been the easy one.

This time, the choice was between a house that seemed more secure on the surface, and a tavern that also appeared secure, but not as secure as the walled house. It seemed to be merely a question of degree. Recalling what had happened in the last encounter, the players would now suspect that the gamemaster was tempting them with the walled house in favor of the tavern, but the choice that was apparently more dangerous the last time had been the wrong choice, so now the stone tavern seemed more tempting. However, the gamemaster had fooled them once before, and would obviously now try to fool them again, so they would pick the walled house, after all. And it would not be the right choice.

"I think I prefer the stone tavern," Sorak said after pretending to consider his choice for a moment.

"No, not I!" the dwarf fighter replied. "I do not believe that is the proper choice at all. It is the walled house for me."

"I cast my vote for the walled house, as well," the templar said, nodding agreement with the dwarf fighter.

"And I, also," said the cleric firmly.

"I favor the tavern," said Valsavis.

"Three against two," the dwarf fighter said, shaking his head. "You are outvoted."

"Is there anything in the rules that says we must all make the same choice together every time?" Sorak asked, breaking character for a moment to ask for clarification.

The gamemaster raised his eyebrows. "No," he

replied, "there is not, unless I have specified it in setting forth the situation."

"I will choose the tavern then," said Sorak.

"And I will go there with him," said Valsavis.

"And the rest of you?" the gamemaster asked, again revealing nothing by his tone.

"It is their funeral," said the dwarf fighter. "I still choose the walled house."

The others all agreed and made the same choice.

"Interesting," said the gamemaster with a faint smile, still giving away nothing. "Very well, then. The dwarf fighter, the templar, and the cleric proceed to the walled house, while the druid and the mercenary part company with them to go inside the tavern. The first three reach the walled house, open the heavy iron gate, which takes an effort, as the hinges are very old, and they enter the courtyard, carefully closing and fastening the gate behind them. There does not appear to be anything of any interest or significance in the courtyard, so they proceed to the front door." He paused. "What happens now?" he asked.

"Detect magic," said the cleric quickly.

"You detect none," said the gamemaster flatly.

"I examine the door carefully to see if it contains any nonmagical traps," the cleric said, then quickly added, "I had learned to do so from watching the thief before."

"You find none," said the gamemaster.

"I *find* none, or there *are* none?" asked the cleric.

"You find none, and there are none," said the gamemaster.

"Very well, we go inside," the cleric said, satisfied.

"The templar, the cleric and the dwarf fighter open the door and go inside," the gamemaster continued, "closing it behind them and throwing the heavy bolt.

It takes an effort to move the old bolt, but after a few moments, they manage to force it through. They are now in the dark central hall of the house. All around is dust and sand and cobwebs. It is very difficult to see." The gamemaster paused again and raised his eyebrows in a questioning manner.

"I light a torch I have brought with me," said the templar.

"Very well," the gamemaster said. "The torch is lit. Before you is a wide and winding staircase that leads to the upper floors and the towers at the east and west wings of the house."

He paused again and looked at them expectantly.

"I think we should go up to one of the towers," said the templar. "It would afford us a better view of the outside, and we would be in a more defensible position."

"But which tower?" asked the cleric. "The one at the east wing? Or the west?"

"Perhaps it doesn't make a difference," said the dwarf fighter.

"Perhaps it does," the cleric replied.

"It is not yet sundown," said the templar, "so we are still safe from the undead. And we have fastened the iron gate and bolted the heavy wooden door. If, by some chance, there are any undead within the house, they will not be about yet. We still have some time to search. We could split up and check both towers to see which would be the more secure. And I have brought more torches with me," she added quickly.

The gamemaster nodded, indicating that was accepted.

"Very well then, I shall elect to check the east tower," said the dwarf fighter.

"You are stronger and more able than I," the cleric said. "I will go with you."

"And I will examine the west tower," said the templar, "after giving you two a torch to take with you."

"Very well," the gamemaster said. "You have split up. You take the winding stairs and ascend to the upper floors. The templar takes the corridor leading to the tower in the west wing, while the cleric and the dwarf fighter take the opposite corridor, leading to the tower on the other side. Simultaneously, you arrive at the tower entrances, which have heavy wooden doors."

The gamemaster paused.

"We listen at the doors very carefully," the templar said.

"You hear nothing," said the gamemaster.

"We check for hidden traps again, as we saw the thief do," said the cleric.

"You find none," said the gamemaster.

They tried to think of various things that they could do to determine if there was anything dangerous on the other side of the doors, but the gamemaster replied the same way each time. Finally, the doors were opened, and they went through. The gamemaster told them that they encountered winding stairs leading up to the tower rooms. They exercised all possible caution going up them, checking for traps, stairs that might collapse underneath them, every possible trick they thought the gamemaster might throw at them, but meanwhile, Sorak realized that they were using up whatever daylight still remained to them. And he knew that when they reached the rooms at the tops of the towers, the sun would have gone down.

There were, of course, undead in the towers. The

players fled from them, but the entire house was full of undead, who had been lying in the other rooms, waiting for the night. The cleric protested that no magic had been detected, and the undead were animated by magic. True, the gamemaster replied, unperturbed, but the cleric had only cast a detect magic spell on the front door. Besides, the magic that animated the undead did not come into play until after sundown, and the cleric had not bothered to detect magic again after the first time.

With each encounter, dice were rolled, scores were checked, and one by one, the players died. Finally, only the templar remained, and she made it all the way to the front door, only to discover that the bolt they had managed to force through with so much difficulty would not open for her. And the undead were closing in by the dozens. She rolled to see if she would be able to open the bolt before they reached her. She rolled low, and her character died.

Exasperated, the player who had assumed the character of a templar glanced at Sorak and Valsavis, pointed at them, then turned to the gamemaster. "What about them?" she demanded. "You haven't said what happens to them!"

The gamemaster merely shrugged. "Very well. They entered the tavern, locked the heavy wooden door from the inside, and spent an uneventful night listening to the undead howling in the streets. Eventually, they fell asleep and when they woke up, it was morning."

"That's *it?*" the templar said with disbelief.

"They chose wisely," was all the gamemaster said in reply.

"Gith's blood!" the templar swore in frustration. "This is a stupid game!"

She threw down her dice and left the table.

"We seem to have an empty chair," the gamemaster announced, calmly, glancing at the onlookers.

"I will join the game," Ryana said as she sat down.

The other two players elected to remain. They paid ten ceramics apiece for the privilege of creating new characters and remaining in the game, though they lost not only their previous wagers, but all of their experience points as well, since their characters had died. As new characters, they were now starting out afresh, as was Ryana.

The dwarf fighter unimaginatively chose to remain a dwarf fighter. He was now simply a different dwarf fighter, and he had to roll to determine the strengths and abilities of his new character. He came off rather worse than he had the first time, which did not please him at all, and he continued to play in a surly mood.

The cleric decided to become a thief this time. She rolled, and her new character turned out to have better strengths and abilities than her last one. She seemed happier about this, even though she had lost heavily with her wagers as a cleric.

"And what character class will you choose?" the gamemaster asked Ryana.

"I will be a priestess," said Ryana.

"You mean a templar," said the gamemaster.

"No, I mean a priestess," she replied firmly. "I could never be a defiler, not even in a harmless game."

"Ah," said the gamemaster, nodding. "I see. Well, I suppose that is permissible. But you shall not have any strengths and abilities beyond those listed in the cleric class."

"That is acceptable to me," Ryana said. She rolled. She came out with the highest scores of all. The game continued.

This time, the dwarf fighter and the new thief paid closer attention to what Sorak and Valsavis chose to do. The gamemaster continued to spin out the adventure for them. As they moved through the city, searching for the fabled lost treasure, they encountered one trap after another. They encountered a nest of deadly crystal spiders. They were faced with banshees, who could go abroad during the day. They had to fight rival treasure seekers and fire drakes and elementals. With each encounter, however, the Guardian probed the gamemaster's mind and determined what awaited them, and each time Sorak made the wisest choice. And on those occasions when no safe choice was available, the Guardian gave the dice a small assist when Sorak rolled, and he emerged from the encounters unscathed and successful in his wagers every time.

Valsavis followed his lead, wagering heavily, while Sorak wagered more conservatively. Ryana, too, followed his lead, and did not wager a great deal, but her telekinetic skills enabled her to control the dice every time she rolled, as she had when she had scored so high in her character's strength and ability.

The other two players died before very long. Others took their places at the table. Eventually, their characters died as well. Some stayed and created new characters, others left to play at other games, but Sorak, Valsavis, and Ryana continued to score well and win their wagers, accumulating more experience points with each encounter. Eventually, they found the legendary "Lost Treasure of Bodach," but near the end of the game, Sorak realized that the gamemaster had become suspicious of them, and so when there were only three encounters remaining, he "died."

Ryana followed his lead and died in the next encounter. Valsavis lasted through to the end, despite not having Sorak's example to follow. Since he had been wagering heavily throughout the game, he walked away from the table with a small fortune. Sorak and Ryana had their winnings, too, which were not affected much by their loss near the end, though they lost on the bonus that their experience points would have awarded them. The gamemaster announced the beginning of another adventure quest as they left the table and headed toward the bar.

"Well, that was certainly a rather interesting sort of game," Valsavis said.

"You did very well," Ryana said.

"I would have preferred it if it were the real thing and not simply an imaginary game," Valsavis said nonchalantly. "That would have been much more stimulating, I think."

Sorak gave him a sidelong glance, but did not rise to the bait. As they approached the bar, they suddenly became aware that a number of the burly guards had fallen in behind them.

"Your pardon, gentlemen and lady," one of them said, "but the manager would deem it an honor if you were to join him for a drink."

"Certainly," said Valsavis. "Bring him over."

"He invites you to join him in his private chambers," said the guard.

"And what if I said that I prefer to have my drink here, at the bar?" Valsavis asked.

"Then I would assure you that you would find the manager's private stock of superior quality," the guard replied.

"Fine," replied Valsavis, "send some of it over."

"The manager has impressed upon me the sincerity of his request," the guard said, "and therefore, I sincerely urge you to accept his gracious invitation."

"And what if we refuse?" Valsavis said.

The guard hesitated slightly. "Sir," he said in an even tone, "I perceive that you are an able fighting man. Doubtless, you have a wealth of experience in your chosen trade. My salary here is not so great that it makes me relish the prospect of going up against a warrior who, in all probability, is at the very least my equal, and quite possibly my superior in skill. I am also not desirous of seeing other patrons injured inadvertently if such an unpleasantness should come to pass. I ask you, therefore, once again, with utmost humility and respect, to accompany me to the manager's private chambers, and to note that there are, at this very moment, half a dozen crossbows aimed in your direction, held by the finest elven archers that money can buy. And I can assure you, with no fear of being proven wrong, that each of them can hit a kanna seed at thirty paces with six arrows out of six."

Valsavis raised his eyebrow. "What, only thirty paces?"

"We will go with you," Sorak said, taking Valsavis gently by the arm. "Won't we, Valsavis?"

The mercenary glanced at Sorak's hand upon his arm, then looked up at Sorak's face. Sorak met his gaze unflinchingly.

"As you wish," Valsavis said. He gave a slight bow to the guard. "We have decided to accept your employer's gracious invitation."

The guard returned the bow without a hint of irony. "My profoundest thanks, good sir. If you would be so kind as to follow me, please?"

The guards led their charges to the stairway leading

up to the gallery. The crossbows of the archers never wavered from them for an instant. Most of the other patrons were so intent upon their games that they never even noticed, but a few did, and anxiously followed them with their gazes, hoping to see something dramatic. However, they were doomed to disappointment.

The guards ushered them into the manager's private chamber at the rear of the gallery. The room was brightly lit with oil lamps, and the whitewashed walls were hung with expensive-looking paintings of desert landscapes and village street scenes. There were several plants in large, ceramic containers set about the office, and the oiled, wood-planked floor was covered with an exquisite Drajian rug in muted tones of red and blue and gold. Three handsome, carved agafari chairs were placed in front of the manager's large and ornate desk, on which there was a glazed ceramic tray holding a cut-glass decanter of wine and three goblets.

The manager of the Desert Palace sat behind his desk, but stood as they came in. He appeared to be in his late middle years, with dark hair liberally streaked with gray, which he wore down to his shoulders. He was clean-shaven, and his features were soft and delicate-looking. He wore a simple black cloth tunic and matching breeches, with no weapons or ornamentation.

"Come in," he said, in a quiet, pleasant voice. "Please, sit down. Allow me to offer you some wine."

"If you do not mind, I would prefer water," Sorak said.

The manager raised his eyebrows slightly. "Some water for our guest," he told a beautiful young serving girl.

"I will accept the wine," Valsavis said.

"And you, my lady?" asked the manager.

"I would like some water, too," Ryana said.

The serving girl brought a pitcher of cold water and poured for them, then poured a goblet of wine for Valsavis. She served them, and then quickly left the room. The guards remained behind them, standing as impassively as statues.

"You seem to have done quite well in your gaming tonight," the manager said.

Valsavis merely shrugged.

"I fear that we lost near the end," said Sorak.

"Yes," the manager replied. "But only because you chose to lose on purpose. We *have* had psionicists in here before, you know. Admittedly, most were not as gifted as you are."

"I am no psionicist," Valsavis said, frowning.

"No," said the manager, "I do not think you are, good sir. But your friend, here, is. And so, I will wager, is the lady. You *are* villichi, are you not?" he asked Ryana.

She was surprised. "Most people cannot tell," she said.

"Yes," said the manager, nodding, "you do not have the features one normally associates with the sisterhood, but you are unusually tall for a human female, and your physical attributes are . . . well, rather remarkable. Clearly, you have had a lifetime of intense training. And your mastery of mind over matter is most impressive. My gamemaster was not convinced that you were cheating until five encounters from the conclusion of the game. I must admit that I am rather surprised to find a priestess at the gaming tables, and in such . . . irregular circumstances . . . but then that is purely your concern." He glanced at Sorak. "And as for you, sir, I must confess to unabashed and open admiration. Your skills are astonishingly subtle."

"What gave me away?" asked Sorak.

"The game itself, my friend," the manager replied. "We are experienced gamers here in Salt View. We pride ourselves on being the acknowledged masters of our trade. Our games are most carefully designed. No one has ever survived to complete an entire quest adventure. You, sir," he added, with a glance at Valsavis, "have the distinction of being the very first to have done so. And you managed it by following your friend's lead and having some good luck at the end. Only a psionicist could have successfully survived as many encounters as your companion did."

"So?" said Valsavis.

"So it was cheating," said the manager.

"And I suppose you want your money back," Valsavis said.

"I wouldn't dream of asking for it," said the manager. "You have the look of a man who would not surrender it without a fight. I prefer to avoid violence, myself. I am not a strong man, as you can plainly see, and my guards are more accustomed to dealing with the occasional inebriated trader or disenchanted aristocrat than a seasoned warrior such as yourself. I merely wanted to congratulate you on your winnings—however ill-gotten they may have been—and to inform you that you are welcome to partake of any recreations our fine establishment has to offer for the remainder of the night, completely free of charge. On the sole condition that you avoid the gaming tables.

"My staff has been advised that they are closed to you. Of course, I would not object if you chose to leave and go elsewhere, but you will find that within the hour, every gaming house in Salt View will be alerted to your presence. We have, of course, many interesting diversions here, and you will be free to take advantage of them. You may find our fighting rings of interest, or perhaps our theater, which is superlative. But in any event, I extend to you the hospitality of the Desert Palace for the remainder of the night, and pray that you return our courtesy with courtesy in equal measure."

"I have no interest in keeping the money I have won unfairly," Sorak said. "And I can speak for the lady, as well. Valsavis speaks for himself, though we would hope that he follows our example. For our part, we would be pleased to return all the winnings."

"In that case, I suppose you may as well have mine, too," said Valsavis dryly, throwing the heavy purse containing his winnings on the manager's desk.

The manager frowned slightly. "I must admit, I am puzzled at your willingness to return the money. May I ask why?"

"I was hoping to see how you would try to take it from me," said Valsavis.

"Somehow, that does not surprise me," said the manager. Then he glanced at Sorak and raised his eyebrows.

"I merely found the game itself of interest," Sorak said. "I had never seen such an unusual game before. I worked for a time in a well-known gaming house. My duties were to expose cheats and cardsharps, and I was merely curious to see how you did so here."

The manager raised his eyebrows. "Had you but asked, my friend, and told me of your credentials and experience, I would have been only too glad to show you. And if you were looking for employment, there would have easier ways of making an impression. Tell me, where did you work before?"

"In Tyr, in a gaming house known as the Crystal

Spider."

"I am familiar with it," said the manager, nodding. "May I ask your name?"

"It is Sorak."

"Indeed?" the manager said, with some surprise. "You are the one they call the Nomad?"

Now it was Sorak's turn to be surprised. "How is it that you know of me?"

"Word travels fast in certain circles," the manager replied. "And I make it my business to find out about skillful individuals in my profession. You made quite a lasting impression in Tyr, it seems." He glanced at Sorak's sword. "I have heard about your sword, as well. A unique weapon in more ways than one, I'm told. If you seek employment, I would be privileged to make you an offer. And I am sure that positions could be found for your companions, as well."

"Once again, I cannot speak for Valsavis," Sorak said, "but although I thank you for your generosity, it is not employment that I seek, but merely information."

"If I am unable to provide it," said the manager, "I shall endeavor to find someone who can. What is it you wish to know?"

"I would like to know where I can find a druid known as the Silent One," said Sorak, slipping back to allow the Guardian to probe the manager's mind. However, it turned out to be entirely unnecessary.

"Is that all?" the manager asked. "Well, nothing could be simpler. You will find the Silent One in the Avenue of Dreams, on the south side of Main Street. Look for an apothecary shop known as the Gentle Path. The owner of the shop is named Kallis. Tell him that I sent you. The Silent One has quarters just above his shop."

"You have my thanks," said Sorak, surprised that the information had come so easily.

"Your gratitude may yet be premature," the manager replied. "The Silent One does not welcome visitors, and in all probability will refuse to see you. Are you quite certain I could not tempt you with an offer of employment? I am certain you would find the terms most generous."

"Another time, perhaps," said Sorak.

The manager pursed his lips thoughtfully. "I can easily guess the reason why you seek the Silent One," he said. "You would not be the first, you know. I think that I may also safely predict that you will receive no assistance from the Silent One. However, if you are determined to pursue your course, and choose to press on regardless, then I fear that there may never be 'another time' for you."

"I *am* determined to pursue my course," said Sorak.

"Pity," said the manager. "You seem much too young to die so mean a death. But if you are determined to pursue oblivion, then so be it. The choice is yours to make. The guards will show you out. I must see to the entertainment of the living. There is little reason to be concerned about the dead."

SIX

The Avenue of Dreams was a narrow, twisting street, little more than an alleyway that wound its way south from Main Street. Unlike the neatly white-washed buildings at the center of Salt View, the buildings here were plastered with a light earth-toned coating, and none were taller than two stories. They were well maintained, though they showed their age. The windows all had wooden shutters to protect against the heat, and there were no covered walkways, though most of the buildings had covered entrance portals.

The street was dark here, illuminated only by the moonlight and some oil lamps by the doorways. Here, too, the street was paved with dark red bricks, but it was old paving, and many of the bricks had settled or risen slightly, giving the street an uneven, gently undulating surface.

They were approaching what must once have been the center of the old village, before it grew into the small, desert gaming and entertainment mecca it had now become. Sorak was reminded slightly of the warrens in Tyr, except that here there were no wooden shacks in danger of collapse at any moment, and no refuse littered the streets. The buildings were constructed of old sunbaked adobe brick, with all the corners gently rounded, and there were no beggars crouched against the building walls, holding out their grimy hands in supplication. There were also no prostitutes in this part of the village, which seemed unusual considering the number of them they had seen on Main Street, until Sorak realized that the Avenue of Dreams offered a different kind of temptation altogether.

"What is that strange, sickly-sweet odor?" asked Ryana, sniffing the air.

"Bellaweed," replied Valsavis with a grimace.

Ryana glanced at him with surprise. "But I have seen bellaweed before," she said. "It is a small, spreading desert vine with coarse, dark-green leaves and large, bell-shaped white blossoms. When dried, they have some healing properties, and yet they smell nothing like this."

"The blossoms themselves do not," Valsavis agreed. "But the plant has other uses of which the villichi sisterhood is doubtless well aware. However, you obviously had not been taught that yet."

"What sort of uses?" she asked, curious. She had thought that, by now, she had learned all of the medicinal properties and other uses of most plants that grew on Athas.

"When dried and finely chopped, the coarse leaves of the bellaweed plant are mixed with the seeds the plant produces, which are pulverized into a powder," Valsavis explained. "The mixture is then soaked in wine and stored in wooden casks. Pagafa wood is generally used, as it imparts a special flavor to the blend. It is allowed to marry for a period, and when the process is complete, the final product is a fragrant smoking mixture. It is packed in small amounts into clay pipes, and after it has been set alight, the smoke is drawn deeply into the lungs and held there for as long as possible before it is expelled. After a few such puffs, the smoker begins to experience a pleasant sense of euphoria. And after a while, one begins to have visions."

"So it is a hallucinatory plant?" Sorak asked.

"A particularly dangerous one," replied Valsavis, "because its effects are so deceptive."

"How so?" asked Ryana as they walked down the twisting street, the heavy scent wafting out of building doorways and windows.

"The euphoria you feel at first is extremely pleasant and soothing," said Valsavis. "Your vision blurs slightly and everything takes on a sort of softness, as if you were staring at the world through a fine, sheer piece of gauzy fabric. You then experience a pleasant warmth that slowly suffuses the entire body and produces a comfortable lassitude. Most people feel a slight dizziness at first, but this sensation quickly passes. You become very relaxed, and feel detached from your surroundings, and you think that never before have you experienced such a quiet and peaceful feeling of contentment."

"That does not sound particularly dangerous," said Sorak.

"It is much more dangerous than you think," Valsavis said, "precisely because it seems so harmless and so pleasant. If you smoke only one pipeful and stop there, never to touch the noxious stuff again, you will probably escape serious harm, but that is not so easily accomplished. All it really takes is just one pipeful—not even that, merely a deep puff or two is usually sufficient—and a strong craving for more is produced, a craving that is extremely difficult to resist. A second pipeful will only increase the level of pleasure and start to produce the visions. At first, they will be only mild, visual hallucinations. If you are looking at someone seated across from you, for instance, they might suddenly appear to be floating a few feet above the floor, and their features may appear to change. The effect varies with the individual. You might see your mother or your father, or the person may take on the aspect of a spouse or lover, someone who has always been foremost in your mind. You will see swirling colors in the air, and the dust motes will appear to dance and sparkle brilliantly. And the more you smoke, the more vivid these visions will become. After a third pipeful, unless your will is very strong, you will usually become completely disconnected from your immediate surroundings."

"How so?" asked Sorak. "You mean, you fall into a trance?"

"In a manner of speaking," said Valsavis. "You will remain awake, but you will enter a dreamscape peopled by the creations of your own mind, which has been greatly stimulated by the pernicious smoke. You will see fantastic things that defy reality. You may find, in this dreamscape, that you are capable of flight, and spend your time soaring like a razorwing through a world of indescribable wonder. Or you may find yourself capable of magic, like no wizard who has ever lived, and you will feel omnipotent in your imaginary surroundings. You will never want the experience to end and, when it does, you will only want to repeat it again and again. Your ordinary life will suddenly seem dull and flat and lusterless by comparison. And by this time, the drug will have permeated your being, and resisting it will be next to impossible.

"The more you smoke the bellaweed," Valsavis continued, "the more you become disconnected from the reality of your existence. The visions will become real to you, instead, and life without the bellaweed takes on the aspect of a nightmare, which you are driven to escape at any cost. You will sell all of your possessions, degrade yourself, perform any task at all that will bring you money so that you may buy more bellaweed and find sweet refuge in your visions. However, while bellaweed stimulates the mind to create these fabulous visions, it also dulls the wits. When not under its influence, you will often find all but the simplest tasks too difficult to perform. Your movements will become sluggish and stupid, and you will lack the wit even to steal in order to support your craving.

"And there are some," Valsavis went on, "who enter their dreamscapes never to leave again. Those people are, in many ways, the more fortunate ones among the doomed victims of the dreadful drug because they never truly realize what has happened to them. To those who fall under the thrall of bellaweed, ignorance can, indeed, be bliss. The rest become so completely dependent on it that nothing else will seem to matter, and in time, when their fortunes are depleted and they have sold everything they owned, they will sell themselves and live out the remainder of their lives in slavery, inexpensive for their masters to keep because they are easily controlled and require very little in the way of food and lodging. So long as they have bellaweed to smoke, they will meekly go about their work, suffering any indignity, while they gradually waste away."

"How horrible!" Ryana said, aghast.

She glanced around with a new sense of foreboding. The buildings all around them were small emporiums dedicated to the pursuit of this deadly and virulently addictive euphoria. And now they realized why the few people they saw on the streets moved so listlessly.

"If we remain here long enough," Valsavis said, "the odor of the smoke upon the air will begin to seem more and more pleasant, and it will start to affect us the way the smell of fresh-baked bread affects a starving man. We will start to feel a strong urge to enter one of these emporiums and sample some of this strangely compelling smoke. And if we were foolish enough to succumb to the temptation, we would be greeted warmly, and ushered to a comfortable sitting room where pipes would be provided for us, at a cost so very reasonable that no one would think to object, and that would be the beginning of the end. We would discover that the second pipeful would cost us more, and the third more still, and the price would always escalate. Before long, we would be taken from the luxurious comfort of the sitting room and led to tiny, cramped rooms in the back, lined with crude beds made of wooden slats and stacked to the ceiling so that six people or more could lie on them as if they were trade goods stored upon shelves in a warehouse. But by this time, we would not object. Eventually, we would say anything, do anything, sign any piece of paper that would bring us just one more pipe. And before long, the slave traders would come and purchase us by lots."

"How do you know all this?" Ryana asked, glancing at the mercenary uneasily. His story sounded all too unpleasantly vivid, as if he had experienced it himself.

"Because, in my youth, I once worked for such a slave trader," said Valsavis. "And that was enough to destroy in me forever any temptation to draw the odious smoke of bellaweed into my lungs. I would much sooner open my wrists and die bleeding in the street. If there is one thing that experience has taught me over the long years, it is that any attempt to bring peace, joy, or satisfaction into your life through artificial means is a false path. One finds those things through looking at life with clear and sober eyes, meeting its adversities and overcoming them through will, effort, and determination. Only there does true satisfaction lie. The rest is all as illusory as the visions produced by the sweet-smelling smoke of bellaweed. All shadow and no substance."

"Let us be quit of this dreadful place," Ryana said. "I do not wish to smell the odor of this deadly smoke any longer. It is already starting to smell pleasant, and now the very thought sickens me."

They hurried on through the Avenue of Dreams, leaving the sickly smelling smoke behind. Before long, they came to an even older section of the village, where the buildings showed greater signs of age. They passed through a small, square plaza with a well in the center of it, and continued on down the twisting street. Here, the buildings were smaller and packed closer together, many no more than one story tall. Most of these buildings appeared to be residences, but there was the occasional small shop selling various items such as rugs or clothing or fresh meat and produce. A short distance past a small bread bakery, they came to a narrow, two-story building with a wooden sign hanging over the entrance on which was painted, in green letters, the Gentle Path. Below the name was the single word Apothecary.

It was late, but there was a lamp burning in the front window, which had its shutters opened to admit the cool night breeze. They came up to the front door and found it unlocked. As they opened it, it brushed a string of cactus rib pieces suspended over the entrance, which made a gentle series of clicking noises, alerting the proprietor that someone had come in.

The shop was small and shaped in a narrow rectangle. Along one wall there was a wooden counter, on which stood various instruments for the weighing, cutting, crushing, and blending of herbs and powders. Behind the counter, there were shelves containing rows of glass bottles and ceramic jars, all labeled neatly and holding various dried herbs and powders. There were more such shelves across the room, from floor to ceiling, and many of these held bottles of various liquids and potions. Strings of herbs hung drying from the ceiling, filling the shop with a wonderful, pungent smell that completely banished the lingering memories of the sickly-sweet odor of bellaweed smoke.

A small man dressed in a simple brown robe came through the beaded curtain at the back, behind the far end of the counter. He came, shuffling as he walked, holding his old, liver-spotted hands clasped in front of him. He was almost completely bald, and he had a long, wispy white beard. His face was lined and wrinkled, and his dark brown eyes, set off by crow's-feet, had a kindly look about them.

"Welcome and good evening to you, my friends," he said to them. "I am Kallis, the apothecary. How may I serve you?"

"Your name and the location of your shop was given to us by the manager of the Desert Palace,"

Sorak said, "who asked that we mention him to you."

"Ah, yes," the old apothecary said, nodding. "He sends me many clients. He is my son, you know."

"Your son?" Ryana said with surprise.

The old man grimaced. "I had him late in life, regrettably, and his mother died in birthing him. He chose not to follow in his father's footsteps, which has always been something of a disappointment to me. But one's children always choose their own path, whether one approves of it or not. Such is the way of things. But then, you did not come here to hear the ramblings of a garrulous old man. How may I help you? Is there some ailment you seek to cure, or perhaps you wish a liniment for sore and aching muscles? A love potion, perhaps? Or a supply of herbal poultices to take with you on your journey?"

"We came seeking the Silent One, good apothecary," said Sorak.

"Ahhh," said the old man. "I see. Yes, I suppose I should have guessed from your appearance. You have the look of adventurers about you. Yes, indeed, I should have known. You seek information concerning the fabled lost treasure of Bodach."

"We seek the Silent One," Sorak repeated.

"The Silent One will not see you," Kallis replied flatly.

"Why?" asked Sorak.

"The Silent One will not see anyone."

"Who is going to stop us from seeing the Silent One, old man? You?" Valsavis said, fixing the apothecary with a steady gaze.

"There is no need to be threatening," Kallis replied, saying precisely the words that Sorak had been about to speak. "I am clearly not going to stop you from going anywhere you wish. You are big and strong, while I am small and frail. But if you tried to force your way in, it would not serve you well, and you would find that leaving Salt View would be far more difficult than it was for you to come here."

Sorak placed a restraining hand on Valsavis's shoulder. "No one is going to use any force," he reassured the old apothecary. "We merely ask that you tell the Silent One that we are here, and request an audience. If the Silent One refuses, we shall leave quietly and bother you no more."

The old man hesitated. "And who shall I say is requesting this audience?"

Sorak reached into his pack and pulled out the inscribed copy of *The Wanderer's Journal* that he had received from Sister Dyona at the villichi convent. "Tell the Silent One that we have been sent by the author of this book," he said, handing it to the old man.

Kallis looked down at the book and saw its title, then looked up at Sorak. It was difficult to judge anything by his expression. Sorak slipped back and allowed the Guardian to probe his mind. What the Guardian saw there was skepticism and caution.

"Very well," said Kallis. "Please, wait here."

He disappeared behind the beaded curtain.

"This all seems pointless," said Valsavis. "Why not simply go up there and see the old druid? What is to stop us?"

"Good manners," Sorak said. "And since when has our private matter started to concern you? What is *your* interest in all of this? You came to Salt View merely for the entertainment, or at least, so you said."

"If you are going to search for the lost treasure of Bodach, then I am interested—for all of the obvious reasons," said Valsavis. "Granted, you have not invited me to come along with you, but you must see that it would be in your best interests to have an experienced and skillful fighter by your side in the city of the undead. And if what they say about the treasure is true, then there is more than enough to split three ways and still leave us all rich beyond our wildest dreams. Aside from which, you owe me, as you yourself admitted. It was I who found you and tended to your wound when the marauders left you for dead, and it was I who helped you rescue Ryana from their clutches. Moreover, there are all my winnings that I was forced to leave behind back at the gaming house."

"No one forced you, Valsavis. You could easily have kept your winnings, though you would not have won them without me," Sorak said. "The manager said that he would not try to force you to return them."

"Perhaps," Valsavis said, "but after the noble example you two set by returning your winnings, I could hardly fail to do the same, now could I?"

"I thought money was not important to you," Sorak said. "Did you not say that all an excess of money brought a man was trouble?"

"Perhaps I did say that," Valsavis admitted, "but it is one thing not to wish to steal another's sword, however fine a weapon it may be, and quite another to win a treasure by risking life and limb. One act is craven, while the other is heroic. And at my age, I must think about how I shall spend my rapidly approaching declining years. A share of the lost treasure of Bodach, even if it were just a small share, would insure my comfort in my final days. Or is it that you are greedy and wish to keep all of it for yourselves?"

But at that moment, before Sorak could reply, Kallis returned. "The Silent One will see you," he announced. "This way, please."

They went through the beaded curtain and followed him through a supply room in the rear of the shop and up a flight of wooden stairs to the second floor. It was dark up there, with only one lamp burning at the head of the stairs. Valsavis tensed, not knowing what to expect. They walked down a short, dark corridor and stopped before a door.

"In here," said Kallis, beckoning them.

"Open it and go through first, old man," Valsavis said.

The apothecary merely looked at him for a moment, then sighed and shook his head. He opened the wooden door and went through first. They followed him, Valsavis keeping his right hand near his sword.

Behind the door was a room divided into two sections by an archway. The front part of the room contained a small, cone-shaped, brick fireplace in which a small fire burned, heating a kettle. The walls were bare, and the floor was wood-planked. Bunches of herbs hung drying from the beamed ceiling. There were two small and crudely built wooden chairs and a small round table made from planks. On it sat a candle in a holder and some implements for cutting and blending herbs and powders. There was a small sleeping pallet by the wall and a shelf containing some scrolls and slim, bound volumes. The room held no other furniture or items of decoration.

On the other side of the archway was a small study, with a writing desk and one chair pushed up against a bare wall. There were no windows in the room. A solitary oil lamp burned in the study, illuminating a white-robed figure with very long, straight, silver hair, who was seated at the desk, facing away from them.

"The Silent One," said Kallis, before he turned and left the room, closing the door behind him.

The Silent One stood and turned around.

"Gith's blood!" said Valsavis. "It's a woman!"

The silver hair hanging down almost to her waist more properly belonged to a woman in the twilight of her life, but the Silent One looked scarcely older than Ryana. Her face was ethereal in its fragile beauty, unlined, with skin like fine porcelain, and her eyes were a bright, emerald green, so bright they almost seemed to glow. She was tall and slender, and her posture was straight and erect. When she moved, as she came toward them, it was with a flowing grace. She almost seemed to float across the floor.

She held out the copy of *The Wanderer's Journal* that Sorak had given Kallis. "I believe this is yours," she said in a clear and lilting voice. "You come with impeccable credentials."

"But . . . you can speak!" said Valsavis.

She smiled. "When I choose to," she replied. "It is far easier to avoid unwelcome conversation when people do not think I have a voice. Here, I am known as the Silent One, and all save old and faithful Kallis believe I cannot speak. But now you know the truth, and you can call me by my name, which is Kara."

"No, this is some trick," Valsavis said. "You cannot possibly be the Silent One. The druid called the Silent One went to Bodach and returned nearly a century ago. The story itself is at least that old. You are far too young." He glanced at Sorak and Ryana. "This woman is an imposter."

"No," said Sorak. "She is pyreen."

Valsavis stared at him with astonishment. "You mean . . . one of the legendary peace-bringers?" He glanced uncertainly at the Silent One. "A *shapeshifter?*"

"I am not as young as I appear to be," Kara replied. "I am nearly two hundred fifty years old. However, for one of my people, that is still considered very young."

"I have heard stories of the pyreen," Valsavis said, "but I have never met or even seen one, and I do not know of anyone who has. For all I know, they are nothing but a myth, a legend. If you are truly one of the pyreen, then prove it."

She gazed at him for a moment without saying anything. Finally, she said, "I have no need to prove anything to you. The Nomad knows who and what I am. And that is all that matters."

"We shall see," Valsavis said ominously, drawing his sword.

"Put away your blade, Valsavis," Sorak said curtly, "unless it is mine you wish to cross."

Their gazes locked for a tense moment. Then slowly, Valsavis returned his sword to its scabbard. No, he thought, now was not the time. But soon. Very soon. The pyreen merely stood and watched them, unperturbed.

"Permit me," said Ryana, stepping up to the pyreen and taking her hand, then dropping to one knee and bowing her head.

Kara placed a hand upon her head. "Rise, priestess," she said. "There is no need to pay me formal homage. Rather, it is I who should pay homage to you, for the task that you have undertaken."

"You know why we came?" Sorak said.

"I have been expecting you," the pyreen replied. Her gaze shifted to Valsavis. "But not him."

"I am traveling with them," said Valsavis.

Kara glanced at Sorak and raised an eyebrow.

"For the moment," Sorak said.

"If that is your choice," was all she said.

"They say you know where the lost treasure of Bodach may be found," Valsavis said.

"I do," Kara replied. "In Bodach."

"We did not come here to hear you speak in riddles, woman," said Valsavis irritably.

"*You* did not come here to hear me speak," she said.

"By thunder, I have had enough of this!" Valsavis said.

"Keep your peace, Valsavis," Sorak said calmly but firmly. "No one has made you spokesman here. Remember that you *asked* to come. And as of yet, we have not refused you."

Valsavis gave Sorak a sidelong look, but said nothing more. It would not serve to antagonize the elfling now, he thought, governing his temper with difficulty.

"I know why you have come," said Kara, "and I know what you seek. I will go with you to Bodach. Meet me here an hour before sunset tomorrow. It is a long, hot journey across difficult terrain. We shall do better if we travel by night." And with that, she turned around, went back to her writing desk, and sat down with her back to them. The audience was over.

"Thank you, Kara," Sorak said. He opened the door and let the others out. Kallis waited for them downstairs as they came through the beaded curtain.

"Good night," was all he said.

"Good night, Kallis," Sorak said. "And thank you."

"So," said Valsavis, when they were once again back out in the street, "we leave tomorrow night, with the not-so Silent One to guide us."

"The way you acted in there, we are fortunate that

she agreed to guide us," said Ryana angrily. "One does not threaten a pyreen, Valsavis. Not if one has an ounce of wit about him."

"I will believe she is one of the pyreen when I see her shapeshift, and not before," Valsavis said dryly. "I do not make a habit of taking things on faith."

"That is because you *have* no faith," Ryana said. "And so much the worse for you."

"I have faith in what I can see and feel and accomplish," said Valsavis. "Unlike you, priestess, I did not grow up sheltered in a convent, fed on a diet of foolish hopes and dreams."

"Without hopes and dreams, foolish or not, there can be no life," Ryana replied.

"Ah, yes, of course," Valsavis said. "The vain hopes and dreams of all preservers, that one day Athas will be green and live again." He grimaced. "Take a look around you, priestess. You have traveled clear across the Tablelands from your convent in the Ringing Mountains, and you have crossed the Great Ivory Plain. You have seen Athas firsthand. Just what are the odds, do you think, of this desolate, desert world ever being green again?"

"So long as people believe the way you do, Valsavis, and think only of themselves, the odds are very slim," Ryana replied.

"Well, then at least you have learned that much practicality," Valsavis said. "As you learn more, you will find that most people think only of themselves, for in a world as harsh as this, there is neither the time nor the luxury to think of others."

"Indeed," said Sorak. "I wonder why you stopped to help me, then."

"It cost me nothing," said Valsavis with a shrug. The elfling was being very clever, using the priestess to draw him out. He would have to watch himself more carefully. "As I said before, it provided an interesting diversion on an otherwise uneventful journey. So you see, Nomad, as it turns out, I was really only thinking of myself. If it had proved an inconvenience for me to stop and help you, rest assured I would have passed you by without a qualm."

"I am truly comforted by that thought," said Sorak wryly.

Valsavis grinned. "Well, as things turned out, your companionship has served me well. A new adventure beckons, with the promise of wealth that will see me through my old age in comfort. I think that I shall build myself a new home, perhaps even right here in Salt View. Or perhaps I will take permanent rooms at the Oasis. A man could do much worse. I will be able to afford the constant company of beautiful young women to take care of me, and I shall never have to worry about where my next meal is going to come from. I may even buy the Desert Palace, so that I may amuse myself by ordering about that sly rasclinn of a manager and have a place where I can always come for entertainment free of charge."

"It might be more prudent to find the treasure before you start to spend it," Ryana said.

"What," said Valsavis, raising his eyebrows in mock astonishment, "and give up all my hopes and dreams?"

Ryana shook her head. "You can be a most irritating man, Valsavis," she said.

"Yes, women often find me irritating," he replied. "At first. And then, despite themselves, they find that they are drawn to me."

"Truly? I cannot imagine why," Ryana said.

"Perhaps you will soon find out," Valsavis said.

She gave him a sharp glance. "Now *that*," she said, "would fall into the category of foolish hopes and dreams."

Valsavis grinned and gave her a small bow. "Well struck, my lady. A good riposte. But the match is not yet finished."

"For you, it ended before it could even begin," she said.

"Did it, now?" Valsavis said. "Is that so, Nomad? Have you already staked your claim?"

"I have no claim upon Ryana," Sorak said. "Nor does any man on any woman."

"Indeed? I know many men who would dispute that curious assertion," said Valsavis.

"No doubt," said Sorak. "But you might try asking women."

"When it comes to women," said Valsavis, "I generally do not make a habit of asking."

"That I can believe," Ryana said.

Suddenly, Sorak stopped and put his arm out to hold back the others. "Wait. It seems that we have company," he said.

They had entered the small plaza with the well, beyond which lay the bellaweed emporiums. Four shadowy figures stood at the far end of the small plaza, blocking their way. Eight more had entered the plaza from the alleys to either side, four from the left, four from the right.

"Ah, what have we here?" said Valsavis. "It would appear that the night's entertainment is not yet over." He drew his sword.

"Smokers in pursuit of means to buy more bellaweed?" wondered Sorak.

"No, not these," Valsavis said. "There is nothing listless in their movements. And they seem to know what they're about."

The men stood, surrounding them. One of the four in front of them spoke. "One of our hunting parties failed to return to camp," he said, immediately solving the question of who they were. "We went out to search for them and soon discovered why. We found their bodies, and then followed the trail left by their assassins. It led us here. We also found the stable where their kanks were sold. The man who purchased them was . . . persuaded . . . to provide a detailed description of the sellers. Curiously enough, they looked a great deal like you three."

"Ah, so then those were your friends that we butchered back there?" said Valsavis.

"You admit it?" the marauder said with some surprise.

"I am not especially proud of it," Valsavis said with a shrug. "They barely gave me cause to work up a good sweat."

"Well, I think we can manage to exercise you somewhat better," the marauder said, drawing his obsidian sword with one hand and his dagger with the other. "After all, we are not asleep."

"Nor were your friends when we killed them," said Valsavis. "But they sleep now, and you shall join them soon enough."

"Kill them," the marauder said.

The bandits started to converge on them, but Valsavis moved with absolutely blinding speed. Almost faster than the eye could follow, he drew a dagger with each hand and flung them out to either side. Two of the marauders fell, one on the left, one on the right, even as they were drawing their weapons. Each man had a dagger through his heart. Neither of them even had a chance to cry out.

But as quickly as Valsavis had moved, Sorak moved even faster, except it wasn't Sorak anymore. The Shade had come storming up from his subconscious—dark, malevolent, and terrifying, charging toward the four men at the far end of the plaza.

For a moment, they were too startled to respond. There were a dozen of them against three. And suddenly, in the space of an eyeblink, two of their number had fallen, and instead of being the attackers, *they* were being attacked.

The first thing the four men at the far end of the plaza realized was that one of their intended victims was actually *charging* them. And then, in the seconds before he was upon them, they realized something else, as well. They realized what it meant to be absolutely terrified. Death was coming at them. The feeling was sudden, inexplicable, and overwhelming. They went cold, and it was as if a huge fist had grabbed each of them by the guts and started squeezing.

They had no way of knowing that the Shade was a unique and horrifying creature, that basic, primal, bestial instinct contained subconsciously within all men, only in this case, fully developed into a discrete persona—and capable of intense, psionic, emotional projection. The Shade *literally* instilled terror.

Two of the marauders began to back involuntarily away as the Shade charged across the plaza toward them. They were still in that momentary state, between full realization of what they were feeling and running in blind panic, when their leader shoved them forward, yelling, "*Get him, you fools!* He's just one man!"

For an instant, the spell was broken, and then, even as it took hold once again, it was too late to run. The juggernaut charging across the plaza was upon them, and they suddenly found themselves fighting for their lives. The only trouble was, their obsidian weapons shattered with the first stroke against the stranger's blade.

Valsavis tried to step forward to protect Ryana, but she merely shoved him aside and said, "Take the ones on the right!"

As she moved toward the three marauders on her left, Valsavis directed his attention toward the three on the right. They had already moved to within striking distance, and they were infuriated that he had already killed two of their number. Since the Shade's projection was not being directed at them, they attacked Valsavis without hesitation.

He parried the first stroke with one of his own and had the satisfaction of seeing the marauder's obsidian sword break against his stronger, iron blade. A downward, sweeping slash finished the man, and then only two were left. They struck simultaneously. Valsavis could not parry both blows at once. He blocked one, twisting and deftly slipping the second thrust, kicking the man in the groin as he did so. The man made a gasping, squealing sort of sound and doubled over. Valsavis felt a dagger scrape along his side and smashed the marauder in the face with his elbow. As the marauder cried out and staggered back, Valsavis ran him through. That left only the man he'd kicked in the groin, and he was in no shape to offer any resistance. Valsavis raised his blade and brought it down, finishing him off. He then turned to help Ryana, but saw that she was in no need of his assistance.

One marauder was already lying in a pool of his own blood. She ran the second one through even as Valsavis turned toward her. And it took her less than a moment to finish off the third. Valsavis watched with open admiration as her blade executed its delicate and lethal dance. The marauders were no competition for her. She had quickly dispatched two, and now the third was on the retreat, desperately trying to parry her flurry of strokes, but he was hopelessly out of his depth. It ended quickly; one thrust, and it was over.

Valsavis glanced toward the far end of the plaza. The last he had seen of Sorak, he was suddenly charging the four men at the other end. Now only one remained, the leader. Valsavis heard the man scream once, and then the scream was abruptly cut off and Sorak stood alone.

Valsavis heard the sound of running footsteps and turned, raising his sword to meet the threat, but it wasn't more marauders. It was a squad of the town guards, mercenaries by the look of them, and they seemed to know their business. They did not simply come charging in blindly. Instead, as they entered the plaza from a side street, they fanned out quickly and covered the area with their crossbows. Valsavis slowly sheathed his blade and held his hands out away from his sides.

Ryana came up beside him and did likewise. Sorak approached them across the plaza, moving slowly, his blade sheathed. He was carefully keeping his hands in plain sight.

The mercenary captain quickly glanced around the plaza, taking in the situation. "What happened here?" he demanded.

"We were attacked," Ryana said. "We had no choice but to defend ourselves."

The mercenary leader looked around. "You three did all this by yourselves?" he asked in disbelief.

"I saw it all," cried a voice from a window on the

second floor of a building facing onto the plaza. "It happened just the way she says!"

Someone else who had apparently witnessed the fighting from the safety of his building added his voice in agreement. "It was a dozen against three! And I have never seen anything like it!"

"Nor have I," the mercenary captain said, apparently convinced by this corroboration. Several people started coming out into the street, staring at the scene with fascination, but the mercenaries held them back.

"Do you have any idea why these men attacked you?" asked their captain.

"They were marauders," said Sorak. "Some of their comrades had attacked us on our way here and we fought back. These men trailed us and came looking for revenge."

"It seems they found more than they had bargained for," the mercenary captain said. He signaled his men to lower their bows. "I will require your names," he said.

They gave them.

"Where are you lodging?" the mercenary asked.

"The Oasis," Sorak said. "But we were planning to leave Salt View tomorrow. Unless, of course, there is any difficulty about that."

"No difficulty," said the mercenary captain. "Witnesses have borne your story out. I am satisfied that it was self-defense. And it would seem unlikely that three would try to ambush twelve," he added wryly. "Though I daresay, given the results, it certainly appears that you could have pulled it off."

"We are free to go, then?" Sorak asked.

"You are free to go," the mercenary captain said. He turned and beckoned to one of his men. "Go and get the charnel wagon to remove these bodies."

As they crossed the plaza, heading back toward Main Street, Valsavis glanced down at the corpses of the marauders Sorak killed. He noticed two very interesting things. Each of their weapons had shattered, as if made of glass. And each man had an expression of stark terror frozen on his features. It was only the second time that Valsavis had seen Sorak in action. The first time, the marauders had been taken by surprise, and they had been drinking heavily. This time, however, they had come sober and prepared to fight—for all the good that it had done them. He was beginning to understand why the Shadow King felt anxious about this elfling.

There was something very special about that sword of his, quite aside from its obvious rarity. When he had first seen it, Valsavis had noted the hilt, wrapped with precious silver wire, and the unusual shape of the blade, but though he was curious to see the elven steel, he had never removed it from its scabbard. He had lived a long time, and he owed his survival not only to his abilities as a fighter, but to his sense of caution. It was said to be a magic blade, and Nibenay himself believed it. Valsavis chose the prudent course. Until he had learned more about the nature of its enchantment, he had simply held it carefully by its scabbard and laid it aside, without examining it. Whoever had enchanted the sword could easily have warded it as well, to prevent its falling into the wrong hands. And besides, he was no thief. To take a weapon from a man honorably slain in combat was one thing; to steal it while he lay helpless would have been craven.

What then, was the precise nature of the sword's enchantment? Both times he had seen Sorak use it, the weapons of his antagonists had shattered against its blade. For obsidian weapons to break on iron or steel was not uncommon, but for them to shatter as they had was very unusual, indeed. So perhaps that was its special property. No ordinary weapon could stand up against it. That meant he would not be able to fight Sorak the same way he fought other men. When the time came, he would either have to make certain that Sorak did not have the sword, or that his own weapon did not come in contact with it.

Then there were those expressions of terror on the faces of those men that he had slain. What could account for that? Marauders were not men easily frightened, much less terrified. Veela had told him that the elfling was a master of the Way. If so, then it was possible that he had the ability to psionically project terror at his antagonists. Coupled with the enchantment of the elven blade, that would make him not merely a formidable opponent, but an indomitable one. Yet, he had to have a weakness, all men did. Obviously, there was the priestess, but aside from her, there had to be something inherent in the elfling himself that would make him vulnerable. Until he found out what that was, he would have to play the game very cautiously.

As for the priestess . . . Valsavis had never seen a woman fight like that before. And he had seen women fight. He was well aware that villichi priestesses were trained in combat, but they usually preferred to use psionics to disarm their enemies or otherwise subdue them. Ryana had waded into the fight without even using her psionic ability, as if she had relished the prospect of taking the marauders on blade to blade. And the way she had dispatched them was magnificent. He could not have done better himself. This was a woman well worthy of respect, he thought. Beautiful, intelligent, and deadly. He found it an exciting combination.

"You fight well," he told her.

"Yes," she replied. "I do."

Valsavis grinned. "We make a good team," he said. She glanced at him sharply, and he quickly added, "The three of us, I mean. If this is any indication of how things will go in Bodach, we should all be rich before long."

"You will find it is far easier to kill the living than the undead," she replied flatly.

He gazed at her with interest. "You sound as if you speak from experience," he said.

"Have you ever fought undead before?" she asked.

"No," Valsavis said. "I have fought men, elves, giants, dwarves, even halflings and thri-kreen, but never yet undead. I imagine it should prove an interesting experience. I am looking forward to it."

"I am not," Ryana said. "It is not an experience most sane people would be eager to repeat."

"And yet you travel with Sorak to Bodach," said Valsavis, glancing at the elfling, who walked slightly ahead of them. "I find that curious. I had always thought villichi priestesses and druids lived a life of austere simplicity, dedicated to the spiritual path. Seeking treasure seems somewhat out of character."

"Everyone chooses his own path," Ryana replied. "As you have chosen yours."

"And what of Sorak? Is this path of your choosing, or his?"

"What difference would that make to you?" she countered.

"I was merely interested."

"I see," she replied. "Is it the treasure of Bodach that interests you, or me?"

"And just supposing I said it was both?" Valsavis asked.

"Then I would reply that you could only hope to gain one," she said, and quickened her pace to catch up with Sorak.

"Perhaps," Valsavis said softly to himself. "And then again, perhaps not."

SEVEN

It was late when they arrived back at their rooms at the Oasis. Ryana removed her sword belt and flopped down wearily on her bed. Sorak stood by the window, looking out at the night thoughtfully.

"Valsavis is going to be a problem," Ryana said, as if reading his thoughts.

"Yes, I know," Sorak replied, still gazing out the window.

"He wants me," said Ryana dryly.

"I know that, too." His response was flat and unemotional, merely a simple acknowledgment of her statement.

She glanced at him, puzzled. "And how does that make you feel?" she asked, carefully keeping her voice neutral. She did not want anything in her tone to dictate the nature of his response.

He turned to look at her. "Do you want to hear me say that I am jealous?" he asked.

"I want to hear you say how it makes you feel," she replied.

"It makes me feel cautiously optimistic."

She stared at him with open-mouthed astonishment, unable to believe what she'd heard. Of all the

167

responses he might have given, that was the last one she could ever have expected. "*What?*"

"I am still not completely certain," Sorak replied, turning back to stare contemplatively out the window, "but I am growing more and more convinced that Valsavis is an agent of the Shadow King. And if so, then his attraction to you could serve as a distraction from his true purpose. That would be very useful for us."

"Is that all I mean to you?" Ryana asked with a stricken expression. "I am merely of value as a *distraction* and nothing more?"

He turned back to face her. "Forgive me," he said, contritely. "I did not mean it that way at all." He exhaled heavily. "You know very well how I feel about you, and you know how much you mean to me. But I have no reason to feel jealous of Valsavis. I know what sort of man he is, and I know *you*, Ryana. Regardless of your feelings toward me, I know that you could never feel anything for such a man."

"He may not care about how I feel," she replied, wryly. "In fact, I doubt it would make much difference to him at all."

"Perhaps not," Sorak said. "A man such as Valsavis usually takes what he wants with no thought for the desires of others. But you are far from a helpless female, and even given that, I have no intention of leaving you unprotected. I think we have both learned our lessons in that regard, thanks to the marauders. But I suspect that Valsavis has never met anyone like you before." He smiled. "If, in fact, there *is* anyone else like you. Valsavis is a man who thinks very highly of himself. He certainly does not think much, if at all, of others. I would guess that women have either given themselves to Valsavis easily and willingly in the past, or else he simply took them by force. Either one would represent to him merely the satisfaction of his animal desires. Neither would represent a challenge, and challenge, above all, is what truly drives Valsavis. I doubt he cares about much else."

"So then I represent a challenge to him, is that it?" Ryana asked.

"I would certainly think so," Sorak said. "You are beautiful, but Valsavis has doubtless had beautiful women before. You are also highly intelligent. Most intelligent women would know to stay well away from someone like Valsavis, but a few might easily have been tempted by what they perceived as his aura of danger and unpredictability. They, in their turn, might have regarded *him* as a challenge. And the results, of course, would have been predictable, whatever their expectations may have been. But you are also a fighter, perhaps the most skilled female fighter he has ever seen. Villichi priestesses are known for being expert in the arts of combat, and you were the best back at the convent."

"Second best," she corrected him. "I never could match you at swordplay."

He shrugged. "Either way, you have mastered a skill to which Valsavis has devoted a lifetime of study. Whatever else he may be, he is first and foremost a warrior. And you are not only intelligent and beautiful but a warrior, as well, perhaps his equal in ability. I think that to a man such as Valsavis, that would represent an almost irresistible challenge. I suppose it's possible he might try to take you by force, just to see if he could. But then, if he were successful, that would only lessen the thrill. How much more challenging to see if he could win you over, especially when he knows that you are already devoted to someone else."

"Someone who is also a warrior, and the object of his mission," said Ryana.

Sorak nodded. "Yes, if he is an agent of the Shadow King, as we suspect."

"Either way, I do not like this at all," she said. "We are facing enough danger as it is without having him around."

And a voice within each of their minds suddenly spoke, saying, "*I agree.*"

They stared at each other with surprise, and in the next moment, a small, desert dust devil came spinning into the room through the open window. Sorak moved back quickly, startled as it blew past him and alighted on the floor, a small, funnel-shaped whirlwind of dust and sand that, in the next instant, lengthened and expanded, transforming itself into Kara, the pyreen known as the Silent One.

"Forgive the intrusion," she said, "but I had to speak with you in private. I do not trust this man, Valsavis. I was told to expect you two, but not him."

"Then you have communicated with the Sage?" asked Sorak eagerly, recovering from his surprise at her sudden and dramatic appearance.

"Say rather that he has communicated with me," Kara replied. "I promised him that I would help you, but I promised nothing about Valsavis. His thoughts are inaccessible to me, and I regard that as a warning. There is an aura of malevolence about him, and of duplicity. I do not want him with us. Therefore, we are leaving now, instead of tomorrow evening."

"We do not trust Valsavis either," Sorak told her. "We believe that he may be an agent of the Shadow King. Nevertheless, I thought that it would be easier to keep an eye on him if he were with us rather than trailing us. Valsavis is an expert tracker. He will doubtless follow us to Bodach. We cannot prevent him."

"That is all the more reason to start now and place as much distance between us as possible," Kara replied.

"I am in complete agreement with your assessment of him," said Sorak, "but we should consider that his sword arm could come in useful in the city of the undead."

"If it were not used against us," the pyreen replied. "I might be willing to take that chance on my own behalf, but not where the Sage may be concerned. If Valsavis is an agent of the Shadow King, then surely he must have some means of reporting to him. The Breastplate of Argentum is a powerful talisman. The Shadow King would know that and would do anything to insure that the Sage did not acquire it." She shook her head. "No, I shall not take the risk. We must leave at once without alerting Valsavis."

"Then we are ready," Sorak said, picking up his pack and shouldering it. Ryana buckled on her sword belt and shouldered her own pack. They headed toward the door.

"No," said Kara. "Not that way. If you are seen leaving, then someone could alert him."

"Yes, you're right, of course," said Sorak. "I would not put it past him to have bribed someone to watch our comings and goings and report to him. We shall use the window, as you did, and sneak out over the garden wall. Where shall we meet you?"

"Outside the east gate of the village," Kara replied.

"Good," said Sorak. "Our kanks are stabled there. We can pick them up and—"

"No," said Kara, "leave them. Kanks would leave an easy trail to follow, especially for an expert tracker."

"But if we go on foot, then he will catch us easily," Ryana protested, not adding that she was not looking forward to crossing the southern half of the Ivory Plain and going all the way around the inland silt basins on foot.

"We are wasting precious time," said Kara in a tone that brooked no disagreement. "Meet me outside the east gate as soon possible."

And with that, she spun around once, twice, three times, and became a dust devil once again that whirled out through the window and over the garden wall.

"Perhaps she knows a short cut," Sorak said.

"To Bodach?" said Ryana. She grimaced. "I have seen your map. It is an even longer journey there than it was to here from Nibenay."

"Well, you will recall the map was not entirely accurate," said Sorak, though he knew it was a rather lame response. "In any case, she is our guide, and we must place ourselves in her hands."

He swung out through the window. Ryana followed, and they quickly crossed the garden, keeping well away from the main path by the entrance. They reached the wall, and Ryana made a saddle of her hands, giving Sorak a leg up. Once he reached the top of the wall, he held his hand down to her and helped her up. They dropped to the street and quickly lost themselves among the nighttime crowd.

It did not take them long to reach the east gate of the village. Ryana cast a longing glance at the stables as they passed them, thinking how much more comfortable it would have been to ride a kank than go again on foot across miles of hot salt. They had filled their waterskins at a public well on their way out of the village, but with a journey as long as they had ahead of them, Ryana knew that it would not be enough. Fortunately, however, they would be traveling with a pyreen this time. If anyone could find water in the dry wasteland between Salt View and Bodach, Kara could.

There was no sign of Kara at the gate, however. But then Sorak recalled that she had told them to meet her *outside* the village gate. They went through and stopped to look around, yet the pyreen was nowhere to be seen.

"Now what?" said Ryana, with a worried look.

"She said that she would meet us here," said Sorak.

"So? Where *is* she?"

"She will be here," Sorak replied confidently.

"I certainly hope so," said Ryana dubiously.

"She is pyreen," said Sorak with conviction. "She would never let down fellow preservers. Especially those who served the Sage. Perhaps we should continue on ahead for a short distance."

"Only what if she comes after we've gone and waits for us by the gate?" Ryana asked.

"A shapeshifter will have no difficulty finding us," said Sorak. "She will assume we must have gone on."

"Very well, if you say so," Ryana replied, but she had her doubts, and the prospect of the long journey ahead, on foot and without a guide, was not a pleasant one.

They started walking down the trail leading away from the village. After a few moments, they became aware of something moving off to their right. They heard the rapid pattering of small paws, and Sorak, with his superior night vision, could make out a creature running on all fours a short distance away, parallel to their course.

"What is it?" asked Ryana.

"A rasclinn," Sorak said.

"Here?" said Ryana, with surprise. "In the flat-lands?"

"Somehow, I do not think this one is an ordinary rasclinn," Sorak replied.

And sure enough, the creature trotted ahead of them and crossed their path, then stopped on the trail. A voice in their minds said, *This way. Follow me.*

They left the trail, following the rasclinn as it trotted off into the scrub brush. They had to run to keep after it. After a short while, in addition to the faint sounds made by the rasclinn as it trotted through the desert scrub, heading toward the foot of the lower slopes of the Mekillots, they heard other sounds, as well. Loud, rustling sounds ahead and to their left, in a small grove of pagafa trees.

"What is that strange, rustling noise?" Ryana asked.

Sorak frowned. "I do not know," he said.

"You don't think it's a trap?"

"I cannot believe a pyreen would lead us into a trap," said Sorak. "She is sworn to the preserver cause."

The rustling sounds were growing louder as they approached.

"I do not like this, Sorak," said Ryana apprehensively.

A moment later, Sorak said, "Antloids."

Ryana stopped. "Antloids?" she said with some alarm.

"There is no need to fear," he said. "The antloids are our friends, remember?"

She recalled how Screech had once summoned the

antloids to help rescue her and Princess Korahna from Torian and his mercenaries, and her apprehension abated somewhat, though it did not disappear entirely. And a moment later, they reached the grove of pagafa trees, where Kara waited for them, having shapeshifted back to her natural form.

In the shelter of the grove, a dozen or more antloids were hard at work, stripping branches from the pagafa trees and bringing them to another group of antloids, who were using their mandibles to weave them together with the thick, strong, fibrous leaves of desert dagger plants, which grew to a height of ten feet or more, with long, wide, blade-shaped leaves up to five or six feet in length. Some of the antloids were gathering the leaves, picking them off the nearby plants at the foot of the slopes, and bringing them to the others, who used their mandibles and claws to tear them into long and narrow strips. These strips were then used to fasten the branches of the pagafa trees together into a sort of mat about five feet wide by eight feet long. As they approached, the antloids were finishing the task, weaving the last strips together and fastening them carefully, sealing the ends with their sticky spit, which hardened into a gumlike substance.

"This is why you did not need the kanks," said Kara as the antloids finished their work on the mat. "And now you will see why Valsavis, however skilled a tracker he may be, will find no trail to follow."

Ryana stared at the mat without comprehension. "I do not understand," she said. "Surely you do not mean for us to *drag* that cumbersome thing behind us to obliterate our trail?"

"No," said Kara. "I mean for you to ride upon it."

"Drawn by the antloids, you mean?" Sorak said.

He shook his head. "That would never work. Valsavis could follow that trail as easily as he could follow the course of a well-established caravan route."

"Through the air?" said Kara with a smile.

"Through the *air?*" Ryana repeated, her eyes widening.

"Why walk when you can fly?" asked Kara.

"Fly?" Ryana said. "On *that*? But . . . *how*?"

"Borne up by the wind," said Sorak, suddenly understanding what Kara planned. "The wind of an air elemental."

"*You?*" said Ryana, staring at Kara with astonishment. "But . . . forgive me—not to doubt your powers, my lady, but to hold us up for such a distance. . . . Even a pyreen would surely find that taxing beyond her abilities."

"If I were to do it by myself, no doubt I would," said Kara. "But though a pyreen can shapeshift into the form of an elemental, a pyreen can also *raise* elementals. Observe. . . ."

She closed her eyes and tilted her head back, spreading her arms out from her sides. They saw her lips moving soundlessly, and though her face bore an expression of calm serenity, they could tell that she was concentrating intensely. They could both *feel* it.

A stillness descended on the pagafa grove. There was utter silence. There was no chirping of small insects, no cries of night birds, not even the faintest breeze. It was as if the entire world had suddenly stopped to draw breath. And a moment later in the distance, in the air above the mountains looming over them, there was the rumbling sound of thunder. It was the still before a desert storm. A few more moments passed, and then they felt the coolness of a strong breeze on their faces as it swept down from the heights above them. The thunder rolled once more, and dark clouds roiled in the moonlit sky. The breeze grew stronger, whipping their hair back from their faces. In the distance, they heard a whistling sound as the winds gathered.

"Now," said Kara, beckoning them toward the mat the antloids had constructed. "Take your places."

Ryana glanced down at the small, crudely woven platform of pagafa branches and dagger plant leaves held together, literally, with nothing but spit, and suddenly the very last thing she wanted to do was sit down upon it.

"Quickly," Kara urged them.

"Come on," said Sorak, taking her hand and pulling her toward the platform.

"Sorak . . . I'm afraid."

"There is nothing to fear," he said. "I will be with you. Kara will not let us fall."

His calmness and his complete sense of certainty eased her apprehensions. She stepped onto the mat with him and eased herself down upon it, sitting cross-legged. She swallowed hard and held tightly onto his hand, not wanting to let go. He squeezed her hand reassuringly.

"Trust the Way," he said. "Believe in the Path of the Preserver."

"I do," she whispered. "I believe."

The wind grew stronger. The thunder rolled. Sheet lightning flashed in the desert sky above them, giving off a spectacular display of natural pyrotechnics. The wind shrieked as it swept down off the mountains, plucking at their hair and clothing. Ryana closed her eyes.

"*Sorak!*" she cried.

"I am here," he said, squeezing her hand, his voice

instilling calm.

The wind was now blowing with hurricane force. Ryana held onto Sorak's hand and clutched at the mat with her other hand. She forced herself to open her eyes, and what she saw was so incredible that she couldn't have closed them again even if she tried.

Kara stood several feet away from them, her head tilted back, her arms outspread, her long, silver-gray hair and her white robe billowing around her in the wind. And as Ryana watched, the wind actually became *visible*, took on form, swirled around and around her like a whirlpool, then coalesced into three separate funnel shapes, much larger than mere dust devils, more like the funnel clouds of desert tornados, only smaller and more dense. And in those whirling, roiling funnel clouds, gathering greater and greater force as they spun around and around and around, Ryana could suddenly make out *features*.

She stared with disbelief, having heard stories of natural elementals before, but never having actually seen one, much less *three*. Within those whirling funnel clouds of gale-force wind, she could see, indistinctly, the rough approximation of *eyes*, and *mouths* that seemed to shriek like banshees.

She tightened her grip on Sorak's hand, holding onto it with all her might, and she felt an incredible pressure in her chest. She tried to breathe, but she couldn't seem to draw any air into her lungs. And as Ryana watched, unable to tear her eyes away, much as she wanted to, Kara began to spin around and around and around, her arms outstretched, twirling with wild abandon, like an elven dancing girl. Her shape grew indistinct. It seemed to blur as she spun around, faster and faster. Her form became even more blurred until she completely disappeared from view and became a whirling funnel cloud herself, just like the three elementals that hovered all around her.

And then those four funnel clouds all came together and twisted violently, bending underneath the woven mat they sat upon and lifting it into the air.

Ryana felt the platform lurch suddenly beneath her, and then it lifted and began to turn, slowly going around and around as the force of all that wind gathered beneath it. She somehow found the strength to close her eyes once more, squeezing them shut tightly, and she held onto Sorak's hand with all the force that she could muster. If he said anything to her, she could not hear it for all the shrieking of the howling wind.

The platform was raised higher and higher, until it cleared the tops of the trees in the pagafa grove and went up higher still, turning around and around as it rose twenty feet above the ground, then thirty, then forty, and higher still, until finally, Ryana forced herself to open her eyes once more and saw the desert spreading out far below her.

She saw the village of Salt View from a height of several hundred feet above the ground, the neatly whitewashed buildings, illuminated by torchlight and braziers in the streets, looking very small and not quite real. And then the wind beneath them shifted and they began to move forward, gathering speed as they were swept out across the white, salt desert far below them.

They were *flying*, buoyed up by the winds, the air elementals Kara had raised and joined with. The crudely woven mat they sat upon floated like a feather on the strong winds, tilting forward slightly as they were blown away from Salt View and across the southern part of the Great Ivory Plain, toward the inland silt basins in the distance. All around them, the night sky was lit up with sheet lightning, illuminating their way, and thunder crashed with a deafening roar as the elemental storm swept across the desert with increasing speed.

Ryana suddenly let go of Sorak's hand and threw her arms up into the air, crying out with sheer delight. Her fear was gone, replaced by an exhilaration the like of which she had never felt before. She threw back her head and laughed with an unrestrained joy that permeated every fiber of her being. She felt marvelously free. She turned toward Sorak and threw her arms around him. And he held her close, and she knew that whatever trials lay ahead of them, she would face them at his side, unafraid and filled with a sense of determination that came of knowing, without the faintest scintilla of a doubt, that the path she had chosen was the right one, the one she had been born to follow.

Unable to restrain herself, she shouted out over the shrieking wind, "I love you!"

And she felt his arms tighten around her, and heard him say into her ear, "I know. I love you, too."

And that was all that mattered.

*　*　*　*　*

Valsavis awoke in the morning, shortly after sunrise. He sat up in bed and looked down at the curvaceous young woman lying beside him, who had come to massage his muscles with her strong and skillful hands when he came back from the fight with the marauders in the Avenue of Dreams. She had stayed to cater to his other needs, as well, and had done so eagerly and expertly.

She was just twenty years old, young enough to be his daughter—no, his granddaughter, actually—and her svelte and lean young body looked beautiful and inviting as she lay there in the early morning sunlight, the covers thrown back. For a moment, Valsavis simply stared at her as she slept, one leg straight, one slightly bent, the gentle curve of her hips accentuated by her position as she lay upon her side, a slight smile on her lips. He looked at the fullness of her shapely, young breasts; the firmness of her youthful body; and the clarity and smoothness of her skin, which had responded with a trembling eagerness to his caresses as they had made love throughout the night.

Valsavis recalled how she had moaned softly, her eyes closed, her lips parted as she had gasped for breath, saying his name over and over again. And for all her beauty, for all the fierce passion of her youth, for all the tenderness that she had lavished on him, a tenderness the intensity of which had told him that this time it was much more than merely a service she performed for money, for all the kisses she had covered him with, kisses that had all the fervor of a young woman truly awakened for the first time to the joys of physical fulfillment with a man who knew, from long experience, how to bring out the full intensity of passion in a woman—for all that, as immediate and powerful as all those sensations had been—all Valsavis had been able to think about as he coupled with her was Ryana.

It was the villichi priestess he had imagined staring down at him, her expression filled with passion and longing. It was *her* body he had imagined pressed against his, *her* voice he had heard, saying his name over and over again. The beautiful young woman was, unknowingly, merely a surrogate for what he had really wanted and, to his immense frustration, knew he could not have.

And as he looked down at the young woman now—whose name he could not even recall—as he watched her lying there peacefully, the embodiment of youth and passion, a dream most men his age would sell their souls for, Valsavis felt a disappointment and a longing he had never known before. He tried to superimpose upon her sleeping features the face of the young villichi priestess and he knew that until he had the real object of his desires, he would never truly know what it meant to feel complete satisfaction. For the first time in his life, Valsavis felt a *need* for a woman. And only one would do.

Anything else was just a fantasy. This young woman, lovely as she was, had been no more than a substitute that left him feeling, for all her genuine emotion, loss and hunger that demanded satisfaction. And no mere substitute, no matter how young and beautiful and passionate, no matter now genuine her feelings and responses may have been, would answer to his need.

Valsavis quietly got out of bed and quickly started getting dressed. Tonight, he thought, they would leave for Bodach. They would go to meet the Silent One, who would guide them through the city of the undead. He still did not really believe that she was what she claimed to be, but either way, it didn't really matter. The lure was Bodach, and both the riches and the terrors it contained. For most men, this would have represented a doom that would have frozen their blood in their veins. For Valsavis, it only meant a way to feel more stimulation, a challenge to all of his abilities and skills, an adventure to make his blood boil and make him feel alive. He was looking forward to it.

He tried to imagine what it would be like, fighting the undead. No warrior could face a more dangerous or fearsome opponent. It would be the ultimate test of a man who had devoted his life to being tested. And it would mean a resolution, one way or the other. If Sorak found the talisman known as the Breastplate of Argentum, then Valsavis would have to take it from him. He would have to best a Master of the Way, an elfling with powers of endurance and strength rivaling those of the finest human warriors, an opponent with a magic sword capable of cleaving through any obstacle or weapon—and an enemy who had the one thing that Valsavis wanted most of all, the loyalty and affections of a villichi priestess who could hold her own with any man, and who was worth whatever pains it took to capture her devotion.

Valsavis looked down at the beautiful young girl sleeping peacefully in his bed and decided that no substitute would ever do again. It had been pleasant, but the pleasure had been ephemeral and, ultimately, unsatisfying. There was only one woman he had ever met who was truly worthy of him; one woman who could challenge him on every level. There was only one woman worth winning, no matter what the cost. And her name was Ryana.

When the time came, Valsavis thought, he would kill the elfling. But the priestess he would claim as his own reward, as the Shadow King had promised. And if he could not have her, he decided, she would have to die. I *will* have you, Ryana, he thought, if it takes both my life and yours. One way or the other, he thought, you are going to be mine, either in bed or on the field of battle. Resign yourself. It is inevitable.

He finished dressing and buckled on his sword belt.

It would not be long before they met the Silent One and departed on their journey across the Great Ivory Plain to the city of the undead. He decided that he would go to their room and invite them to join him for breakfast. They had much to talk about.

He was certain they suspected him, but he also knew that they could ill afford to dispense with his skills when it came to surviving what they would have to face in Bodach. Yes, indeed, he thought, regardless of whether they trusted him or not, they needed him. And so long as that was the case, he had the upper hand.

There was no answer when he knocked at their door. The image suddenly came to him of the two of them in bed together, and he felt his anger rise. With difficulty, he fought it down. No, he thought, not yet. Not yet. Now is not the time. But soon. He knocked once more. No answer. He placed his ear against the door. Could they have failed to hear? It seemed unlikely. Both were seasoned desert travelers, which meant they were light sleepers. In the desert, one had to come awake at once, alert and ready, if one wanted to survive.

He knocked again. "Sorak!" he called out. "Ryana! Open the door! It's me, Valsavis!"

There was no response. He tried the door. It was unbolted. He swung it open. There was no one inside the room. He noticed that the window shutters were open. And then he noticed that their packs were gone and the beds had not been slept in. He hurried quickly to the dining room, but there was no sign of them there among the other patrons having breakfast. He ran back to the lobby.

"My two companions," he said to the clerk, "the ones I paid you to keep a watch on . . . have you seen them?"

"No, sir," the clerk replied. "Not since last night, when they came in with you."

"They did not leave?"

"If they have, sir, they did not go by me, I assure you. But you could check with the gatekeeper."

Valsavis did just that, but the man at the gate had not seen them, either. Valsavis recalled the open window shutters in their room and went back into the garden. He stepped off the path and moved among the plants until he came to the outside of Sorak and Ryana's room. He checked the ground below the window, then swore softly. They had left by the window. Probably last night, while he had foolishly sported with the girl. He followed the trail to the wall. That explained why the gatekeeper had not seen them. He saw clearly where Ryana had stood to give Sorak a leg up, and then where she had scuffed her foot on the wall as he had helped her to climb over.

He immediately hurried back to his room and threw his things together, then left the inn, running down to the Avenue of Dreams. He ran past the bellaweed emporiums and through the plaza where they had fought the marauders. Nothing remained now to indicate the struggle except some dried bloodstains on the bricks. He came to the apothecary shop and threw open the door.

"Apothecary!" he called out. "Old man! Damn you, whatever your name is, where *are* you?"

Kallis came out through the beaded curtain. "Ah," he said, on seeing Valsavis, "back so soon? I had heard there was some trouble last night. You were injured perhaps? You seek some healing salve?"

"Damn your salves and potions!" said Valsavis. "Where is the Silent One?"

The old man shook his head. "Gone," he said.

"Gone *where?*"

"I do not know," said Kallis. "She does not always confide in me, you understand."

"I think I can guess where she has gone," Valsavis said through gritted teeth. "When did she leave?"

"I really cannot say," Kallis replied. "I have not seen her since last night, when you were here with your friends."

"What about the others? The two that I was with last night. Did they return?"

"No," said Kallis, shaking his head. "I have not seen them either. However, I can see that you are rather upset and agitated. That is not healthy for the constitution, you know. Are you quite certain I cannot interest you in some—"

But Valsavis was already going out the door. Cursing himself for a fool, he ran toward the stables by the east gate. The stablekeeper had not seen them, either. The kanks they had ridden were still there in their stalls. And none of the kanks they had sold were gone yet, either. Doubtless, the marauders had intended to claim them when they returned, but they had not been able to return. Valsavis quickly checked the other stables in the area, in case they had sought to trick him by obtaining mounts elsewhere. However, no one at any of the other stables had seen Sorak and Ryana, nor anyone answering to the description of the Silent One.

Was it possible? Valsavis wondered. Could they have actually proceeded on *foot?* They might have thought the kanks would leave an easier trail for him to follow, but then he already knew where they were going and, mounted, he could catch them quickly if they had gone on foot. Surely, they had to realize that, he thought. Why would they go on foot? It just did not make any sense.

He stepped outside the gate. With all the traffic going in and out, it was impossible to pick up their trail on the road leading up to the village gate. But at some point, he realized, they had to leave the road and head south, across the plain, toward Bodach. He went back to the stable to get his kank and the supplies that he stored there. It would take some time to replenish them and draw enough water from the well to fill all of his skins, but if they had gone on foot, as seemed to be the case, then catching up to them would pose no problem.

It was a much longer journey to Bodach from Salt View than it was to Salt View from Nibenay. They did not have quite as long a stretch of the Ivory Plain to cross as they headed south, but when they reached the inland silt basins that blocked their way, they would have to turn either to the east or to the west and go around them. It made no real difference which direction they chose, either way was about the same distance. They would have to go all the way around the silt basins and along the spit of land that separated the basins from the Estuary of the Forked Tongue, which meant they would have to make a wide, long sweep around to the peninsula that projected into the silt basins. At the tip of that peninsula lay Bodach. They would have to follow that route, going around one way or the other, unless, Valsavis thought, they had some means of crossing the silt basins. But he did not see how they could.

The silt basins were deep and wide, broken up by several desert islands in the center on which nothing could be found but sand. Nothing grew along their banks, not even the sparest desert vegetation. It was one of the most desolate and barren areas on Athas. There was no way they could construct a raft and pole their way across, because there would be nothing to construct it from. And there was no one there to ferry them. Not a soul lived around the silt basins, or anywhere else within miles of Bodach.

The only other possibility was for them to make their way to the small village of North Ledopolus, on the north bank of the estuary, and perhaps find a raft there that they could take across, but then they would have to drag the raft with them all the way to the silt basins, and making the detour to North Ledopolus would take them just as long as it would take to reach Bodach by land.

No, Valsavis thought, they would have to go around the silt basins, and on foot, the journey would be brutal and extremely time-consuming. What could they possibly be thinking? Unless, perhaps, there was something he simply did not know.

He replenished his supplies and drew more water, then mounted his kank and started out the gate. The road from the east gate of the village led back to the canyon pass through the Mekillots. They would have to leave the road sometime before they reached that pass. And they had not gone out the west gate. He had described them in detail to the gatekeeper at the east gate, and the man had remembered seeing them leave just after he began his shift the previous night. He insisted that they had gone out on foot.

It was still early in the morning. The gatekeeper was just getting ready to go off shift when Valsavis questioned him, which meant that they had left late last night. At most, they could have no more than six or seven hour's head start. And they would be traveling without having had any sleep. Valsavis shook his head, bewildered. They must have lost their minds. It seemed unbelievable that they could be so foolish. What did they hope to accomplish by this? Did they really think that they could lose him this way?

He followed the road leading back to the pass, riding slowly, watching to either side to see where they had gone off. Logic dictated that they would have gone off to the left and headed straight south, but they might have tried going off to the right and doubling back, just to throw him off the trail. After he had ridden a short distance, Valsavis found the spot where they had left the road. And it was to the *right*. He grinned. Just as he had anticipated. They had doubled back. Did they really hope to fool him that way?

However, his grin soon faded when he saw that their trail led not back the way they came, on a course doubling back parallel to the road, but *north*, toward the slopes of the lower foothills. They were going in the exact opposite direction, toward the mountains! *Why?*

After a while, he came to a pagafa grove, and there the trail simply ended. He dismounted and looked around, puzzled. He carefully checked the entire area. There were antloid tracks everywhere. Could they have fallen prey to antloids? Again, that did not seem to make sense. They were not inexperienced city dwellers. Far from it. They would not have simply stumbled upon a group of antloids. And antloids did not generally go out of their way to attack humans. Or elflings, for that matter. Workers did not attack at all, and soldier antloids attacked only if they felt their warren was being threatened, or if they had a queen with them.

It was said that pyreens had an affinity with nature's

creatures, but then the trail he had followed showed only two sets of tracks—Sorak's and Ryana's. There was no sign of the Silent One. Valsavis looked around. The branches of the nearby trees were stripped, and some of the dagger plants had leaves removed, as well. The ground all around the area, and especially in the center of the pagafa grove, showed a great deal of activity. What had the antloids been doing? And why had Sorak and Ryana come here?

In addition to the branches that had been neatly stripped off by the antloids, there was also evidence of branches that had been torn off and broken by a violent storm, but it was a storm that appeared to have been extremely localized. Such things were known to happen in the desert, Valsavis realized, but it was curious that it should have happened here, with all these other curious signs. He frowned. Exactly what *had* happened here?

He went back over the trail that Sorak and Ryana had left behind. They had been running. That much was clear. He could tell from the weight distribution. But why? To get to the grove? What was their hurry? Unless, Valsavis thought, they had been running to *keep up* with someone . . . or some*thing*. He crouched and carefully examined the trail. Yes, there it was. A rasclinn's track. But what was a rasclinn doing here in the flatlands? This was not their normal habitat. On the other hand, he thought, perhaps this was no ordinary rasclinn. Maybe the Silent One really *was* a pyreen, a shapechanger.

He followed the rasclinn's trail. It was harder to spot than the trail left behind by Sorak and Ryana, but there was no question about it. The trail led directly to the grove, then disappeared, just as Sorak

and Ryana's trail had disappeared. But where? And
how?

Valsavis knew there had to be an answer. It had to
be in the signs. Antloids working at some strange and
unknown task, leaving behind evidence that was completely out of character for their natural behavior; a
rasclinn leading Sorak and Ryana to the grove, and
then vanishing without a trace. Sorak and Ryana also
vanishing without a trace. And signs of a violent
storm. A very intense and very localized storm. Or
else . . .

"An elemental?" said Valsavis aloud. He swore
softly. All the available evidence seemed to point to
the same thing. The Silent One really *was* a pyreen, a
shapechanger able to influence the behavior of beasts
and raise air elementals. But to what purpose? And
what had the antloids been working at?

He wandered around the scene some more. The
ground had been disturbed, not only by the antloids
moving back and forth, but by the churning of the
storm, as if a small tornado had touched down. Or
perhaps several small tornados. Several elementals? It
was possible. How many had she raised?

Something on the ground caught his eye, and he
stooped to pick it up. It was a piece of dagger plant
leaf, but it had been torn very carefully lengthwise,
peeled to make a strand. . . . A strand, he thought. It
would be a very strong strand. Something that could
be used to bind together the branches the antloids
had snipped off from the pagafa trees. . . .

"A *raft?*" he said aloud.

And suddenly, it all came together. Sorak and
Ryana had come to the grove, and there was no sign
of a trail leaving it. It was as if they had simply disappeared into thin air. Or else *flown* up into it! Raised

up by elementals conjured by the pyreen.

With disgust, Valsavis tossed the strand of dagger plant leaf back down onto the ground. Of course, he thought. Now it all made sense. So that was why they had left the kanks behind. They had not gone on foot, after all. They had a much faster means of travel, on a wooden raft constructed by the antloids at the pyreen's direction and held up by the air elementals she had raised. And that also neatly solved the problem of taking all that time to circumvent the silt basins. They didn't need to go around the basins. They would simply fly over them. There would be no catching them now, he realized bitterly. He had failed. And it was his own fault. He had underestimated them. He had grown overconfident. Now he would have to pay the price.

Well, he thought, never let it be said that Valsavis did not accept responsibility for his mistakes. He raised his hand, gazing at the gold ring on his finger. For several moments, he stared at it, concentrating. Then his hand began to tingle and the golden eyelid opened.

"*You have something to report?*" the voice of the Shadow King asked within his mind.

"Yes, my lord. I fear that I have failed you."

There was a momentary stillness in his mind. Then the voice spoke once more. "*How?*"

Valsavis quickly told the Shadow King what he had discovered, without omitting his responsibility in allowing them to get away. When he had finished, the Shadow King did not reply at once. The golden eye stared at him for a long moment, then blinked once.

"*You have made a mistake, Valsavis,*" Nibenay said. "*Fortunately, it may not be irreparable. See that you do not make one again. Remain where you are. I shall send you a means to follow them.*"

The golden eyelid closed.

A means to follow them? Valsavis wondered what Nibenay had meant by that. How could he possibly follow them? Could the Shadow King bestow upon him the ability to fly? And at such a distance? Nibenay was a powerful sorcerer, but surely not even he could cast a spell clear across the Great Ivory Plain and the Mekillot Mountains! Obviously, however, he intended to do *something*. And he was apparently willing to forgive him for his mistake. That was no small thing. One thing was for certain. Nibenay would not forgive him twice.

Remain where you are, he had said. Well, he could do that. Especially since there did not seem to be anything else he *could* do. But how long was he to remain? Until Nibenay did whatever it was he was going to do, quite obviously. Valsavis had not had any breakfast yet. He went to his kank and took out some of his provisions, sat down on the ground and began to eat.

An hour later, he was still waiting. Most of a second hour lapsed. And then a shadow passed over Valsavis. He looked up. The shadow passed over him again. It was a roc. The huge bird was fifty feet long from head to tail feathers, with a wingspan of over one hundred feet. It circled, cried out once, and swooped down.

Valsavis grabbed for his sword. Then he realized that the creature was not stooping at him. It was gliding in for a landing. This was the means to follow them that Nibenay had sent, all the way from the Barrier Mountains. Valsavis grinned. The creature landed and stood there, cocking its huge, fearsome looking head at him.

"One moment, my feathered friend," Valsavis said, as he removed some of the supplies from his kank and slung the pouches over his shoulders. He would have to leave the rest behind, along with the kank, of course, but he could only take what he could carry. It would suffice. He no longer had to cross the desert and go around the inland silt basins. He would fly over them, just like Sorak and Ryana and the pyreen.

He climbed up onto the massive roc's back, straddling its thick neck with his legs. The huge bird cried out and beat its giant wings, lunging up into the air. The others would arrive in Bodach, thinking they had lost him, confident that he could never catch up to them in time.

Valsavis smiled. They would be wrong.

EIGHT

As they flew on the rushing wind, the moonlit desert spread out all around them, a wide and all-encompassing vista. The light of the twin moons, Ral and Guthay, sparkled on the salt below, giving the Ivory Plain a ghostly and ethereal appearance. It was much cooler at this higher altitude, and the wind rushed through their hair and clothing, making them shiver as they huddled together on the airborne raft.

"It's so beautiful!" Ryana said, enchanted by the sight despite the cold. At first, she had been frightened as the ground had dropped away, receding farther and farther below them, and she could not resist the rising panic that they were going to fall. But the air elementals were strong, and with Kara there to hold them together and guide them, Ryana soon relaxed and gave herself completely to the experience.

Beside her, she heard a sudden burst of utterly joyous and completely unrestrained laughter, and she glanced at Sorak to see his face shining with delight. His lips were stretched wide in a grin of pleasure, his nostrils flaring, his entire face animated in way that told her this wasn't Sorak anymore, but Kivara, his mischievous, childlike, female entity, whose personality was ruled by

195

the thrill of novelty, the hunger for pleasure and stimulation of sensation.

"I'm flying!" she shouted, happily. "Oh, Ryana, this is wonderful!"

Despite knowing that this was not really the Sorak that she loved, but another personality entirely, Ryana could not help feeling a lightness at seeing "him" so transported. Normally taciturn and stoic, sometimes grim and often moody, Sorak had never really given himself over to the emotion of joy. Perhaps because whatever part of him could do that had been the basis for what became the entity Kivara. She had none of his other qualities. They were two completely different people, of different ages, different genders even, who just happened to share the same physical body.

Kivara was like an irrepressible young girl ruled only by her passions and her curiosity. She didn't know any better and seemed to lack the ability to learn. Or perhaps she simply didn't care. Of all the personalities who made up the tribe of one that she knew as Sorak, Kivara was the most unpredictable.

The Guardian could always be counted on for her wise and thoughtful council and strong, maternal, stabilizing influence. The Ranger rarely spoke and remained largely self-contained, the hunter and the tracker, the strong and able male who played the role of the provider.

Lyric was the innocent, the naive and playful child who was content to look at the world with constant wonder and express himself in song. In some ways, he was the male counterpart to Kivara, save that he lacked her stubborn willfulness and amoral instincts. Of all Sorak's personalities, Lyric was the closest to the Inner Child, who slept cocooned deep in the collective subconscious of the tribe.

The Shade was the complete opposite side of that coin, the dark and menacing, terrifying, beastlike entity contained within all men, submerged for the most part deep within Sorak's subconscious, emerging without warning only when the tribe was severely threatened. Sometimes Sorak could control him. More often, he could not. Rarely did Sorak even remember what had occurred while the Shade took control of his body, but Ryana had seen on a number of occasions what the Shade could do, and it was frightening.

Screech was that part of Sorak that was closest to the animal kingdom, an evolutionary throwback to a time when they all were little more than animals themselves. He could commune with beasts and speak to every Athasian species in its own language, understanding their instincts and behavior and capable of mimicking their behavior patterns.

Eyron was, in some ways, the most human of Sorak's varied aspects, even though Sorak had no human blood. At least, Ryana thought, not to her knowledge or his. Eyron was coldly pragmatic, the thinker and the planner among them, but his nature was often cynical and pessimistic. He was the cautious side of Sorak's personality, developed into a discrete identity. Much of the time, Eyron could be supremely aggravating, especially given his intelligence, but he was a vital part of the whole, without which Sorak would have been incomplete.

And then, of course, there was the mysterious Kether, whom none of the others could explain. Kether was a part of them, and yet not a part of them. Sorak insisted that Kether did not spring from within him, but came, somehow, from without, an

ethereal and powerful, serene and spiritual other-
worldly entity that came upon him like a visitation
from some other plane of existence. But Kivara. . . .

Ryana knew that there was never any way of predicting what Kivara was liable to do. The Shade was
easily the most frightening of Sorak's personalities,
but at least Ryana knew what to expect of him. With
Kivara, she was never certain, and so Kivara made
her feel the most uneasy. She did not come out often,
but when she did, her behavior was usually willful
and irresponsible. And Ryana suddenly realized that
a fragile wooden raft, held together by nothing more
than dagger plant fibers and antloid spit, buoyed up
high above the ground by the swirling vortices of air
elementals, was hardly the best place for Kivara to
emerge suddenly and assume control of Sorak's body.

"Look at me!" Kivara shouted, leaping to her feet
and throwing out her arms like wings. "I'm a bird!"

The raft gave a lurch as the balance shifted, and
Ryana became alarmed. She grabbed Kivara by the
leg. "Sit down, you little fool!" she shouted. "You
want to upset the raft and send us both plummeting
to the ground?"

"What's the matter?" asked Kivara tauntingly.
"Afraid?" It was Sorak's voice, only it was pitched
higher, and it had a completely different quality—coy
and mischievous, challenging and stubborn. It was
the voice of a child dancing on the edge of a precipice,
completely oblivious to the risk it faced.

"Yes, I am afraid," Ryana replied, "and so would
you be if you had any sense! This raft is all that keeps
us from plunging to our deaths. Now sit down and
stop acting like a child!"

"Oh, pooh!" Kivara said, petulantly, but she sat
down again. Actually, she *plopped* down, simply drop-

ping to a sitting position the way children often do, and the raft gave another violent lurch. Ryana grabbed her for support as the raft rocked dangerously on the wind currents, and Kivara giggled.

"I ought to pull your breeches down and spank you!" said Ryana, angrily.

"Oooh, that sounds like fun!" Kivara countered, giving her a coy sidelong glance. "Why don't you?"

Ryana glared at her. "Because I know you too well, that's why. You would never feel it. The moment I began to warm your bottom, you would duck under and I'd find myself in the embarrassing situation of spanking Sorak."

"Oh, you never know, he might enjoy it," said Kivara. "And so might you, for that matter. Maybe it's what you really want."

"Ohhh, you're insufferable!"

"And you just don't know how to have any fun."

"*Fun?*" Ryana said. "Do you even have any idea what we are doing? Where we are going?"

"What difference does it make?" Kivara asked, looking around at the spectacular view spreading out below them. "*Look* at this! Is it not incredible?"

"Kivara, we are on our way to Bodach, the city of the undead," Ryana said firmly.

"Undead?" Kivara said, glancing at her uncertainly.

"Yes, undead. An entire city of them. There will be hundreds, perhaps thousands."

"Well, what we going *there* for? That's stupid!"

"We have to go there to find a talisman known as the Breastplate of Argentum and take it to the Sage."

Kivara made a face. "Him, again. All we ever do is go here, go there, running all over this dreary desert like a stupid erdlu, and for what? What has the Sage ever done for us?"

Ryana tried to fight down her mounting irritation. In the past, whenever Kivara had come out, the others would allow her some freedom, but her unpredictable and willful nature eventually made it necessary for the Guardian to exert control and force her to duck under once again. Lately, however, the last several times Kivara had come out, she had resisted the efforts of the Guardian to hold her in check. It was a worrisome development. And Ryana did not wish to antagonize Kivara at this point by calling for the Guardian. This was certainly not the place for Kivara to respond with one of her violent temper tantrums.

"The Sage works for us all," Ryana explained patiently. "He is the only power that stands between us and the dragon kings, the only hope for the future of our world. And he is the only one who may be able to help Sorak learn the truth about himself."

"Well, I don't see why that matters," said Kivara stubbornly.

"It matters to Sorak," replied Ryana, struggling to control her temper. Kivara could be absolutely infuriating.

"It wouldn't change anything, you know," Kivara replied. And then she gave Ryana an uneasy sidelong glance. "Would it?"

"I do not know," Ryana said. "That is a question the tribe shall have to answer for itself when we confront the Sage. Wouldn't you want to learn where you came from?"

"Why? I am already here."

That was, of course, vintage Kivara, thought Ryana. Living only in the present. "Perhaps it does not mean anything to you," she said, "but it is important to Sorak to know and understand his origins. And perhaps to some of the others, as well."

"Important enough to risk going to a place full of undead?" Kivara said. She shook her head. It looked odd to see him evidence her mannerisms. Even though Ryana had grown up with him, it was something she had never quite gotten used to completely. It always threw her off a bit.

"That is not the only reason, as I told you," said Ryana. "We go to Bodach in the service of the Sage."

"This is boring," said Kivara, her limited attention span used up. "I don't wish to talk about it anymore."

"What would you rather talk about?"

"I don't know. It's not much fun talking to you. You never have anything interesting to say. You never like to have any fun."

"I like to have fun as much as anyone," Ryana said. "However, there is a time and place for such things."

"Only you never seem to find the time or the place," Kivara replied petulantly. "Look at what we're doing, Ryana! We are *flying!* We are as high as birds! Does it not make your spirit soar?"

"Yes," said Ryana, "but if I only pay attention to the soaring of my spirit, then I may do something careless, and we will both fall to the ground and to our deaths. That is something that you need to learn, Kivara. There is nothing wrong in taking joy in your emotions and in the thrilling sensations you experience, but not at the expense of your better judgment. Because if you do, then you lose all sense of perspective and self-preservation."

"That is what the Guardian is for," Kivara said indifferently. "I cannot be bothered with such things. Not when I am flying!" And she jumped to her knees, throwing out her arms once more. The raft once again rocked dangerously on the wind funnel that bore them up, and Ryana grabbed her for support.

"I think that will be quite enough," the Guardian said, taking over from Kivara. The voice was still Sorak's, but the tone was completely different. The pitch had dropped slightly, and her voice was one of calm control and reassurance. Ryana could imagine Kivara protesting loudly within Sorak's mind, but the Guardian had emerged now and taken firm control. "Forgive me," she said. "She slipped out."

"It's all right, Guardian," said Ryana. "No harm done."

"I am not so sure," the Guardian replied. Her tone sounded slightly concerned. "Kivara is growing more and more difficult to control. Each time she comes out, she more stubbornly resists going back under. She appears to be growing stronger."

"You think there is a chance that you may lose control?" Ryana asked, unnerved by the idea.

"I do not know for certain," the Guardian replied. "I certainly hope not. That would upset the balance of the tribe."

"It could upset a lot more than that," Ryana said, looking down at the raft uneasily. "She isn't bad, I know that, but the trouble is she simply does not *think*."

"She is very young," the Guardian replied. "And in a full grown male body, at that. That makes things more difficult."

"That's putting it mildly," Ryana said. "Well, we can always look on the bright side. At least we've lost Valsavis. There is no way that he can possibly catch us now."

"Are you quite certain?"

Ryana shrugged. "Even mounted on a fast kank, it

would take him days just to reach the silt basins, and then he'd still have to go all the way around them to reach the peninsula where Bodach lies. By the time he gets there, we will surely have completed our task."

"Perhaps," the Guardian replied. "But then what? Bodach is still a long way from anywhere. If I recall the map in *The Wanderer's Journal* correctly, the nearest settlement to Bodach is North Ledopolus, and the nearest city would be Balic, but it lies on the opposite shore of the Estuary of the Forked Tongue. We would still have to cover a great deal of ground to reach civilization, and that would give Valsavis more than ample opportunity to close the distance between us."

"I had not thought of that," Ryana said with concern. "Has Sorak considered this?"

"He has considered it," the Guardian replied, nodding. "For the present, he is primarily concerned with surviving the undead in Bodach and finding the Breastplate of Argentum. And that will certainly pose challenges enough. Valsavis can be dealt with later, but you must not think that we have seen the last of him. He is too clever and resourceful a man to be so easily discounted. True, he will have a long journey to Bodach, but there is no telling how long it may take us to find the talisman. And we have no way of knowing how much of our time will be spent dealing with the threat of the undead. All Valsavis has to do is head for Bodach, since he already knows that is our destination. And he also knows that the only way back to civilization from Bodach is to the west."

"We could just fly right over him," Ryana said.

"Perhaps," the Guardian said. "But we do not know that Kara would be willing to convey us to our next destination. She has already undertaken much on our behalf. Or on behalf of the Sage, I should say. Either way, it would not be fair for us to expect any more from her. If she chooses to return to Salt View once she has done her part in conveying us to Bodach, that is certainly her right."

"Yes, of course," Ryana said. "I understand."

"Don't worry, little sister," Sorak said, emerging suddenly. "We will manage. We always have."

She smiled, pleased to see him back again, especially after her unsettling experience with Kivara. "Did you have a nice nap?"

"Yes. I truly needed the rest. But what of you? You have not slept."

"You think I could *sleep* under these circumstances?" she said.

"I suggest you try," he said. "You will need all of your strength and energy when we reach Bodach."

"It should be morning when we get there," she said. "The undead will be at rest."

"Yes," said Sorak. "If we are fortunate, we may complete our task in time and leave Bodach before nightfall. But we must not count on that. We cannot afford to assume anything. You really must try to get some rest. At least for several hours."

She glanced around uncertainly. "Sleep on a tiny wooden raft hundreds of feet above the ground, buffeted by the wind?" She shook her head. "Well, I can try, but in truth, I do not think that it will do any good at all."

"Here," he said. "I will hold you. Try to get some sleep."

She snuggled into his strong arms. It felt good to be there.

"Close your eyes," he said.

She took a deep breath and shut her eyes. Sud-

denly, she heard a gentle humming in her mind, very
low at first, then rising slowly, until the voice of Lyric,
singing beautifully, not aloud, but in her mind, filled
her with his song. She held her breath for a moment
in amazement and delight. She had never known that
he could do that. Then she sighed and settled into
Sorak's arms, secure in their embrace as Lyric sang to
her, a gently soothing, haunting melody for her and
her alone. The rocking motion of the raft upon the
wind seemed almost like the rocking of a cradle. She
smiled as she lay in Sorak's arms, her mind filled with
Lyric's song, and soon she drifted off to sleep and
dreamt of the verdant valleys and forests high in the
Ringing Mountains. And the winds continued to
blow them toward the city of the undead.

* * * * *

"Ryana," Sorak said, squeezing her gently. "Wake
up."

Her eyelids fluttered open, and for a brief moment,
she did not remember where she was. She had gone
to sleep with Lyric's beautiful voice singing in her
mind and had dreamt of her young girlhood at the
villichi convent in the Ringing Mountains.

In her dream, she had been no more than seven or
eight years old, her body still awkward and coltish,
her sense of wonder at the world she lived in still
undiminished and untainted by its harsher realities.
She had dreamt of running down the forest trails
around the convent, her long hair streaming behind
her in the breeze as her feet pounded on the sun-
dappled ground. She had run with all the exuberance
and joy of youth, trying to keep up with Sorak, who
even then could outsprint her easily with his elvish

speed and endurance. It had seemed, then, that they would live out their whole lives that way, studying and training at the convent, nurtured by the loving bond of the villichi sisterhood, bathing in the bracing cold waters of the small lagoon fed by the stream running down from the mountains, running through the peaceful, green valley with its sheltering canopy of trees, sharing simple pleasures and true contentment. It had been a happy and uncomplicated time. And as she awoke, she realized that it was gone forever, faded just like her dream.

"We have arrived," said Sorak.

She sat up and followed his gaze. They were being blown across the inland silt basins and, ahead of them, now clearly visible, was the ancient, ruined city of Bodach.

It was shortly after sunrise. From the height at which they flew upon their wooden raft, Ryana could see the peninsula jutting out into the silt basins from the north bank of the Estuary of the Forked Tongue, where it met the Sea of Silt. Near the tip of the peninsula, the spires of Bodach rose high above the surrounding countryside. Ryana caught her breath.

At one time, it must have been a truly magnificent city, testimony to the accomplishments of the ancients. But as they approached, they could see that it now possessed merely a shadow of its former glory. Many of the buildings were crumbling into ruin, and the once sparkling edifices were now scarred and worn by blowing sand. There were ancient, rotting wooden docks extending out into the silt basins, where boats had once been moored when the basins and the sea were water instead of slowly shifting sand and dust. At one time, during an earlier age, a time that no one now living on Athas could remember, the

city had stood almost completely surrounded by
water, a bastion of commerce and flourishing culture.
Part of the spit of land now extending to the east
must once have been submerged, forming a protected
bay that opened out onto the sea.

Ryana tried to imagine what it must have looked
like then, with triangular-sailed dhows gliding across
the sparkling, blue water of the bay, pulling into the
docks and unloading their cargoes. She tried to imagine the bustling crowds around the docks; the merchants loading up their wares to take to market; the
fishermen sorting and cleaning their catches and
hanging out their nets. As they started to descend,
she could see the city streets, once paved with brick
and cobblestones, now covered with blowing sand
that had piled up into dunes against the building
walls. She could see the large and ornate fountains in
the plazas, many of them surmounted by beautiful
stone sculptures that had once spouted water in
graceful arcs, all of them now dry and filled with
sand. The streets were totally deserted. There was
not a sign of life anywhere. And, of course, she
thought, there wouldn't be. It was now a city of the
undead.

Legend had it that those who first came to Bodach,
seeking the fabled treasure of the ancients, fell under
a curse the long-dead sorcerers had left behind. They
now roamed the streets at night, dead but animated,
held in thrall by the curse of the ancients and doomed
to spend eternity protecting the treasure they had left
behind. They had come to plunder, and they stayed
to act as terrifying sentinels, preying on all those who
came in their way. And in this manner, over the centuries, their numbers had grown until Bodach was
now a city populated by an army of undead, deserted

by day and crawling with horror by night.

As their little raft descended farther, skimming over the rooftops and weaving among the crumbling spires and towers, Sorak and Ryana stared down silently at the deserted streets below. The ruined city was filled with an eerie and disquieting stillness. Nothing stirred down there. Not even a rodent or an insect. Whatever lay in wait for them, it lay in hiding.

The raft descended as the force of the funnel-clouds holding it aloft gradually abated, and one by one, the air elementals dispersed, peeling off and disappearing into the distance with a sound like wind whistling through a canyon. Finally, only Kara remained, and she lowered them gently to the ground in a large, central plaza of the ruined city. The raft settled with a slight bump and Sorak stepped off first, followed by Ryana, as the swirling vortex that whirled scant feet away slowed and gradually dissipated, revealed Kara standing in its place. She took a deep breath and exhaled slowly and wearily. Even with the help of the elementals, it was obvious that the journey had taken a great deal out of her.

Sorak glanced up at the sky. They had perhaps twelve hours before the sun began to set once more and the darkness unlocked the full extent of Bodach's terror.

"Are you well, my lady?" Ryana asked Kara with concern.

The pyreen smiled, wanly. "Yes. Merely tired."

"Perhaps if you took some time to rest—"

The pyreen shook her head, emphatically. "No. There *is* no time. I do not have much to fear from the undead. I can avoid them easily enough. But you will be vulnerable when darkness falls. We must try to find the talisman by then and be gone."

Sorak recalled the last time he had faced undead. It had been back in Tyr, when a defiler templar had raised them from their graves and sent them out against him. He had managed to summon Kether barely in the nick of time, and the mysterious spiritual entity had somehow defeated them through the use of powers Sorak could not even begin to comprehend. He had no consciousness of what happened when he manifested Kether, nor did any of the others. And he did not know if Kether had prevailed over the undead because he had been stronger or because he had found a way to neutralize the spell that animated them. Either way, it had happened only once, and he could not be sure it would happen here in the same way. Fighting dozens of undead was one thing, especially when he had the preserver wizards of the Veiled Alliance to help him. Fighting hundreds, perhaps even thousands, of them was something else again.

"Do you know where the Breastplate of Argentum is to be found?" he asked Kara.

"I know where the treasure is," she replied. "However, if it is not among the treasure, then we may have to search the entire city."

"But that could take weeks!" Ryana said.

"Days, perhaps," the pyreen replied. "I do have the ability to detect magic, and that should help us greatly in our search. It was how I knew not to trust your friend, Valsavis."

"He is no friend of ours," Ryana said.

"Wait," said Sorak. "You mean you detected magic on him?"

Kara nodded. "I could not tell specifically what sort, without being obvious, and that would have alerted him. But there was a strong aura of defiler magic about him."

"The Shadow King," Ryana said. "That settles it. There can be no doubt about Valsavis now, not that I ever had much to begin with."

"Well, we do not need to concern ourselves about Valsavis now," said Sorak. "There is no time to waste. We had best be about our business."

"This way," said Kara, leading them across the plaza.

"What if we do not find the talisman by nightfall?" asked Ryana as they followed her.

"Then we must allow enough time for us to leave the city and be well way from it before darkness falls," said Kara, "so that we may return and continue our search again in the morning. Of course, that is no guarantee that the undead shall not follow."

"But if they do not know that we were here—" Sorak began.

"They know," said Kara, walking quickly. "They know even now. They can sense our presence."

Ryana glanced around uneasily.

Kara led them across the plaza, from which three streets led off in different directions. Suddenly, Ryana had an eerie sense of deja vu. As they crossed the plaza, she realized that this was exactly like the game they'd played back at the Desert Palace in Salt View. One street led off the plaza to the left, curving slightly, so that they could not see what lay around the bend. Another street led straight away from them, offering an unobstructed view for several hundred yards. And the third street led off to the right . . . and part of it was blocked by rubble. It seemed too much for coincidence.

"Sorak . . ." she said.

He nodded. "I know. It is just like that game we

played back in Salt View."

"It seems exactly the same," Ryana said. "Exactly, right down to the pile of rubble there. But how can that be?"

Sorak glanced toward Kara, walking ahead of them with a purposeful stride. "Perhaps she had something to do with it," he said. "The manager of the Desert Palace was the son of Kallis, the apothecary, above whose shop she lives."

"You think she purposely designed the game to mirror the reality?" Ryana asked. "But why?"

Sorak shook his head. "I do not know. And I do not know that she designed the game. It is possible that she told Kallis about her journey here all those years ago, and that he may have told his son, perhaps in the form of a story. And perhaps his son recalled it when he designed the game. It could be as innocent as that."

"Or else there could be a purpose to it," said Ryana.

"Yes, I suppose there could be," Sorak said. "Time alone will tell."

"Could the Guardian probe Kara's mind?"

"A pyreen?" Sorak shook his head. "Not without her being aware of it. It would be foolhardy to attempt using psionics on a pyreen. They are masters of the art. And there could be no greater display of disrespect."

"No, I suppose not," Ryana acknowledged. "But I would feel much better if I knew what to expect."

"*Expect the unexpected,*" came a voice within both their minds. Kara stopped and turned to smile at them. "The ears of a pyreen are even sharper than the ears of elves," she said.

They continued walking. Kara chose the street that

led to the northeast.

"I meant no offense, lady," said Ryana.

"I know," said Kara. "Your reaction is quite understandable, under the circumstances."

"But the game, my lady . . ."

"I know about the game," she said. "And you were right. There is a purpose to it. There are many adventurers who come to Salt View hoping to seek me out and pry the secret of the treasure from me. They do not know, of course, that the Silent One can speak, or that she is pyreen. They have only heard the story, since elevated into legend, that I have been to Bodach, that I had found the treasure and survived. They assume that I am some old woman who had embraced the druid vows after her ordeal, and they imagine they can prevail upon me to write down what I know."

"So the game is an attempt to draw them out so they can be identified," said Sorak.

"More than that," said Kara. "There is no adventurer who can resist the lure of Salt View's entertainments. And 'The Lost Treasure of Bodach' is played in each of Salt View's gaming houses. Who would not be tempted, if that was what they came to seek? And by the way they play, the gamemasters can evaluate their responses. You would be surprised how much can be learned about an individual by watching how they play."

"And what did you learn about us from the way we played?" Sorak asked. "I assume that word had somehow reached you concerning us long before we reached the apothecary shop."

"Indeed," she said. "I had been told to expect you long before you arrived in Salt View, but I needed to be sure you were the ones. I did not wish to expose

Kallis to unnecessary risk."

"You care for the old man," Ryana said with a smile.

"Of course. He is my husband."

"Your *husband?*" Ryana was shocked.

"Do not be deceived by appearance," Kara said. "Remember that I am far older than he is, but I am pyreen, while he is human."

"Then, that would mean that the manager of the Desert Palace is your son?" Ryana asked.

"No. Kivrin is the son of Kallis and his first wife, who died in giving birth to him. But he is my adopted son, and has taken the vows of a preserver."

"Why marry a human?" Sorak asked. "Why even live in Salt View? I have always thought pyreens avoided humans."

"Most pyreens do," she replied. "There are not many of us left. And while we are strong and long-lived and have abilities superior to those of humans, we are not invulnerable. We do not take unnecessary chances, but each of us has a purpose to which we devote our lives. Mine requires that I live in Salt View."

"Why?"

"You will soon learn that for yourselves," she answered enigmatically.

"And Kallis?" asked Ryana.

"Even a pyreen can get lonely," Kara said. "Kallis is a good man, and his heart is pure. His wife's death left a great void within his life. I have done my best to fill it."

Sorak stopped suddenly before an old building that somehow looked familiar, even though he had never before seen it. And then he realized what it was. "The stone tavern," he said.

Kara smiled. "Yes. But unlike the game scenario, we will not seek shelter here."

They continued on. "And there is the walled home of the aristocrat," Ryana said, as they turned a bend in the street.

"Filled with the undead?" asked Sorak.

"Perhaps," said Kara. "They do move around, you know."

They bypassed it and continued on.

"There is one thing I have been wondering," said Sorak as they walked down the twisting, sand-blown street. "Why did you come to Bodach in the first place? What use would a pyreen have for treasure?"

"None," Kara replied.

"Then . . . why?"

"I came seeking something else," she said. "The *true* lost treasure of the ancients."

"The true lost treasure?" Sorak said, puzzled. "That would seem to imply that there is a false one."

"Yes," Kara said, enigmatically. "It would, indeed."

"Why do I feel suddenly as if I am back in the Desert Palace, playing the same game?" asked Sorak.

"Every game is a test," said Kara. "A test of skill, of luck, of perspicacity. Some games are merely more difficult than others."

"So this is a test, then?" Sorak said.

"Did you not know that when you came?"

"Whose test? Yours? Or the Sage's?"

"It is *your* test," Kara said, looking at him.

"And what if I should fail?"

"You mean you did not consider that before?" she asked.

Sorak said, "I have considered it at length."

"Good. One should always give considerations to one's actions."

"Is there a purpose to these riddles?" asked Ryana irritably.

"There is a purpose to everything," said Kara. "We must turn right here."

They proceeded down another street, deeper into the heart of the ruined city. Sorak asked no more questions. Kara had made it clear that he would discover the answers for himself in due time. She was here to provide guidance, not answers. So be it, he thought. He had come this far, there was no turning back now.

As they walked down the narrow, twisting, turning streets, Sorak recognized many scenes from the game he had played back at the Desert Palace. It was almost as if he could hear the voice of the gamemaster describing them in detail.

"*You come to a juncture where two streets branch off, one ahead of you and to the left, one ahead and to the right. Directly to the left and right there are two dark and narrow alleyways. You cannot see where they lead. Which course do you take?*"

They took the street ahead and to the left. By now, several hours had passed. Sorak wondered why she had chosen to set them down where she did when they had this far to walk. He saw no reason why she could not have landed the raft closer to whatever their destination was. The streets were certainly wide enough, and they had passed through several plazas that would have served equally well to land the raft. He was tempted to ask, but didn't. There had to be a reason. Perhaps he could figure it out for himself.

It was after noon by the time they reached a large building with a columned portico in front of it. There was a wide flight of stone steps that ran all around the front of the building, leading up to the arched entryway. Kara turned and started to ascend the steps.

"Is it here?" asked Ryana. "Is this the building where they kept the treasure?"

"One of them," said Kara.

"I am tired of these riddles!" said Ryana, forgetting her respectful tone in her exasperation. "We have wasted half the day! We could easily have landed right *here*, instead of on the other side of the city! Or is it that you *want* us to waste time, so that we may encounter the undead? Is *that* part of the test, too?"

Kara suddenly held up her hand for quiet, cocking her head and listening intently. "This way, quickly!" she said.

They hurried up the steps. No sooner had they stepped under the shelter of the columned portico than a large shadow passed over the plaza. A loud, screeching cry pierced the air, and they heard the beating of gigantic wings.

The creature came swooping down over the city, casting its huge shadow over the spot where they had stood moments earlier. The ominous sound of its wingbeats filled the air. Its shrill, reverberating cry echoed off the building walls as it passed overhead, momentarily blotting out the sun with its huge bulk.

Ryana glanced up. "A roc!" she said with astonishment as the creature passed over them. "But what is doing *here*, so far from the mountains?"

"It was sent by the Shadow King," said Kara. "And it brings your old traveling companion, Valsavis."

Sorak suddenly understood. "You knew that Nibenay would help him find a way to follow us," he said. "That is why you left the raft on the other side of the city, to make him think that we are somewhere in that vicinity. You meant to throw him off and buy us time."

"If he is, indeed, as good a tracker as you say," said Kara, "then it will not take him much longer to find us than it took us to reach here. And there is still much left to do. Hurry. There is not much time left."

She stepped through the archway and disappeared into the shadows of the building.

NINE

"Why must we be so afraid of Valsavis?" asked Ryana, her voice echoing in the darkness of the cavernous building. The sound of it startled her slightly, and she lowered her voice. "He may be skilled and dangerous, but could he really hope to stand against the three of us?"

"It is not Valsavis we must fear, but his master, Nibenay," said the pyreen as she led the way. "That Valsavis was able to follow us so quickly proves what I had suspected all along. The magic I detected on him was some means for him to communicate with Nibenay. And with Valsavis here, the Shadow King has never been closer to uncovering the secret of the Sage."

"Then the Sage is *here?*" said Sorak with amazement. "In *Bodach?*"

"No," said Kara from the darkness just ahead. "But the secret to finding him is here."

Ryana had no idea what that meant. She could barely see ahead of her, but she held onto Sorak's arm, knowing he could see easily in the darkness, as could Kara. For his part, Sorak's view was very different. He followed Kara down a wide, tiled corridor, past fluted stone columns that held up the roof high overhead. He had no idea what sort of building this once was. Some meeting hall, perhaps, or noble's palace. Many of the tiles on which they walked were cracked, and some were missing. Here and there, the floor had buckled, and several times they stepped around some rubble where pieces of the ceiling had dropped down. He hoped the roof would not fall in on them. Near the entrance, sand had blown into the building, but now that they had gone farther inside, there was merely a thick layer of dust upon the floor. And after they had gone a little farther, he suddenly heard the last sound he would have expected to hear in such a place.

"Water!" he said.

"*Here?*" Ryana said with disbelief, but a moment later, she could hear it, too. The unmistakable, old, familiar, trickling sound of water, like that of a babbling brook.

Ahead of them, Kara stopped and held her arms out, bent at the elbows, palms facing upward. She mumbled a spell under her breath, and there was the rushing sound of air being displaced, followed by a sudden spark of brightness that grew rapidly until it formed into a swirling ball of flame about the size of a large melon. Kara brought her arms up, moving them inward, then fanning them out, and the fireball divided into four smaller fireballs that whooshed across the room in four different directions, landing in four ancient iron braziers that suddenly erupted into flame, illuminating the large chamber in which they stood.

Sorak caught his breath, and Ryana gasped with astonishment at what they beheld. In front of them, taking up almost all of the floor space in the chamber, was a large, rectangular pool of water that sparkled in the firelight. In the center of the pool, there rose a stone fountain that sprayed water up into the air, recirculating and filtering the water in the pool. There was no way of telling how long it must have been here. Centuries, at least. And probably much longer.

"But . . . how can this be?" Ryana said with disbelief. It seemed to defy all rational explanation. "It is impossible!"

"You see it with your own eyes, do you not?" asked Kara, turning toward them.

"It must be some sort of trick," said Sorak, "an illusion. One cannot always believe what one sees. How could there still be water in this pool after so many years? How could it still remain so clear? Where does it come from?"

"It comes from an underground spring deep beneath our feet," said Kara, "under many layers of rock. The ancients truly had accomplished marvels in their time, during the age of science. This building was once a public bath. The fountain draws the water up from deep beneath the ground, and it is filtered by a system of porous rock that still serves its purpose after all these years. On the surface, Bodach appears to be a dead and ruined city, but there are many wonders to be found here if you know where to look, not the least of which is this."

She walked over to the wall and reached into one of the recesses spaced at intervals around the pool and containing ornamental statues. She pulled a concealed lever. There must have been some sort of hidden counterbalance, for it moved easily. The arc of the fountain grew smaller, and after a moment, became no more than a trickle. And as they watched, the water in the tiled pool began to drain away. The water level dropped by inches, then by a foot, then farther still, and they could see something beneath the surface that they had not seen before for the darkness of the ceiling tiles, which reflected in the surface. As the water level dropped still farther, something metallic gleamed beneath it, and suddenly both Sorak and Ryana realized what they were seeing as the water drained away.

It was the fabled lost treasure of Bodach. As the water receded, they saw that the treasure filled the entire pool. It was an absolutely priceless hoard. They stared, open-mouthed, as thousands upon thousands of gold and silver coins gleamed in the soft firelight, among rubies, sapphires, emeralds, diamonds, amethysts, and other precious stones. There were jewel-encrusted weapons scattered throughout the pile of riches, glittering necklaces and tiaras and brooches, bracelets and arm bands, chains of office and medallions, ceremonial armor made from precious metals, a fortune that made those of the richest sorcerer-kings of Athas pale by comparison. In a world where metal of any kind had become so scarce that weapons made of iron commanded prices few could afford, here was a mountainous horde of precious metals and jewels that rivaled even the most fanciful depictions of the treasure in the legends.

"I cannot believe my eyes," said Sorak, staring at the hoard with fascination. "Is all this *real?*"

"Yes, it is real," said Kara. "Gathered over the years from all over the city and placed here by the undead, who were driven by some vague instinct left over from their days among the living, when they came to Bodach seeking riches, and found instead an eternal living death. Each night, if there is no prey within the city for them to pursue, they shamble through the ruined buildings and the cellars and the storehouses, seeking the wealth they once came here to find. An old chest of jewels in the residence of some long-dead aristocrat, a ceremonial golden dagger in a dusty council chamber, found by some animated corpse and polished lovingly, then brought here and dumped with all the rest. Bit by bit, the horde accumulates. It is much larger now than when first I came."

"But . . . why do they bring it here?" asked Sorak.

Kara shrugged. "I cannot say. The undead are not rational creatures. Their minds, if they have not rotted away, are incapable of coherent thought. They are like simple beasts, driven by hunger and by instincts they cannot truly understand. If they were not so horrifying and so dangerous, they would be pathetic."

"And the Breastplate of Argentum is somewhere among all *this?*" said Sorak, aghast. "How could we ever find it?"

"It was not here when I first came to Bodach," Kara said. "Of course, I was not searching for it then, but for something else entirely. However, when I found this precious horde, I detected nothing magical within it. Since then, they may have found the talisman and brought it here. They would not know what it was. To the undead, it would merely be a breastplate made of silver. But if it is here, at least it will not be near the bottom of the pile."

"But even so, finding it among all this would take forever!" said Ryana with a sinking feeling as she realized the sheer impossibility of searching through all the treasure piled before them. "And we have only hours until nightfall!" The task seemed utterly impossible and hopeless. "We shall never find it if it lies buried among all this!"

"Perhaps not," said Kara. "But this had to be the first place for us to look. If there is now a magical talisman within this horde, I shall know it in a moment. But I can detect only the aura of its magic. I cannot be absolutely certain it is the talisman we seek. Still, it would have enormous power, and that should help identify it."

She closed her eyes and held her hands out toward the treasure horde, palms facing down. Sorak and Ryana held their breath as Kara slowly moved her hands in a gradual, sweeping motion.

"Yes," she said, after a moment. "There *is* something . . . something very strong. . . ."

"Where?" asked Sorak, scanning the pile anxiously.

"A moment," Kara said, trying to localize the aura she was picking up. She opened her eyes. "There," she said, pointing. "At the far end of the pool, near the righthand corner."

Sorak and Ryana ran to the area she indicated and stared down at the pile of treasure in the nearly drained pool. "I do not see anything that looks the way it was described," said Sorak. "Can you pinpoint the location more precisely?"

Kara came over to them. "I will try," she said. She closed her eyes and held her hands out once again. "There," she said, pointing to an area roughly four feet out from the side of the pool.

Sorak started to lower himself over the side, but Ryana stopped him. "No, not like that," she said. "It would take forever to sort through it all by hand, and you may cut yourself on something in the pile. It would be much better if we used the Way."

"Of course," he said with a grimace. "How stupid of me. In my enthusiasm, I simply was not thinking."

They both stood beside the pool. Ryana closed her eyes and concentrated as Sorak slipped back and allowed the Guardian to come forth. Kara stood by, concentrating on the magical aura of the talisman to help guide them in their efforts.

For a moment, nothing happened, and then several of the objects on top of the pile of treasure shifted slightly with a clinking sound. Then they rose up into the air, as if something had forced them up from underneath, and the next moment, it was as if another fountain had suddenly been turned on, an invisible fountain that spewed pieces of the treasure horde up into the air, flying outward from the spot Kara had indicated and landing atop the treasure pile several feet away.

As the Guardian and Ryana combined their telekinetic powers, jewels and coins seemed to erupt into the air, sparkling in the firelight from the braziers. Necklaces and rings and bracelets made of gold and silver and studded with precious stones flew up and landed a short distance away, raining down upon the pile of treasure with metallic, clinking sounds. As bits and pieces of the treasure horde were thrown up into the air, Sorak, Ryana, and Kara watched for the glint of silver breastplate made of chain mail.

Sorak was reminded of the exercises they had done as children back at the villichi convent, lifting objects into the air with the power of their minds and holding them there for as long as they could, juggling balls and making them describe graceful arabesques in midair. As a boy, he had found those exercises difficult, frustrating, and pointless, and could never move so much as one little ball with the power of his mind, no matter how hard he concentrated. He would exert himself until his face turned red and sweat started to break out on his forehead, all to no avail, only to execute the exercise successfully the moment he gave up.

He had not known then that it was not he but the Guardian who was doing it, that he himself had no psionic powers, but that others of the tribe did. He had not yet known about the tribe then. All he knew back then was that there were periods when he seemed to black out, often to awaken somewhere else, with no memory of what he had been doing or how he got there. With the help of Varanna, High Mistress of the villichi sisterhood, he had discovered the truth about his other personalities, and she had helped him forge a link with them so that they could all work together instead of competing for control of the same body. The Guardian, as the strong, maternal, balancing force among them, had worked together with Varanna to help the tribe find a sense of unity and cohesiveness.

Now, all Sorak had to do was slip back slightly so that he was still aware of what was going on but watching, with no real control over his body, as the Guardian came to the fore and brought her strong psionic powers into play. With Ryana adding her ability to the Guardian's, object after precious object sailed up into the air, as if some indefatigable invisible worker were throwing up shovelfuls of treasure that spun, glittering, through the air. Precious coins that had not been minted in any Athasian city for countless generations because of the rarity of metals pattered down by the dozens like gold and silver raindrops. Daggers made of elven steel, a long and complex forging process that had been forgotten for several thousand years, came up from the shining horde and fell again, to be buried once more under hammered gold tiaras and silver girdles, intricately worked pieces of ceremonial armor. All gave testimony to an age when Athas had been a very different world, indeed, abundant in the natural resources that had provided the metals and the gems for the construction of these ornaments by master craftsmen, whose descendants saw such materials only rarely, in the form of ancient, cherished heirlooms handed down through the generations among the old families of the wealthy aristocracy.

A depression began to form in the area of the pool that they were excavating in this unique manner. Bits of treasure started sliding down into it, only to be thrown up again and hurled aside. The tinkling and chinking of metallic objects made a strange, ethereal sound as it continued, like some giant, many-stranded wind chime being blown about. And then Kara cried out, "*There!*"

One by one, the pieces of treasure filling the air fell to the surface of the pile until only one object remained, held up by the power of the Guardian's psionic talent. And among the other objects making up the treasure horde, this one looked dull and ordinary except for one thing that set it apart from all the other pieces they had seen.

It was a breastplate made of small, intricate links of gleaming, silver chain mail, not really a proper breastplate at all, since no metal plate was used. It seemed a peculiar and impractical piece since it was designed in such a fashion that it covered only the chest, leaving the back, arms, and shoulders unprotected. It looked like ceremonial armor, the wearer's back remaining comfortably bare beneath a light cape or cloak. The breastplate was constructed to be fastened around the neck and waist, covering only the front part of the upper torso from the waist to the collarbone. But there was one thing about it that set it apart from all the rest of the glittering objects in the treasure horde. It glowed with an eldritch, bluish light.

As it came up from the pile, its glow was not immediately perceptible, merely a faint, blue aura that could have been nothing more than a trick of the firelight from the braziers. But now, as it floated in midair above the treasure horde, they could see that it was, indeed, glowing with some inner power of its own.

"The Breastplate of Argentum," Kara said softly. "I have heard of it in legends, but I had never truly thought to see it for myself."

The talisman floated over to Sorak, guided by the Guardian, and she then slipped back as he came to the fore once again. The glowing talisman dropped into his waiting hands. It was heavier than it looked.

"What is its purpose?" Sorak asked, staring down at it. "What is the nature of its spell?"

"Put it on," said Kara with a smile.

Sorak glanced up at her uncertainly, then did as she had told him. He fastened it around his neck, then again at the waist, feeling the weight of it . . . and something else, as well. As he put it on, his chest began to tingle strangely, as if with hundreds of tiny, minute pinpricks. It was not painful, but it felt similar to the sensation he'd experienced when he sat too long in one position and his legs would fall asleep. The sensation spread quickly to his arms and legs, and the blue glow grew brighter for an instant, flaring briefly, then subsiding as it seemed to fade into him. And when blue glow of the talisman faded from sight . . . so did he.

"*Sorak!*" Ryana cried out with alarm. It had happened quickly. Just a brief flaring of the blue glow, and then he faded away, completely disappearing from sight.

"What is it?" his disembodied voice asked, speaking from where he had stood a moment earlier, and apparently still stood, though Ryana could not see a thing. It was as if he wasn't even there.

"*Sorak?*" asked Ryana, straining to catch some glimpse of him. She could tell from the sound of his voice that he stood right in front of her, but she saw absolutely nothing.

"What?" he asked again. "What's wrong, Ryana? You seem alarmed. What is the matter?"

She stretched her hand out tentatively until she felt it come in contact with his face, and then she jerked it back again.

"What are you doing?" he asked irritably. And then, realizing that something was wrong from the expression on her face, he nervously added, "Has something happened to me?"

"You're . . . you're not there!" she said with astonishment.

"What are you talking about? Of course, I am here. I am standing right in front of you! Can't you see me?"

"No," she said, in a small, frightened voice. "You have become invisible!"

For a moment, he was silent. He raised his hand up in front of his face. He could see it clearly, but apparently, Ryana could not see a thing. He stepped around quietly behind her. She continued staring at the spot where he had stood a moment earlier. He tapped her on the shoulder. She gasped and spun around, her gaze searching for him in vain.

"You *really* cannot see me?" he asked.

She shook her head. "No," she said, her voice barely above a whisper.

"Kara?" he asked. "Can *you* see me?"

"I can hear you," she replied, her senses being sharper than any human's. "I can hear the faint fall of your footsteps, and in the stillness, I can hear your breathing. But I cannot see you. No one can, Sorak, not so long as you wear the Breastplate of Argentum."

"A talisman of invisibility!" said Sorak with wonder. He tiptoed around behind Ryana and once again tapped her on the shoulder. She jerked around, startled.

"Stop that!" she said. "Where *are* you?"

He chuckled. "This is fun," he said.

"Well, I don't think it's very funny," she replied, irritably. "Take it off!"

"Not yet," he said, and Ryana heard the soft fall of his footsteps as he moved around her. "This is a strange and wondrous experience! I feel no different, save for a momentary, curious tingling sensation that I felt when I first put it on. I see everything clearly, just as before. I look down at my legs, and I can still see them. I hold my hand up before my face, and I can see it, too. But you and Kara see nothing? Not even the faintest disturbance in the air?"

Ryana shook her head. "No, not a thing," she said. "And it is most unsettling. I wish that you would take it off."

"What about the undead, Kara?" Sorak asked. "Would I be invisible to them, as well?"

"Most of the undead no longer have eyes," said Kara, "yet still they 'see,' in a manner of speaking. They would sense your presence. Unfortunately, the Breastplate of Argentum would not safeguard you from them."

"Pity," Sorak said. "Does it do anything else?"

"Not to my knowledge," Kara replied. "But it is imbued with an ancient, eldritch power that perhaps the Sage would use in some other way. I cannot tell. I am a pyreen and a druid, not a sorceress. Only the Sage could tell you what use he would make of its enchantment."

"Where *is* the Sage?" Ryana asked her. "Do you know? Can't you tell us? Is he near?"

"No," said Kara. "He is very far away. But in another sense, he is nearer than you think."

Ryana sighed with exasperation. "Do you never reply with anything but riddles, my lady?"

Kara smiled. "Sometimes," she said. "And speaking of time, we had best be on our way if we do not wish Valsavis to find us."

"He has already found you," came a familiar voice, echoing through the chamber.

Kara and Ryana turned quickly to see Valsavis step into the room, his sword drawn.

"Did you really think you could leave me behind so easily?" he said. "And did you truly believe you could mislead me by leaving your flying platform in plain sight on the other side of the city? Or did you forget that a roc can spy its prey from a great distance, hundreds of feet above the—" and then his words caught in his throat as he saw the treasure horde spread out before him in the pool. "Gith's blood!" he swore.

Ryana gazed at him impassively from the other end of the chamber. "Yes, Valsavis," she said. "You have found the fabled, lost treasure of Bodach. And you are more than welcome to it. It should make you rich beyond your wildest dreams. Richer than any aristocrat, wealthier even than any sorcerer-king, including Nibenay, your master. Though, of course, how you will transport it may prove something of a problem."

As she spoke, Sorak, still wearing the enchanted talisman, quietly began to circle around the pool.

"Where is the elfling?" Valsavis said, recovering from his astonishment.

"Who?" asked Ryana innocently.

Valsavis glanced quickly around the chamber. "He is here somewhere," he said. "If you think to trick me, then—" and suddenly he paused, listening intently.

Sorak glanced down at his feet and silently cursed. His foot had struck a bracelet that had landed on the lip of the pool and knocked it in. It fell into the treasure pile with a clinking sound.

"Are you jumping at shadows now, Valsavis?" asked Ryana, seeking to distract him. She could not tell where Sorak was, but she could guess what he was doing.

"Sorak!" Valsavis called out. "I know you're there! I heard you moving! Come out where I can see you!"

Sorak did not reply. He continued moving toward Valsavis, placing his feet softly and carefully.

"Why do you hide, Sorak?" asked Valsavis, his gaze sweeping the chamber. "What do you have to fear from me? You are a master of the Way, with a magic sword no other weapon can withstand. And I . . . I am only one old man, with no talismans or magic weapons. No psionic powers. Am I such a threat to you?"

"Not you, Valsavis, but your master, the Shadow King," said Ryana, hoping to draw his attention and cover up any sounds Sorak might make.

Valsavis felt a tingling on his left hand as the eyelid of the ring opened.

Kara frowned and quickly held out her hand toward him. "Nibenay is here!" she said with alarm.

"I can sense his presence!"

Sorak slowly drew his sword. And as he did so, Ryana gasped involuntarily. Sorak was still unseen, but Galdra's magic blade was clearly visible. The magic of the Breastplate of Argentum did not affect the enchanted elven steel. And Sorak did not know it.

Valsavis saw the blade approaching, apparently floating toward him of its own accord, and quickly turned to face it, his eyes growing wide with surprise. At once, he took a fighting stance.

"*Sorak!*" Ryana called out. "Your blade! He can *see* it!"

Startled, Sorak stopped, still about eight or nine feet from the mercenary.

"So," Valsavis said, "that is the power of the talisman. It confers invisibility." He snorted with derision. "Were you so afraid to face me that you had to approach by stealth?"

Sorak reached behind him with his left hand and unfastened the breastplate, first at the waist, then at the neck. It fell to the ground at his feet, rendering him visible once more. "Very well," he said. "Now you see me. The next move is yours, Valsavis."

"As you wish," Valsavis said with a smile. And, to their surprise, he sheathed his sword.

Sorak narrowed his eyes suspiciously.

"Now what?" asked Valsavis, raising his eyebrows and folding his muscular arms across his chest.

"What are you up to, Valsavis?" Sorak asked uncertainly.

"I? Why, nothing. I am merely standing here."

"Take care, Sorak!" Ryana shouted. "Nibenay will use him as a conduit for his power!"

"No," said Valsavis. "He shall not. I am no sorcerer, but even I know that such an act would require a great expenditure of power, and the Shadow King hoards his powers jealously. The metamorphosis always remains his first priority. Besides, there is no need for me to depend upon the Shadow King. As you can see, I have sheathed my sword. It has served me well these many years and I have no wish to see it break upon that magic, elvish blade."

"Watch out, Sorak!" cried Ryana. "He has some trick in mind!"

Valsavis shrugged. "No tricks," he said. "Go on, elfling. Now is your chance to be rid of me, once and for all. So . . . strike."

"Damn you," Sorak said, lowering his blade.

Valsavis smiled. "You see?" he said. "I had complete faith in you. You would not hesitate to fight if I attacked. But you would not kill an unarmed man who offers no resistance. That would be murder. Being a preserver does have certain disadvantages."

"What do you want, Valsavis?" Sorak demanded, an edge in his voice.

Valsavis glanced down at the talisman, lying on the tiled floor and glowing faintly. "That . . . for a start."

"You shall not have it."

"Well, perhaps not right this moment, but we shall see," Valsavis said. "You managed to shake me loose once. You shall not do it a second time. I will stay right on your heels until you lead me to your master. And there is absolutely nothing you can do about it."

"I would not be so sure," said Sorak, sheathing Galdra. "You were right, Valsavis. I cannot not kill a man who simply stands there and offers no resistance. But I *can* knock him senseless."

Valsavis grinned and uncrossed his arms, putting his fists on his hips. "*You?* Knock *me* senseless? Now that is something I would like to see."

"Very well, then," Sorak said. "Watch."

He slipped back and allowed the Guardian to the fore. Abruptly, a small, silver coin came flying up out of the treasure horde and spun across the chamber with a soft, rushing sound like an arrow flying through the air. It struck Valsavis hard in the side of his head, just above his ear. Valsavis flinched, recoiling, and brought his hand up to the spot. It came away wet with a drop of blood. Another coin followed, and then another, and another, and another. Bracelets, jewels, golden plates and silver goblets, amulets and more coins followed in rapid succession as Valsavis backed away and brought his arms up to protect his face. More and more pieces of the treasure came flying up out of the pool, hurtling toward him with great speed and force, striking him about the head and body, cutting him and raising painful welts and bruises.

Valsavis staggered backward, crying out, not so much with pain as with rage and frustration. His arms could not ward off all the objects that came flying at him, striking with greater and greater force. He spun around, doubling over, trying to hunch down and make himself a smaller target, all to no avail. The hail of treasure continued relentlessly as Ryana joined her power to the Guardian's, and they hurled one piece after another at him, taking care to make sure that none of them were swords or daggers or other objects that could kill.

Roaring with rage, Valsavis reeled back and slammed into a support column, stunning himself. He dropped to his hands and knees, leaving his head uncovered, and the Guardian took that opportunity to levitate a heavy silver tray and bring it down hard upon his skull. Valsavis collapsed, unconscious, to the tiled floor.

"Well, you did say you wanted to see it," Sorak said, gazing down at him. He stepped forward, walking over the litter of treasure on the floor, and crouched over the prostrate mercenary, looking him over carefully. "Hmmm. That is a rather interesting ring." He reached for it.

"*Don't touch it!*" Kara shouted suddenly.

As Sorak drew back his hand and glanced toward her, startled by her cry, they rushed over to him.

Valsavis lay, stretched out, on the floor. On his left hand, the heavy, golden ring was clearly visible. And from it, a malevolent, yellow eye with a vertical pupil stared out at them. It was the hate-filled gaze of Nibenay, the Shadow King.

"If you touch it, you will establish a link with him," said Kara. "And then you will be lost."

"Then I shall use the Way," said Sorak.

"No," said Kara, putting a restraining hand on his arm. "That will be the same as coming into contact with it. Come away. Leave it alone. To touch it is to be defiled."

"We should at least tie him up so that he cannot follow us again," said Ryana.

"And leave him helpless for the undead to find?" said Sorak. He shook his head. "No. We cannot do that, little sister, tempting as it may be. That would be the same as killing him right now, while he lies senseless."

"That would not stop the Veiled Alliance," said Ryana, a hard edge to her voice. "They would not hesitate to slit the bastard's throat."

"We are not the Veiled Alliance," Sorak replied. "They may be preservers like us, it is true, but they are not druids, and they have compromised the purity of their vows for the expediency of their purpose. That is not our way."

"The Sage does not seem to hold their methods against them," said Ryana.

"Perhaps not," said Sorak. "The Sage needs whatever allies he can find. But do you hold true to your principles for yourself, or for the sake of someone else?"

Ryana smiled wanly. "Those are Varanna's words," she said. "I had lost count of how many times I'd heard them."

"They often bear repeating," Sorak said.

Ryana sighed. "You are right, of course. It would be nothing less than murder to leave him here tied up. Tempting as it may be, it would be no different than executing him."

"No, it would not," said Sorak. "And when it comes to that, what has he really done to merit being killed?"

Ryana glanced at him with surprise. "How can you say that? He serves the Shadow King!"

"Yes," Sorak agreed, "he does. And he has also saved our lives. I might have died with that marauder arrow in my back, or else been eaten by some predator while I lay helpless if he had not given me aid. And he came with me to rescue you from the marauders."

"I would have escaped, regardless," she said.

"Perhaps," said Sorak. "But that does not alter what he did. And do not forget what happened when we were set upon by the marauders in Salt View."

"He only came to our aid because he needed us alive to lead him to the Sage," Ryana said.

"But the fact remains that he did come to our aid, on several occasions," Sorak said. "And all he has really done was follow us."

"And once we had found the Sage, what would he do then?" Ryana asked.

"I cannot judge a man on what he *might* do, or even what it is probable he will do," said Sorak. "I can only judge him by what he has done. That is all any of us can do, Ryana. To do otherwise would be to stray too far from the Path. Further, certainly, than I would be willing to go."

"You are very wise for one so young," said Kara.

"Am I?" Sorak asked. He shook his head. "I am not so sure of that. Sometimes I think that wisdom is merely fear of acting foolishly."

"The knowledge that one *can* be foolish is the first step on the path to wisdom," Kara said. "Now come, quickly. It will be growing dark soon, and it is time for you to see the *true* lost treasure of Bodach."

They hurried outside. It was already late in the afternoon, and the sun was low on the horizon. The shadows were lengthening. And a large bank of dark clouds was moving in from the east, coming in fast over the Sea of Silt.

"A storm is approaching," Kara said apprehensively.

"It is only a desert monsoon," replied Ryana. "It will probably pass quickly."

"I do not think it is the rain she is concerned about," said Sorak. "Those clouds will blot out the sun, and it will grow dark early."

Ryana suddenly understood, and she licked her lips nervously. "The undead will rise."

Kara moistened her fingertip and tested the wind, which had increased significantly. "It is coming in very fast," she said. "Quickly. We do not have much time."

A shadow suddenly fell over them, and a shrill, piercing cry echoed through the deserted streets. They turned quickly. The roc was perched atop the building they had just emerged from, its huge wingspan darkening the plaza. Its giant head bent down toward them as it raised its wings and snapped its powerful beak hungrily.

"Nibenay," said Sorak, quickly unsheathing Galdra. "He still controls the bird."

Ryana barely had time to draw her sword before the roc leapt off the roof and came swooping down at them, its huge, powerful talons outstretched. She dodged to one side, barely avoiding the roc's gigantic claw. She landed on the ground and rolled, coming up with her sword ready.

Sorak had waited until the last possible instant, then darted forward, underneath the roc's outstretched talons. He swung Galdra in a powerful overhand stroke aimed at the giant bird's lower quarters. The blade barely brushed the roc's feathers, cutting several of them as, with a deafening screech, the bird landed just behind him.

"Kara!" Sorak shouted over the deafening screeching of the roc. "Make it stop!"

"It will not respond to me!" cried Kara. "Nibenay's will is too strong! I cannot control the creature!"

"Stay back!" shouted Sorak, circling around the bird as it turned toward them, its wings folded back and up, its huge beak snapping as its head darted back and forth between him and Ryana. It lunged at Ryana. She ducked beneath its snapping beak and swung her sword with both hands. It struck against the roc's beak, and it felt like she had struck a stout agafari tree. The shock of the impact ran all the way down her arms and into her shoulders. For a moment, she felt numb. The bird's head darted down toward her again, and she leapt, diving to the ground and rolling away.

Sorak ran in toward the bird, but before he could strike, it jumped aside, turning as it did so and sweeping out with its wings. One wing caught Sorak in the side, and he fell, almost losing his grip on Galdra. But by that time, Ryana had regained her feet and came in at the roc from the other side, thrusting at its flank.

The giant bird shrieked as Ryana's sword entered its side. The roc twisted toward her, craning its neck around to snap at her. She recoiled, barely avoiding having her head bitten off. Sorak, meanwhile, quickly regained his feet. He took several running steps and leapt, stretching out, diving directly beneath the bird. He swung out with Galdra and the elven steel struck one of the roc's legs, passing completely, effortlessly, through it.

The roc screeched with pain as its leg was severed, and it collapsed to the ground, directly on top of Sorak. Ryana rushed in and thrust at it again, her sword entering the creature's breast as the roc threw its head back and screamed at the sky. Its head arced down to snap at her again, but Ryana leapt aside and came in once more, thrusting deeply just beneath the bird's right wing. The roc emitted a long, drawn-out, ear-piercing shriek and fell over heavily on its side with a loud crash. It thrashed several times, then died.

"*Sorak!*" Ryana shouted. "*Sorak!*"

"Here," he called out.

She ran around to the other side of the bird's carcass. Sorak was dragging himself out from underneath it, freed when the roc fell over. He had been pinned by the bird's crushing weight, unable to move, and Ryana helped him to his feet. He was covered with the creature's blood.

"Are you all right?" Ryana asked him anxiously.

"Yes," he replied, taking a deep breath. "Merely winded. I could not breathe under there."

"Catch your breath quickly," Kara said, coming up beside them. She pointed at the sky.

The storm was moving in fast as the dark clouds scudded across the setting sun, blotting out its light. One large cloud moved across it, darkening the sky, and then the sun peeked out again briefly, and then another cloud moved across, blotting it out once more. There was more light when it passed, and then the main body of the cloud bank swept across the sun, and it disappeared from sight, plunging the streets into darkness.

Night had come early to Bodach.

For a moment, they simply stood there in the sudden darkness, staring at the clouds that had moved in to block the sun. The wind picked up as the storm moved in, blowing dust and sand through the streets in swirling eddies. Lightning flashed, stabbing down at the ground, and thunder rolled ominously. And, in the distance, they heard another sound . . . a long, low wail that rose in pitch and fell again. It seemed to echo down toward them from the deserted streets coming into the plaza, and a moment later, it was repeated, and joined by several more in a grim, chilling, ululating chorus. Night had fallen, and the ancient, ruined city of Bodach was suddenly no longer deserted.

"They rise," said Kara.

TEN

"Hurry!" Kara cried. "There is no time to lose. *Run!*"

She started sprinting across the plaza, toward a street leading off to the left. Sorak and Ryana ran after her. They headed north, down another street that curved around to the left and then ran straight again for a distance of some fifty to sixty yards before it branched off into two forks. Kara went right. They ran quickly, leaping over obstacles in their path, dodging around dunes that the wind had piled up against the building walls and rubble that had fallen into the street from the collapsing buildings.

All around them now, they could hear the blood-curdling groans and wails of the undead as they rose to walk the streets once more. The sounds seemed to be coming from everywhere. They were coming from inside the buildings, and from the cellars under-ground, and from the ancient, long-dry sewers that ran beneath the city streets. Together with the rolling thunder and the rising whistle of the wind, it made for an unwholesome, spine-chilling concert.

"Where are we going?" Sorak shouted as they ran. It had taken him a few moments to reorient himself, and he had abruptly realized that they were running in the wrong direction. "Kara! Kara, wait! The raft is back the other way!"

"We are not going back to the raft!" she called over her shoulder. "We would never reach it in time anyway!"

"But this way leads north!" Ryana shouted, gasping for breath as she ran to keep up with them. She, too, had suddenly realized that the direction they were heading in would take them to the very tip of the peninsula. If they kept going in this direction, they would reach the northernmost limits of the city, and the inland silt basins. And then there would be nowhere left to go. "Kara!" she called out. "If we keep going this way, we shall be trapped!"

"No!" Kara shouted back over her shoulder, without breaking stride. "This way is our only chance! Trust me!"

Sorak realized that they had no other choice now. Kara was right. Even if they turned around at this point, they would never reach the raft in time, nor would there be time for Kara to once more raise the elementals. They would have to go back through the entire city, and it would be a running fight all the way.

The wailing of the undead was growing louder now and ominously closer. Already, he could see several of them come lurching out of the building doorways in the street ahead of them.

Sheet lightning flashed across the sky, briefly illuminating the streets as the shambling, walking corpses came staggering out from their resting places. The wind howled, and there was a deafening clap of thunder that seemed to shake the building walls around them. And then the rain came.

It came down in torrents, with all the strength and

fury of a fierce desert monsoon. Within seconds, they were drenched clear through to the skin. It was raining so hard that it was difficult to see much more than several yards in front of them. Water flowed rapidly down the sides of the buildings and fountained off the rooftops in sheets, cascading to the streets below.

Rivulets formed and ran across the paving bricks, sluggishly at first, then gathering speed and size as the volume of water rapidly increased. Rains were infrequent in the Athasian desert, for the most part coming only twice a year, during the brief but furious monsoon seasons, so the buildings and the streets of Athasian towns and villages were not designed for drainage. If the roof leaked, it made little difference because the storms, though fierce, were usually of short duration, and then the sun came out again and everything dried quickly in the relentless desert heat. If the streets turned into muddy soup, no matter. They would remain that way only for a short while, and then the water would run off into gullies and washes, and in little while, the streets would dry and traffic would make them level once again.

The city of Bodach had been engineered by the ancients to take into account the extremely fierce monsoons that swept across the desert—then the sea—during the very brief storm seasons, but in all the years that the city had been abandoned, the gutters had cracked and been filled with wind-blown sand. The slight grading of the brick-paved streets, designed to allow the water to run off into the gutters at the sides, was not enough to compensate for gutters that no longer functioned.

Sorak and his two companions were soon sloshing through water that ran ankle deep. The hard desert soil beneath the paving bricks could not soak up the sudden volume of water, and so it ran in sheets across the bricks, instead of trickling down into the cracks. The uneven street they ran on became slippery, and to fall or turn an ankle now would mean disaster.

However, the rain did nothing to impede the slow, relentless progress of the undead. Sorak and Ryana saw the dark and spectral figures through the sheets of rain as they came lumbering toward them. More and more of them were coming out into the streets now. Sorak glanced behind him and saw their figures staggering out of the buildings, moving spastically, like marionettes with half their strings cut. And there were walking corpses directly ahead of them, as well. Several came lurching out of building doorways as they ran past.

"We're never going to make it!" Ryana shouted. "Sorak! You have to summon Kether!"

"There's no time!" he shouted back.

To summon the strange, ethereal entity known as Kether, he would have to stop and concentrate, empty his mind and settle his spirit to make himself receptive to the being that seemed to descend upon him from some other plane of existence, and he could not stop for even a moment. The undead were all around them and moving closer. He pulled Galdra from its scabbard. Galdra was now their only chance.

"Stay close behind me!" he called out over the noise of rain and wind and thunder. "And whatever you do, stay on your feet! Don't fall!"

Ryana drew her sword as well, but she knew from hard experience that, at best, it could provide only a temporary respite. The undead were animated by spells, in this case an ancient curse that had survived for several thousand years, claiming more and more victims as time passed. Galdra, with its powerful ancient elven magic could kill them and send them to their final rest, but her sword could, at best, only dismember them. And then the severed, rotting body parts would only come together once again.

Ryana took Kara by the arm and ran to stay close behind Sorak in the blinding rain. Ahead of them, a dozen or more undead were clustered together in the street, staggering toward them with their arms outstretched, their mummified flesh shrunk back to expose brown and ancient bones that glistened in the rain.

Sorak ran to meet them.

* * * * *

Valsavis groaned and opened his eyes. He was dizzy, and his head felt as if it were splitting. He lay among the scattered treasure, a sorcerer-king's ransom in gold and jewels and silver, and he remembered what he said to Sorak about too much wealth bringing a man nothing but trouble. In this case, the axiom had been demonstrated painfully and literally.

"*Get up, you fool!*" Nibenay's angry voice spoke within his mind. "*Get up! They are getting away! Go after them!*"

Valsavis raised himself to his hands and knees, shook his head to clear it, and slowly got to his feet.

"*Hurry, you great, hulking, brainless idiot! You are wasting time! You'll lose them!*"

"Shut up, my lord," Valsavis said.

"*What? You dare to—*"

"I will not find them any easier for your voice yammering in my mind!" Valsavis said angrily. "I need no distractions!"

"*Go!*" said the Shadow King. "*Go quickly! They have the talisman! They must not get away!*"

"They shall not, rest assured of that," Valsavis said grimly. "I have a score to settle with that elfling."

He left the treasure lying there and went outside. The sky was dark. The clouds were sparking with sheet lightning. Thunder rolled. Any minute, it would start to rain. If he was to pick up their trail, he would have to move quickly.

He saw the dead roc lying in the plaza in a giant, dark pool of coagulating blood. Well, he thought, so much for his ride out of here. Nibenay must have had the giant bird attack them, and they had made short work of the creature. But then, what did Nibenay care about his leaving the city safely? Had the Shadow King even paused to consider that when he set the bird upon them?

The thought of leaving the city safely suddenly and unpleasantly reminded him of its undead population. The sky was darkened by clouds. Night had come early to Bodach. And even as he stood there, he heard the wailing start, a chorus of doomed souls crying out their agony.

"*Stop standing there like a stupid mekillot!*" the Shadow King's voice hissed in his mind. "*Find out which way they went!*"

"Be silent, you noisome worm," Valsavis said, not caring anymore how he spoke to the sorcerer. If he could, he would wrench that damnable ring off his finger and fling it as far away from him as he could, but he knew only too well that it would not come off unless Nibenay wished it.

For a moment, the Shadow King actually fell silent, shocked by his response, and then Valsavis felt the tingling in his hand start to increase, and then burn, as if his hand were being held in flame. It began to spread up along his arm.

"Desist, you miserable reptile!" he said through

gritted teeth. "Remember that you *need* me!"

The burning sensation suddenly went away.

"That's better."

"*You presume too much, Valsavis,*" said the Shadow King sullenly.

"Perhaps," Valsavis said. "But without me, what would you do now?" He scanned the plaza carefully as he came down the stairs. There were bloody footprints left by a pair of moccasins going off to the left. He began to run, following them.

The Shadow King fell silent. Logically, without Valsavis, he could do nothing, and Valsavis knew that if there were some threat of punishment hanging over him, Nibenay could wait a long time before he saw the Breastplate of Argentum or learned the secret of where the uncrowned king was to be found. He grinned to himself as he ran down the street that the elfling and the others had taken. It was not every man who could manipulate a sorcerer-king. For all his incredible powers, Nibenay still needed him. And that meant that he, Valsavis, was in control. At least for the moment.

The thunder crashed and lightning stabbed down from the sky. The wailing of the undead grew louder. Things were about to get interesting, Valsavis thought.

He ran quickly down the street, following the path they had taken. They were heading north. He frowned. That seemed very peculiar. Why would they go north? Their flying raft was on the other side of the city. Of course, they must have realized that they could not reach it in time. The streets would be full of undead before they had gotten halfway. So what was to the north? Nothing but the inland silt basins.

That was insane, he thought. Had they lost their senses? All they would succeed in doing was trapping themselves between a city full of the undead and the silt basins. The living corpses would come after them, and they would have nowhere left to go except out into the silt basin, where they would drown in the choking stuff, a death that was certainly no more preferable than being killed by the undead. It made no sense at all. Why would they go that way?

The thunder crashed, filling the city with its deafening roar, and the rain came down in torrents. Valsavis came to a fork in the road. There was no more trail to follow. In seconds, the rain had washed away the already faint traces of roc blood that Sorak had left behind, and there were no footprints to follow on the paved street. Which way had they gone? To the left or the right?

Valsavis suddenly felt a hand grasp his shoulder. He spun around, drawing his sword in one smooth motion, and chopped the arm off the grisly specter that stood behind him, empty eye sockets staring, mummified flesh drawn back from aged bone, nothing but a hole where the nose had once been, a grinning rictus of a mouth whose jaws worked hungrily.

The arm of the corpse fell to the ground, but it did not bleed, and the corpse seemed not even to notice. Valsavis swung at the corpse's face with his fist and knocked its head right off its shoulders. It fell to the rain-slicked street with a thud, its jaws still working. The corpse turned away from him and fumbled for its severed limb with the arm it still had. It found the amputated appendage, picked it up, and simply reattached it. Then it reached for its head.

"Gith's blood!" swore Valsavis.

He swung his sword again in a powerful, two-handed stroke, cleaving the body of the walking corpse in half. The two severed halves of the corpse fell to the street, splashing into the water sheeting over the paving bricks. And, immediately, the two halves started wriggling toward each other, like grisly slugs, and as Valsavis watched, astonished, they rejoined, and the corpse starting searching for its head once more.

"How in thunder do you kill these things?" Valsavis said aloud. He looked up and saw several more dead bodies lurching toward him through the rain. "*Nibenay!*"

There was no response.

"Nibenay, damn you, help me!"

"*Oh, so now it's my help you want, is it?*" said the Shadow King's voice unpleasantly in his mind.

There were more undead coming out into the street around him. And each of them started toward him. Some were no more than skeletons. One came almost within reach, and Valsavis swung his sword again, decapitating the corpse. It simply kept on approaching, headless. He swung his sword again, grunting with the effort, cutting the skeleton in half. The bones fell apart and dropped, splashing, to the flooded street. And then, once more, they began to wriggle back together and reassemble themselves.

"Damn you, Nibenay," Valsavis shouted, "if I die here, then you'll never get what you want! *Do* something!"

He felt something grab him from behind and spun around, kicking out hard. The corpse was knocked back, falling with a splash to the rain-soaked street. But it rolled over and started to come at him once again.

"*Beg,*" said the Shadow King. "*Plead for my help, Valsavis. Grovel like the worthless scum you are.*"

"I'll die first," said Valsavis, swinging his sword once more as the rotting corpses closed in around him.

"*Then . . . die.*"

"You think I won't?" Valsavis shouted, laying about him with his sword as the corpses kept coming, relentlessly. "I'll die cursing your name, you misbegotten snake! I'll die like a man before I grovel at your feet like some dog, and your own miserable pride will deny you what you want."

"*Yesssss,*" said Nibenay, his voice a hiss of resignation. "*I truly believe you would. And unfortunately, I still have need of you. Very well, then—*"

And in that moment, Valsavis felt something crawling up his leg. He screamed with pain as one of the corpses he had felled climbed upon him and sank its teeth into his left wrist. Valsavis cried out, trying to shake it off, but there were still more corpses reaching for him and he had to keep laying about him with his sword to stay alive. He could not stop for a second. Wailing in agony, kicking out at the corpse that had its teeth fastened on his wrist, he could not afford to stop swinging his sword even for an instant to keep the undead from overwhelming him. Each one he struck down only got back up again moments later. And more were closing in. He was fighting for his life, as he had never fought before.

The pain was incandescent as the corpse chewing on his wrist crunched down with teeth that were as sharp as daggers. Valsavis felt the pain washing over him, and he fought with all his might to jerk his left hand free as he kept fighting off the advancing corpses, and suddenly, there was a sharp, snapping, crunching sound, and he was free.

His left hand had been chewed off.

Roaring with both pain and rage, he fought his way through the remaining corpses and ran down the street, through the rain, gritting his teeth against the pain. Blood spouted from the stump of his left wrist. As he ran, he tucked his sword beneath his arm and unfastened his sword belt with his one remaining hand. He shook it hard until the scabbard fell free, then bound it around his arm tightly, making an improvised tourniquet. He twisted it tight, pulling it with his teeth, and then made it fast. His head was swimming. His vision blurred. And, through the rain, he saw more undead stumbling down the street toward him.

Nibenay was gone. Whatever he might have done to help him, there was no possibility of it now. With his left hand gone, the ring was gone, and the magical link was broken. Valsavis stood there in the pouring rain, breathing hard, fighting back the pain, struggling to keep from passing out, and as the walking corpses shambled toward him, he suddenly realized that he had never in his life felt more alive.

His right hand grasped his sword hilt. It felt familiar, natural in his grasp, like an extension of his arm. As the rain came down, soaking him through to the skin, plastering his long, gray hair to his face and running through his beard, reviving him, he threw back his head and screamed in defiance of the death that was lurching toward him. This was the measure of a man; this was the fitting way to die, not with a wheezing, old man's death rattle in a lonely bed, but with a scream of rage and bloodlust. And holding his sword before him, he charged.

*   *   *   *   *

Sorak plowed like a juggernaut through the advancing corpses, swinging Galdra to the left and right. It cut through them effortlessly, and they fell, never to move again, the spell of the enchanted blade more powerful than the ancient curse that animated them. And if Sorak had paused in his plunge through them, he might have heard them sigh with relief as the rain washed away the living death to which they had been condemned.

Ryana clutched Kara's arm, holding her sword in her other hand, glancing around quickly to the left and right, ready to strike out at any corpse that came too near. But something strange was happening. The undead that had been lurching toward her and Kara suddenly turned and started shambling toward Sorak, their arms outstretched, not in a threatening manner, but almost in a pleading one, as if they were beseeching mercy. And she suddenly realized what they were doing.

Having seen Galdra release the others from the spell, these mindless corpses, driven by some fragment of an instinct left over from the days when they were still alive as men, now sought release from living death as well. They were no longer attacking, but instead, they approached Sorak and simply stood there, waiting for him to cut them down. Galdra flashed in the driving rain, again and again and again, and still more of them came, waiting their turns patiently, holding their arms out to him in supplication.

Ryana and Kara both stood leaning on each other in the rain, holding their breath, unable to tear their eyes away from the surreal spectacle. The undead were simply ignoring them, brushing right past them as they moved toward Sorak, then stopped and simply awaited their turn to be struck down, once and forever.

"*Ryana!*" Sorak cried out in exasperation. "I cannot go on! There are too many of them!"

"Cut your way through!" she called to him. "We'll follow!"

Sorak plunged ahead, mowing his way through the corpses blocking his path, and Ryana ran with Kara, hard on his heels. As they broke through and continued down the street, they heard the tormented wailing of the undead rising behind them.

"Which way?" cried Sorak.

"To the left!" Kara called out. "Straight down to the end of the street! You will see a tower!"

They continued on, Sorak cutting down the undead that came into their path. Ryana felt bony fingers clutching at her shoulder, and she turned and swung out with her sword, cutting off the arm that reached for her. It fell to the ground and wriggled like a worm as the corpse continued to stumble after her, holding out its remaining arm, fingers like talons reaching out and grasping vainly at the air.

Ryana felt a momentary pang of regret that she could not free the doomed soul from its torment, but then she thought of all the others it must have killed horribly over the years, and that drove all pity from her mind. If not for Galdra, they too, would have been food for the undead of Bodach.

The rain started to let up as the storm passed over them. Ahead, at the far end of the street, Ryana could make out a tall, stone tower standing at the edge of the city, beside the rotted docks jutting out into the silt. At one time, in an earlier age, it must have been an observation tower, or perhaps a lighthouse to guide ships in to the docks when the silt basins were still full of water.

They ran toward the tower as the rain slacked off to a mere drizzle. Their feet splashed through the street as they ran, and now there were no more undead before them. They heard the wailing behind them, but the tower was merely a short sprint away now. They reached it and plunged inside.

There was no door in the frame, for it had long since rotted away. There was only an open archway, leading into a circular chamber on the ground floor, and a long, spiral flight of stone steps going up.

"We can try to make our stand here," Sorak said, breathing heavily with his exertions as he looked around quickly, satisfying himself that the place was empty. "There is no door, but perhaps we may block off the entryway." He glanced toward the stairs leading to the upper floors. "There may be more of them up there."

"No," said Kara with certainty. "We shall be safe here. They shall not come in."

Ryana and Sorak both looked at her. "Why?" asked Sorak, looking puzzled.

"Because they know not to," Kara said. "We can rest here a moment and catch our breath."

"And then what?" Sorak asked.

"And then we go up," said Kara.

Sorak glanced uneasily toward the stairs. "Why?" he asked her. "Why do the undead know not to come in here? What is up there, Kara?"

"The true treasure of Bodach," Kara replied.

Sorak glanced out the arched doorway, toward the street. Perhaps thirty or forty undead simply stood there, roughly twenty yards away. They came no closer. The rain had stopped now as the storm moved on, and moonlight reflected off the street. Then, as Sorak and Ryana watched, the corpses slowly shambled away into the shadows.

"I do not understand," said Sorak. "They wel-

comed their final death from Galdra, and yet they
seem to fear this tower. What is it about this place?
Why do they keep away from it?"

"You will know the answer to that at the top of the
tower," Kara replied evasively.

Sorak stood, dripping, at the foot of the stairs, gazing up. "Well, I do not relish the climb after all we
have been through, but I have waited long enough for
answers," he said. He glanced at Kara. "Will you lead
the way, or shall I?"

"Go on," she said. "I will follow."

Sorak stared at her uncertainly for a moment, then
started to climb the stairs. Ryana beckoned Kara to
go next. Glancing out the entryway, Ryana took a
deep breath, felt the familiar heft of her sword in her
hand, and followed after Kara and Sorak.

They climbed for a long time. The tower had several levels. The floors on most of them had long since
rotted away. Only bits and pieces of the wood
remained. Cool air came in through narrow windows
in the walls as they climbed. The stone steps were
ancient and worn in the centers by the tread of
countless feet over the ages. How long had it been,
Ryana wondered, since anyone had come this way?
Hundreds of years? A thousand? More? And what
would they find at the top? How could there even be
a top level if all the floors had collapsed centuries
ago?

After a while, she called out to Sorak to stop for a
moment so they could rest. Sorak came back down
several steps to join them. There was room for only
one person to go through the narrow, winding stairwell at a time, so he simply sat down on the steps a
bit above them. Kara sat down just below, and Ryana
gratefully sank to a lower step and leaned back

against the wall.

"How much farther?" she asked wearily. The long run through the city streets and the struggle against the undead had left her thoroughly exhausted. All she wanted to do was lean back and close her eyes and not move another step.

"We are almost at the top," said Kara.

"Well, at least it will be easier going back down," Ryana said with a sigh.

Sorak lifted the Breastplate of Argentum from his pack. It filled the stairwell with its soft, warm blue glow. "Well, we have found what we came here for," he said to Kara. "Now what? What lies ahead at the top of the tower? Another message from the Sage? Another task we must perform for him that will take us to who-knows-what forsaken corner of the planet?"

"That is not for me to say," Kara replied.

"Who is to say, then?" Sorak asked. "How do we find out what to do next? Where to go? Will the Sage contact us in some manner? Have we not proved enough to him by now? I have grown weary of this ceaseless quest!"

"As I told you," Kara said, "you will find your answers at the top of the stairs."

Sorak exhaled heavily. "Fine," he said. "So be it, then. Whatever new tests he will devise to try our worth, we shall undertake them all. We shall not be dissuaded or discouraged. But I cannot help wondering how much more we have to prove to him before he is convinced of our sincerity." He put the talisman back in his pack, stood, and started climbing once again.

With a sigh of resignation, Ryana got up to follow. They climbed on, and suddenly, somehow it started to seem warmer. They could no longer hear the sound of the cold wind wailing outside. And perhaps it was only her imagination, but as they passed one of the narrow windows, Ryana thought she could hear birds singing out there in the darkness. Then, just ahead of them, there was a light. They reached the top of the tower, and as Ryana was coming up behind Kara and Sorak, she heard him swear softly. A moment later, she saw why.

The top of the tower was one large circular room, with carpets on the floor and carved wood furniture placed around it. There was a large table covered with numerous vials and beakers, scrolls and writing quills and inkstands, and a huge round scrying crystal. A fire burned brightly in the hearth built into the wall. All around the circular chamber at the top of the tower, there were large shuttered windows, but the shutters were open, letting in the warm night air. And as Ryana looked out through those windows, she could see the moonlight illuminating not the city of Bodach, or the silt basins beyond, but a lush and verdant valley, beyond which lay a stretch of desert.

A large, six-footed, black and white striped kirre lay on the carpet in the center of the room, slowly wagging its heavy, barbed tail back and forth. It raised its huge head with its ramlike horns, looked up at them lazily, and emitted a deep growl. Sorak and Ryana simultaneously reached for their swords, but a large, hooded figure stepped between them and the beast, shaking its head. It emitted several loud clicking noises.

Sorak stared apprehensively at the hooded figure. It stood just over six feet tall, but its proportions were bizarre. Its shoulders were extremely wide, even wider than a mul's, and its upper torso was huge, tapering to a narrow waist. Its arms were unusually long, ending in four-fingered hands that looked more like talons, and from beneath its robe, there hung a thick, reptilian tail.

"Never fear," said a white-robed figure standing bent over with its back to them, poking at the fire. "Kinjara is my pet, and though she growls, she shall not harm you. Tak-ko, please show our visitors in. They must be very weary from their long journey."

The hooded figure clicked some more, then beckoned them inside. As Sorak approached it, he could see that the face within the hood was not even remotely human. It had a long snout full of rows of razor-sharp teeth, and eyes with nictitating membranes. The creature was a pterran, one of the race of lizard-men that lived in the Hinterlands beyond the Ringing Mountains. Sorak had never even seen one of them before, and he could not help staring. When Ryana first saw the face of the creature she gasped involuntarily.

"Please do not be alarmed at Tak-ko's appearance," said the white-robed figure, turning toward them. "I will admit he looks quite fearsome, but in truth, he is a gentle soul."

Sorak stared at the white-robed man. He looked extremely old, with long, white hair that cascaded down his shoulders, almost to his waist. He was very tall, and very thin, with long and bony fingers. His frame had proportions like a villichi, except that he was male. His forehead was high, and his face was deeply lined with age, but he had bright blue eyes that sparkled with the vitality of youth and intelligence. There was something strange about those eyes, Sorak realized. They had no pupils, and around the sapphire blue of the irises, the whites were faintly tinged with blue, as well. And as he moved, his hair swayed slightly, and Sorak noted his large and pointed ears.

"You see, Tak-ko?" the old elf said to the pterran. "You have lost your wager. They have succeeded after all, just as I knew they would." He turned toward Sorak and held out his hand. "Greetings, Sorak. I am the Sage."

"The Sage?" said Sorak, staring at him with disbelief. After all this time, it seemed difficult to accept the fact that the long quest had reached an end at last. The Sage continued holding out his hand. Belatedly, Sorak realized it and stepped forward to clasp it with his own. "But . . . *you* were the Wanderer? I had always thought the Wanderer was human! Yet, you are an elf!"

"Yes," the Sage replied. "I trust you are not disappointed. You have gone through so much trouble to get here, it would truly be a shame if you were."

He turned to Ryana. "Welcome, dear priestess," he said, extending his hand. Numbly, she took it. "And Kara. How good to see you again. Please, sit down. Make yourselves comfortable. Tak-ko, some hot tea for our guests. They look chilled."

As the pterran went to get their tea, Sorak glanced around at their surroundings. "Where are we?" he said. "Surely, this cannot be Bodach!"

"No, it is not," the Sage replied.

"I . . . I do not understand," said Sorak. He glanced at the pyreen. "Kara, how did we come here? What has happened?"

"That is the *true* treasure of Bodach," Kara said. "The old lighthouse tower is a magical gateway, a portal to another place and time."

"So that is why the defilers have never been able to find you!" Ryana exclaimed, staring at the Sage. "You exist in another time!"

"And even if they suspected that, they would never think to look for the gateway to that time in the city of the undead," Kara said. "It would be the last place a defiler would expect to find preserver magic."

"Please forgive me for having tested you so harshly," said the Sage, "and for having brought you on so long and arduous a journey. However, I fear there was no other way. I had to be absolutely certain of your commitment and resolve. I trust you have brought the Breastplate of Argentum?"

Sorak removed it from his pack.

"Ah, excellent," the Sage said, taking it from him. "And the Keys of Wisdom?"

Ryana removed the gold rings that were the key seals from her fingers and handed them to the Sage.

"Excellent. You have done well. Very well, indeed," he said with a smile. "You have walked the true path of the Preserver. Mistress Varanna would be very proud of you."

Tak-ko brought them their tea. It was steaming hot, brewed from a delicious, fragrant blend of dried herbs.

"I have done all that you have asked of me, my lord," said Sorak.

"Please . . . there is no need for such formality," the Sage replied. "I am merely an old wizard, not a lord of any sort."

"Then . . . what do I call you?"

The Sage smiled. "I no longer use my truename. Even speaking it aloud poses certain risks. Wanderer will do, or you could call me Grandfather, if you like. Either one will serve. I rather like Grandfather. It is a term of both affection and respect. That is, of course, if you have no objection?"

"Of course not, Grandfather," Sorak said. "But, as I said, I have done all that you have asked of me, and—"

"And now you have something that you would like *me* to do for *you*," the Sage said, nodding. "Yes, I know. You seek the truth about your origin. Well, I could help you find the answers that you seek. But are you quite certain that you wish to know? Before you answer, I ask you to consider carefully what I am about to say. You have made a life for yourself, Sorak. You have forged your own unique identity. Knowledge of your past could carry certain burdens. Are you quite sure you wish to know?"

"Yes," said Sorak emphatically. "More than anything."

The Sage nodded. "As you wish. But do finish your tea. It will take a slight amount of preparation."

As the Sage went back to his table, Sorak gulped the remainder of his hot tea. It burned going down, but it felt good after the cold rain. He could scarcely believe that after all this time, he was finally going to learn the truth about himself. He wondered how long it would take the Sage to make his preparations.

The old wizard had untied and unrolled a scroll, and he carefully spread it out upon his cluttered table. He placed small weights at each corner of the scroll, then pricked his finger with a sharp knife and squeezed some blood onto the scroll. Dipping a quill into the blood, he wrote out some runes, then took a candle and a stick of some red sealing wax, holding them over the scroll. Mumbling to himself under his breath, he dribbled a blob of the red wax, leaving an impression of the seal, onto which he then squeezed another drop of blood. He repeated the process three more times, once for each corner of the scroll, using a different one of the seals each time.

As he watched him prepare the spell, Sorak noted once again the peculiar elongation of his form, resulting from the early stages of his metamorphosis. For an elf, it was only natural that he should have been taller than a human, but at a height of approximately six feet, he stood about as tall as Sorak, who did not have an elf's proportions. Then again, the Sage was quite old, and people did grow smaller as they aged: elves were no exception. Still, Sorak thought, when he was younger, he must have been rather small for an elf. Either that, or the metamorphosis had wrought marked changes in his frame. It must have been extremely painful. Even now, he moved slowly, almost laboriously, the way those with old and aching bones moved. With the changes wrought by his transformation, the effect must have been greatly magnified.

The peculiarity of his eyes probably resulted from the metamorphosis, as well. Eventually, they would turn completely blue, even the whites, so that it would appear as if gleaming sapphires had been set into his eye sockets. Sorak wondered how that would affect his vision. His neck was longer than it should have been, even for an elf, but while his arms were also long, they looked more in proportion for a tall human than an elf, likewise the legs. And he walked slightly hunched over, a posture that, along with the voluminous robe, concealed what Sorak saw more clearly now that he stood with his back to them. His shoulder blades were protruding abnormally, giving him the aspect of a hunchback. They were in the process of sprouting into wings.

What sort of creature *was* an avangion? Sorak wondered what he would look like when the transformation was complete. Would he resemble a dragon, or some entirely different sort of creature? And did he even know himself what the end result would be? As he thought of how much he had gone through with Ryana to reach this point, Sorak realized it was nothing compared with what the Sage was going through. All those years ago, when he had been the Wanderer, had he known even then what path he would embark on? Surely, he must have decided even then, for *The Wanderer's Journal* contained clever, hidden messages throughout its descriptions of the lands of Athas. How many years had he spent wandering the world like a pilgrim, writing his chronicle that would, in its subversive way, guide preservers in the days to come? And how long had he studied the forgotten, ancient texts and scrolls to master his art and begin the long and arduous process of the metamorphosis?

No, thought Sorak, what we have gone through was nothing compared to all of that.

He glanced at Ryana and saw her looking at him strangely. She was tired, and she looked it, and as he gazed at her, he realized that he felt profoundly tired, too. They had been through much. His arms ached from wielding Galdra against the scores of undead they had fought their way through. They were cold, and wet, and bone weary, and the warmth of the fire in the tower chamber, coupled with the warmth of the tea the Sage had given them, was making him sleepy, excited as he was at having finally attained his goal. As he watched Ryana, he saw her eyelids close and her head loll forward onto her chest. The cup she was holding fell from her fingers and shattered on the floor.

He could barely keep his own eyes open. He felt a profound lassitude spreading through him, and his vision began to blur. He glanced down at the empty cup that he was holding, and suddenly realized why he was feeling so sleepy. He glanced up at Kara and saw her watching him. His vision swam. She faded in and out of focus.

"The tea . . ." he said.

The Sage turned around and gazed at him. Sorak looked up at him, uncomprehending.

"No . . ." he said, lurching to his feet and throwing the cup across the room. It shattered against the wall. He staggered, then stumbled toward the Sage. "*Why?*" he said. "I have . . . done all . . . that you . . . asked. . . ."

The room started to spin, and Sorak fell. Tak-ko caught him before he hit the floor and carried him back to the chair.

"No . . ." Sorak said, weakly. "You promised. . . . You promised. . . ."

His own voice sounded as if it were coming from very far away. He tried to rise again, but his limbs wouldn't obey him. He saw the pterran gazing down at him impassively, and he glanced toward Kara, but he could no longer make out her features. And then consciousness slipped away as everything went dark and he experienced a dizzying, falling sensation. . . .

ELEVEN

"*Sorak. . . .*" The voice came from all around him. "*Sorak, listen to me. . . .*"

He floated in darkness. He tried to open his eyes but found he could not. He felt somehow detached from his body.

"*Sorak, do not try to resist. There is no need to be afraid, unless it is the truth you fear. The long journey that has brought you here was but the beginning. Now, you are about to depart upon another journey, a journey deep within your own mind. The answers that you seek all lie there.*"

It was the voice of the Sage speaking to him, Sorak realized, coming from a great distance, though he could make each word out clearly. He had no sense of time or place, no feelings of physical sensation. It was almost as if he had drifted up out of his body and was now floating somewhere in the ether, devoid of form and feeling.

"*It will seem as if my voice is growing fainter as you travel farther into the deepest recesses of your mind,*" the Sage said. "*Let yourself go. Release all thoughts and considerations, all worries and anxieties, all apprehensions, all volition, and simply give yourself over to the experience about to unfold for you.*"

Within his mind, Sorak heard Kivara's voice cry out, "*Sorak! I'm afraid! Make it stop!*"

"*Hush, Kivara,*" said the Sage, and Sorak was surprised that he could hear her. Had he spoken Kivara's words aloud in his physical body? Or had the Sage somehow melded with them to guide them on their journey? But then, his voice was growing fainter, just as he predicted.

"*I shall not be going with you,*" said the Sage, confirming what he thought, "*but I shall remain here and watch over you. This is a journey you must undertake alone. A journey deep into your inner self, and beyond. As you travel farther into the depths of your mind, you are going back, back through the years, back to a time before you were born. . . .*"

Sorak felt himself falling slowly, the way a body sinks in water when the lungs are emptied out. The Sage's voice was growing fainter and fainter. . . .

"*You are going back to a time when that part of you that was your father met that part of you that was your mother . . . back to discover who they were and how they met . . . back to when it all began. . . .*"

★　★　★　★　★

The elf tribe had been traveling all winter, and now the hot summer months were fast approaching. They had come east from the Hinterlands, to the western foothills of the Ringing Mountains, through the long and winding pass that had brought them to the eastern slopes. They had no map to follow, but instead, were guided by the visions of their chieftain, who had told them that the journey would be hard, but worth the effort for what they would discover at its end.

Mira and the others knew the visions of their chieftain were true, for he had told them of the mountain pass, and had brought them to it unerringly, just as he had told them of the smoking mountain, which they could now see in the distance from the slopes. Each night, the chieftain gathered his small tribe around him at the campfire, told them what new portents his visions had revealed, and reminded them why they had embarked upon this long and arduous pilgrimage. It was a story that Mira knew by heart, as did all the others of her tribe, who would join in at key parts of the recitation as they sat in a circle round the fire, gazing at their chieftain while, every night, he retold it. It was a way of reaffirming their purpose, and of strengthening their unity in a common cause.

"And so it came to pass that the noble Alaron, last of the long and honored line of elven kings, was cursed by the evil Rajaat, who feared the power of the elves and sought to sow disunity among them," said the chieftain. The tribe listened silently, many nodding to themselves as he spoke. "With his defiler magic, Rajaat cast a spell upon the noble Alaron, so that he could sire no sons, and so the royal line would die out with him. And the evil that he wrought upon our people is with us to this day, may his name live long in infamy."

"May his name live long in infamy," the people of the tribe echoed in grave chorus.

"Rajaat then sowed discord among the tribes, using bribery, deceit, and magic, and in time, he succeeded in driving the tribes apart into many warring factions. Only the noble Alaron continued to resist him, but he was unable to bring the tribes together once again. And so the kingdom fell."

"And so the kingdom fell," the tribe repeated as

one.

"Then the noble Alaron was forced to flee, pursued by Rajaat's evil minions," the chieftain continued. "They caught up to him and the remnants of his tribe at a place known as the Lake of Golden Dreams, and it was there the dream died for our people. A mighty battle followed, and all the tribe was slain. Mortally wounded, the noble Alaron alone escaped into the forests of the Ringing Mountains, and it was there he fell down in despair and waited for death to come and claim him. He had done his utmost, and he had failed, but he had not bowed down before the foe. May his courage be remembered."

"May his courage be remembered," Mira said along with the other members of the tribe.

"And it came to pass that as he lay, dying, a wandering pyreen came upon him and stopped to bring him peace and ease his final moments. My visions have not revealed her name to me, but they revealed how the noble Alaron, with his last breath, gave her his sword, the mighty Galdra, enchanted blade of elven kings. With his last breath, he asked one final boon of her. 'Take this, my sword, the symbol of my once-proud people,' he said to her. 'Keep it safe, so that it should never fall into the hands of the defilers, for the blade would shatter if they tried to use it. I was cursed never to have a son,' he said, 'and a proud tradition dies with me. The elves are now a beaten people. Take Galdra and keep it safe. My life is but the blink of an eye to a pyreen such as you. Perhaps, someday, you will succeed where I have failed, and find an elf worthy of this blade. If not, then hide it from the defilers. I can at least deny them this.'

"And with those words, he died. And so the kingdom of the elves died with him."

"And so the kingdom of the elves died with him," echoed the tribe with sadness.

"And our people became decadent, and the tribes scattered far and wide, most to live as nomads in the desert, raiding and stealing from both humans and each other, forsaking their honor, while others went to reside within the cities of the humans, where they engaged in commerce with them and mixed their blood with theirs and forgot the glory of their once-proud race. And yet, a tiny spark of hope remained, nurtured in the hearts of all our people. That faintly glowing spark became known as the legend of the Crown of Elves, passed on throughout the generations, even though, to most, it was no more than a myth, a story told by elven bards around the camp-fires to while away the lonely desert nights and bring a few moments of solace in the squalid elven quarters of the cities, where our people lived in poverty and degradation. And thus we all recall the legend."

"And thus we all recall the legend," Mira said, along with all the others, who watched their chieftain with rapt fascination as he spoke, his face illuminated by the flickering flames.

"There shall come a day, the legend says," the chieftain continued, "when a chieftain's seventh son shall fall and rise again, and from his rise, a new life shall begin. From this new life will spring new hope for all our people, and it shall be the Crown of Elves, by which a great, good ruler will be crowned, one who shall bring back the elven forest homeland. The Crown shall reunite the people, and a new dawn shall bring the greening of the world. So it is said, so shall it be."

"So it is said, so shall it be," the people chanted.

"And so we gather 'round the fire tonight, as we do

on each and every night, to reaffirm our purpose," said the chieftain. "From the day I fell and struck my head upon a rock in weapons training with my father, chieftain of the Moon Runners, I began to have my visions. I fell and rose again, and from this rise, a new life had begun for me. A new life where I saw visions that would guide my people to the new dawn that was promised. I knew, from that day forth, that it was my fate to seek and find the Crown of Elves, which can only be the legendary Galdra, sword of Alaron and symbol of our people. And I knew, because my visions told me so, that I would one day become chieftain of our tribe and that I, Kether, a chieftain's seventh son, would lead my people on a quest to find the pyreen who held in trust the fabled sword of Alaron.

"We have come far upon that quest," Kether continued, "and now I sense that we are near its end. We have put aside all other concerns and rivalries and passions, we have devoted ourselves to the spiritual purity of the Path of Preserver, and we have embraced the Druid Way, to purge ourselves of violent emotions, petty prides, and selfish motivations. To find the peace-bringer who shall bring the Crown to us, we must first find peace within ourselves, to make us worthy. Each day, we must reaffirm our purpose and pursue it with new zeal. We must bear reverence within our hearts for every living thing, and for our dying world, so that it may one day live again. To this noble end, we dedicate ourselves."

"To this noble end, we dedicate ourselves," the people said, their eyes shining in the firelight.

Kether looked around and saw the way they were all watching him, expectantly. Mira wondered what it must be like to be chieftain and know that everyone in the tribe depended on the wisdom of your leadership. It must be a heavy burden, she thought, but Kether was wise and strong, and he bore it well. He uncrossed his legs and stood, tall and proud, looking around at his people. His long, silvery hair was tied back with a thong and hung down to the middle of his back. His face, sharp-featured, with the high, prominent cheekbones of his people, was striking and handsome. He was young still, and had not yet chosen a wife. Mira was one of several eligible young females in the small tribe, and she wondered if he might one day consider her. She would be proud to bear him strong sons, one of whom might someday take over the leadership of the tribe.

"We have come far, my people," Kether said. "We gather tonight on the slopes of the Ringing Mountains, not far from where the noble Alaron fell all those many years ago. I know that you have all suffered many hardships on this journey, but I sense that it is almost at an end. Somewhere, here in the majestic Ringing Mountains, it is said that the mystical villichi sisterhood maintain their convent. They are long-lived, and they follow the true Path of the Preserver and the Druid Way. If anyone would know where the Crown of Elves is to be found, then surely, it is they.

"Tomorrow, we shall rest, and gather food for the continuation of our journey, and then the next day, we shall head south, toward the higher elevations, where we shall seek the home of the villichi and lay our petition before them. Have faith, my people, and be strong. What we do, we do not only for ourselves, but for all the generations yet to come. Sleep well tonight, and when you dream, dream of a new dawn for our people, and for our benighted world. I wish you peaceful slumbers."

Slowly, the tribe dispersed to their tents, but Mira lingered for a while by the fire, staring thoughtfully into the flickering flames. She wondered, as she often did, what the future held in store for her. She was young, not yet sixteen summers, small and delicate for one of her race, with long, silvery hair, sharp features, and light-gray eyes. Each year, throughout her childhood, she had asked her mother, Garda, when she would grow tall like the others of her tribe, and each year her mother had laughed and said that soon she would start shooting up like a desert broom plant after a monsoon. But in recent years, her mother had stopped laughing when she asked that question, and soon Mira realized that she would never grow any taller than she was now. She would remain slight and unattractive, a runt among her people, and doubtless it was foolish of her to think of being chosen, by anyone, much less by Kether. And if she were not chosen by someone of her tribe, then who else was there?

Her mother was already asleep when she returned to their tent, but though she tried to move quietly, she still woke her when she came in.

"Mira?"

"Yes, Mother. Forgive me, I did not mean to wake you."

"Where have you been?"

"Sitting by the fire and thinking."

"You spend much time alone these days, with just your thoughts for company," her mother said with a sigh. "I know it has been hard for you, my child. Ever since your father went away, I have tried to raise you by myself as best I could, but I know you have been lonely for having been denied a father's love. Forgive me."

"It is not your fault, Mother."

Garda sighed once more as she lay upon her bedroll. "Yes, it is," she said. "Perhaps I should have known better. Your father was not of our tribe, and I knew when I met him that he would not remain with us. He was much like Kether: he, too, was driven to wander, searching for meaning in his life. He never told me he would stay, and I never asked him to. Our time together was brief, but at least I shall always have you to remind me of the love we shared."

"Do you think that he may ever return?" asked Mira.

"I used to ask myself that question all the time," her mother said.

"And now?"

For a moment, her mother remained silent. Then, in a soft voice, she said, "And now, I no longer ask it. Go to sleep, Daughter."

Mira remained silent for a long time afterward, but when her mother's steady breathing told her that she was asleep, she quietly got up again and went outside. Sleep eluded her. Somehow, she felt restless, and she did not know why. She walked out to the edge of the cliff near which they had camped and stared out at the desert to the west, illuminated in the light of the twin moons. In the distance, she saw the smoking mountain, and at its foot, she saw the moonlight reflecting off the Lake of Golden Dreams. It was there that Alaron had fought his final battle, and it was somewhere nearby that he had died.

It did not look very far away, not for an elf. Though she was small, she was still a Moon Runner, and she thought that she could reach the lake in a matter of mere hours. She knew she should not leave the camp, for they were in unknown territory, but she felt a pull that drew her toward the distant lake. It was a site important to the history of her people. How could she not see it close at hand? And its water looked so welcoming . . . it had been a long time since she had bathed. Moistening her lips, Mira gave a quick glance over her shoulder. The camp was quiet, and the fire was dying down. She turned and headed toward the ancient trail that led down from the slopes. And then she began to run.

* * * * *

They met by the Lake of Golden Dreams, on the opposite shore from the mining village of Makla, within sight of the smoking mountain. It was night, and the twin moons, Ral and Guthay, were both full, illuminating the foothills with a silvery glow. It was a warm summer night, and moonlight danced on the placid surface of the lake, making the water sparkle.

She was of the Moon Runners, a nomadic tribe that roamed the Hinterlands and had journeyed far to reach the Ringing Mountains. He was a young halfling, and his name was Ogar. He was the seventh son of his tribal chieftain, born of his seventh wife, and taller than most of the people of his tribe, with the muscular frame, chiseled features, black mane, and the stormy, dark eyes of his warrior father.

He had traveled from the high country down to the lake to fulfill his Ritual of Promise, which marked his passage from adolescence to adulthood. He was to take a mountain cat alone, with just his spear; defeat an enemy in single combat, and bring back a trophy of the contest; then take his vows to the twin moons and sing his Song of Promise. The mountain cat he had already slain, and feasted on its flesh. And the enemy that he had chosen was one befitting the son of a warrior chief. He would slay a human. He had come to the lake shore to look across at the rough mining town of Makla and scout the best approach, and that was when he saw her, alone, bathing in the lake.

He had crept up softly, close to the shore, where she had left her clothes, and watched quietly from cover as she washed her hair in the moonlit waters of the lake. He had never seen a female elf before, and he was struck by her loveliness as the water glistened on her sleek, curvaceous body. She was not as tall as he might have expected, though she stood at least a head taller than him, and he could not tear his eyes away from her. He crouched there by the shore, leaning on his spear, watching as she washed herself. There was something marvelously languid, graceful, and compelling in her movements. She hummed to herself softly as the water trickled off her body and lent her flesh a glittering smoothness in the early light of dawn. And then a twig snapped, and she froze, staring toward the shore with alarm.

Ogar had been so fascinated by her that he had never heard them approach. Neither had she. They had moved with stealth, until a clumsy footstep at the last moment had given them away. And then they rushed her.

It was a small hunting party of humans from the mining village across the lake. There were four of them, and they came charging out into the water, splashing and yelling, two from either side, cutting off all escape. She could have turned and swum straight out into the lake, but either she was paralyzed with shock and fear, thought Ogar, or else she did not know how to swim. She cried out as they closed in and seized her, manhandling her roughly, and from their actions and the expressions on their faces, there was no need to wonder what they intended.

Ogar leapt up from concealment and ran out into the water, holding his spear before him. The four humans were so intent on gratifying their baser instincts and they were making so much noise that they did not hear him approaching, not even when he came splashing through the water toward them. He ran one of them through with his spear and, as the man screamed and died, the others suddenly realized that they were being attacked and turned to face him. As one man turned, Ogar struck him hard in the face with the butt end of his spear, then brought the point down in a vicious, slashing motion across the face of another. The man cried out and lifted his hands to his face as blood flowed freely from the deep gash that Ogar had opened up from his right temple to his left cheekbone, slashing right through the man's right eye.

Without pausing, Ogar plunged his spear into the stomach of the third man and twisted. The man screamed, and instinctively grabbed at the spear's shaft. As Ogar tried to jerk it free, the fourth man drew his obsidian blade, and then the halfling felt the second man, recovering from his initial blow, grab him from behind. He released the spear and slithered down out of the man's grasp, but he had lost his spear in the process, and now was left with only his dagger. As he dropped into the water, slipping out of the human's grasp, he reached behind him quickly and seized the man's ankles, giving a hard jerk. The man fell back into the water, and as Ogar came up with a curse, the fourth man lunged at him with his sword.

Ogar twisted aside, but the blade still struck his shoulder, opening a deep and painful cut. Drawing his dagger, Ogar slashed at the fourth man, but missed, and then quickly ducked as the sword came swinging back in a powerful stroke that would have easily decapitated him had it struck. Moving in under the sweeping blade, he stabbed upward and plunged his dagger into the man's stomach, ripping sideways. The man screamed horribly, clutching at his stomach and trying to hold his guts in.

But as he staggered and fell into the water, Ogar felt an incandescent pain; the remaining human had stabbed him from behind. He spasmed and lunged forward, turning around to meet the threat, but he lost his footing as he staggered, the pain washing through him, and as he fell, he saw the human raising his dagger for the killing stroke.

Then the man grunted and stiffened suddenly as the tip of Ogar's spear burst forth out of his chest. His eyes grew wide and began to glaze as blood spurted from his mouth, and then he fell forward into the water, revealing the naked elf girl standing behind him, with Ogar's spear clutched in her hands. Then Ogar's vision blurred and he lost consciousness.

He awoke much later, with the sun already high in the sky. He was lying on the ground by the lake shore, though he did not remember coming back out of the water. He was surprised to be alive. And then he saw the elf girl.

She had gotten dressed and bandaged his wound with strips torn from her clothing. When she crouched to look at him, her gaze was curious and frank. He thought she had the most beautiful eyes he had ever seen. She crouched over him, looking down, and he gazed up at her with awe. Slowly, he stretched out his hand to touch her, because he wanted to feel her skin, which seemed almost translucent, but he hesitated when he realized what he was doing, and his hand froze in the act.

She reached out her hand and lightly touched his fingertips, caressing, then brought up her other hand and clasped his own in both of hers. She smiled, and slowly pulled his hand toward her. She guided it to touch the smoothness of her cheek, and he marveled at the way she felt. And then she brought it down to touch her breast, all the while gazing deeply into his eyes.

They were two strangers, people of different tribes and different races, who could not even understand one another's language, natural enemies who were, perhaps, too young or too caught up in the magic of the moment to care about prejudice or hatred. Neither of them truly understood what it was that had drawn them together, but from the first moment that their eyes met, something happened, a spark ignited, a bond was forged, and they were no longer a halfling and an elf, but merely two people, a male and a female, each of whom responded to something in the other that mirrored their souls.

* * * * *

"It is time for him to leave us, Mira," said her mother.

They stood at the entrance to their tent as the dark sun sank on the horizon, watching Ogar, who stood alone by the fire, gazing into the flames.

"No!" said Mira, turning to gaze at her mother with alarm. "How can you say that?"

"Because it is true, my daughter."

"But he is one of us now!"

"No," said Garda, "he is not truly one of us and

never can be."

"But he is my husband, and the father of our child!"

"The child is old enough to thrive now," Garda said. "And it is time for Ogar to rejoin his people."

"Would you drive him out, just because he is a halfling?"

"No," said Garda. "That is not our way, Mira, and you know it. Kether has shown us the wisdom of giving up old hatreds. But it has been five years now, and Ogar pines for his tribe and for his homeland. Halflings are strongly connected to their tribe and their land. If he remains with us much longer, he will die."

"Then I must go back with him," Mira said.

"You cannot," her mother replied. "They would not accept you, and they would never accept your son. He would be anathema to them, and they would not allow him to survive. If you were to return with Ogar, it would mean death for all of you."

"What must I do, then?" Mira asked, exasperated.

"You must accept what is," her mother said. "As I had to accept it when your father left us. You have little Alaron. Cherish him, the way that I have cherished you, and be thankful for the love that has produced him."

Mira and Ogar talked long into the night. In the five years they had spent together, they had learned one another's language, and they had grown so close that each had become part of the other. Mira had promised herself she would not cry; she did not want to make the parting any more difficult for Ogar than it already was. They had made love for the last time, and he gave her a bracelet off his arm, a band of bronze engraved with the name and symbol of his clan. In turn, Mira had given him a simple necklace of green and red ceramic beads that she had made and worn. In the morning, when she awoke, Ogar was gone. And then she cried.

*　*　*　*　*

It took a long time for Ogar to reach his people, and while his heart grew lighter with each step that brought him closer to his homeland and his tribe, his grief at leaving Mira and his son, Alaron, increased as well. He had been taught that elves were the sworn enemies of halflings, and yet, even when he had first seen her, he had not been able to look upon Mira as his enemy. Nor had her tribe treated him as a hated adversary. They had taken him in and nursed him back to health, and no one had been more attentive to his needs than Mira, who had remained by his side until he had regained his strength. By then, he knew he loved her, and he also knew that she loved him.

When Mira asked consent from Kether to take him for her husband, Kether had asked only if she truly loved him, and knew that he loved her. No one had raised the question of his race, and no one had treated little Alaron any differently from the other children of the tribe when he was born. How could such people be his enemies?

Ogar had resolved that he would tell his father all about what happened as soon as he returned. His father would be pleased and proud, he knew. His son was not dead, as the tribe must surely believe by now. And Ogar was not only alive, but returning triumphant, having slain not one but three humans— Mira had slain the fourth. He had fulfilled his Ritual of Promise.

But, more importantly, he would bear news that not all elves were the halflings' enemies. He would ask permission from his father to return and bring back his wife and son, so that the tribe could find out for themselves that elves and halflings could live together . . . even love one another.

His tribe had welcomed him on his return, and there was a great celebration, and his father had sat proudly in his chieftain's place as he told how he had slain his mountain cat in single combat, and then how he had slain the humans. But when he told them about Mira, everything had changed.

"Why did you not kill the elf, as well?" his father asked, his face darkening.

"Father, she saved my life," protested Ogar.

"Saved her own life, you mean," replied his father, scowling. "The humans had attacked her, and she merely used you for a diversion so that she could strike. That is the way of elves. They are duplicitous."

"Father, that is not true," said Ogar emphatically. "The fourth human would have killed me had she not come to my aid. He had wounded me severely, and she could easily have left me there to die. Instead, she pulled me out of the water and laid me on the shore, then tended to my wounds. And then she brought me back with her to her own tribe, and they took me in until I had recovered. They could easily have killed me, Father, but they accepted me into their tribe."

"You joined an elven tribe?" his father said, aghast.

"They are called the Moon Runners, Father," Ogar said, "and they are not at all the way we have been taught elves are. They treated me with kindness, and it made no difference to any of them that I was halfling. I lived as one of them."

"As their slave, you mean!" his father said angrily.

"No! Would they allow a slave to marry one of their own?"

"*What?*" his father said, jumping to his feet.

"Mira is my wife, Father," Ogar said. "We have a child. You have a grandson. If you could but meet them, I know that you would—"

"That a son of mine should mate with a filthy elf and beget offspring with her!" his father shouted furiously as the other members of the tribe joined his outraged cry. "Never did I think to live to see this day!"

"Father, listen to me—" Ogar said, but he could not shout over the tumult that his words had prompted.

"You have disgraced me!" his father roared, pointing at him. "You have disgraced the tribe! You have disgraced all halflings everywhere!"

"Father, you are wrong—"

"Silence! You have no place to speak! I would sooner see you mating with an animal than to know you had rutted with an elf! You are no son of mine! You are no proper halfling! You are polluted and disgraced, and we must cleanse ourselves of this disgusting stain upon our tribe! Hear me, people! Ogar is no longer my son! I, Ragna, chieftain of the Kalimor, hereby curse him as anathema, and decree the punishment of death by fire to burn out this disease that has sprung up among us! Remove him from my sight!"

The seized him and dragged him away, kicking and fighting, and bound him securely to a nearby agafari tree while they went to prepare the stake and build the fire. In the morning, they would conduct the Ritual of Purging, where each member of the tribe would formally renounce him and curse his name before their chief, and when the sun set, they would burn him.

Late that night, after they had all retired, Ogar's mother came to see him. She stood before him with tears in her eyes and asked him why he had done such an awful thing, why he had brought such pain into her heart. He thought of trying to explain it to her, but then realized she would never understand, and so said nothing.

"Will you not even speak to me, my son?" she said, "one final time, before I must renounce you to your father?"

He looked up at her then and sought understanding in her eyes. He saw none. But perhaps there was one final hope. "Release me, Mother," he said. "If I have so disgraced the tribe, at least let me go back to those who would accept me. Let me rejoin my wife and son."

"I cannot," she said. "Much as it breaks my heart, your father's word is law. You know that."

"So then you would let me die?"

"I must," she said. "I have your brothers and your sisters to consider. For their sake, I cannot risk their father's wrath. Besides, you would have nothing to return to."

He looked up at her with sudden concern. "What do you mean?"

"Your father has sent a runner to the Faceless One."

"No!" said Ogar with horror. "No, not him!"

"There is nothing I can do," she said. "Your father's will is law. Never have I seen him so furious before. He has sworn that he will undo the disgrace that you have brought upon us, and he will ask the Faceless One to cast a spell against the Moon Runners, killing every last elf in the tribe."

"But they have done nothing!"

"They have defiled Ragna's son," she said, "and through you, they have defiled Ragna. He is set upon his course, and nothing will dissuade him."

"Release me, Mother! For pity's sake, release me!"

"Would you condemn me to the fate you would escape?" she said. "Would you condemn your brothers and your sisters to the flames in your place? How can you ask me such a thing? Truly, you have been defiled by the elves, that you could think of yourself at such a time, at their expense."

"I do not think only of myself, but of my wife and son, and of an entire tribe of people who have done nothing to offend you!"

"So, I see now where your true allegiance lies," she said. "Ragna was right. You are no longer Ogar. You are no longer my son. You care more about a tribe of misbegotten elves than you do about your own family and your people. You are no longer halfling. My son is dead. I thought that he had died five years ago, and I see now I was right. I have already done my grieving. Nothing more remains."

She turned and left him then, though he cried out and strained against his bonds. But they had tied him firmly, and there was no escape.

*   *   *   *   *

They had come down from the lower foothills of the northern slopes to cross a small valley at the desert's edge, beyond which, in a jagged, curving line stretching out as far as the eye could see, lay the highest peaks among the Ringing Mountains. In the distance, as they had started across the valley, they had been able to see the Dragon's Tooth, the tallest peak in all of Athas. Kether had seen it in his vision, and he believed that they would find the pyreen there. When he had told them that their quest was almost at its end, there was great joy among the Moon Runners, and as they began to cross the valley, heading toward the mountains, they had spontaneously burst into song.

Less than an hour later, all of them were dead.

Alaron stood alone among their fallen bodies, stunned and numb and horrified beyond all capacity to endure, unable to understand what had happened to them. His mother lay stretched out at his feet, her eyes wide open and unseeing, her lips pulled back into a rictus of agony that had frozen on her features. He had prodded her and tearfully called her name and screamed, but she had not responded. She would never respond to him or anyone again.

Kivara, too, lay dead, and close beside her, Eyron and Lyric, his three young playmates, who had all fallen writhing and screaming to the ground, clutching at their throats and twisting in agony until they breathed their last. Kether, too, had fallen, and the mighty chieftain was no more. One by one, they had all been struck down by some terrible, unseen force, and now only Alaron remained, somehow unaffected by whatever had struck down the rest of them. Terrified and helpless, he had watched all his people die in excruciating agony.

Now he gazed emptily at the twisted bodies strewn all around him on the sand, and it was a sight too horrible for his young mind to accept. He stood there, breathing in short gasps, feeling a terrible pressure in his little chest, tears flowing freely down his cheeks as he whimpered pathetically. And then something within him snapped.

He turned and started walking out into the desert, not knowing where he was going, not caring, unable even to think. He simply placed one foot before the other, walking with his eyes glazed and unfocused, and after a few steps, his little legs began to move more quickly, and then he began to run.

Half whimpering, half gasping for breath, he ran faster and faster and faster, as if he could somehow outdistance the horror that lay behind him. Farther and farther out into the desert he ran, gulping deep lungfuls of air as an intolerable weight seemed to press down on his chest and something deep within him twisted and churned and writhed. He ran faster than he had ever run before; he ran until his strength gave out completely, but something in his mind broke down long before his muscles ceased responding. He fell, sprawling, face down on the desert sand, his fingers scrabbling for purchase, as if he had to grasp the sunbaked soil to keep from falling off the world.

His father had simply left one day, and now his mother, his guardian and his protector, was also gone forever. Pretty Kivara, his mischievous young playmate . . . gone. Happy, little Lyric, who always laughed and sang . . . gone. Eyron, who was just a few years older and always seemed to know everything better than anybody else . . . gone. Kether, their noble, visionary chieftain . . . gone. Everyone and everything he knew was gone, leaving him alone. Abandoned. Helpless. Why had he survived? Why? Why?

"*WHYYYYYYYYYY?*" his mind screamed, and as it screamed, it shattered, fragmenting into bits and pieces as his identity disintegrated and the young elfling known as Alaron, named after a bygone king, simply ceased to be. And as he lay there, senseless, dead and yet not dead, the fragmented pieces of his mind sought desperately to preserve themselves, and started to reform anew. And as if the cry was heard in a world beyond the plane of his existence, there came an answer. First one, then two, then three, then four . . .

*   *   *   *   *

"I know," he said softly, opening his eyes. He swallowed hard and blinked back tears. "I . . . know."

"Yes," said the Sage, gazing at him with a kindly expression. "Yes, you do. Was it what you wanted?"

"All those years, wondering, yearning for the truth . . . and now I wish I had never found it," he said miserably.

"It was a hard truth that you discovered, Alaron," said the Sage.

"You know my truename?" Sorak said. "But . . . you said that you would not be with me on the journey. . . ."

"Nor was I," said the Sage, shaking his head, sadly. "It was enough for me to know what you would discover. I had no wish to see it for myself."

"You *knew?*"

"Yes, I knew," the Sage replied. "Even though my path in life took me away from them, some bonds can never break. I felt it when she died."

"She?" said Sorak.

"Your mother, Mira," said the Sage. "She was my daughter."

"Father?" said the Guardian, emerging. "Can it be true? Is it really you?"

"Yes, Mira," said the Sage, shaking his head. "You

were but an infant when I left. And I have changed much since that time. I did not think you would remember."

Tears were flowing freely down Sorak's cheeks now, but it was the Guardian who wept. They all wept. All of them together, the tribe, the Moon Runners, who had died, and yet lived on.

"I do not understand," the Guardian said. "How can this be? We are a part of Sorak."

"A part of you is part of Sorak," said the Sage. "And a part of you is Mira, the spirit of my long lost daughter. And a part of you is Garda, my wife, Mira's mother, and Alaron's grandmother.

"The powerful psionic gifts that Alaron was born with, but had not yet evidenced, had forged a strong but subtle bond with you, and with others of the tribe, and he could not accept your deaths, so he would not let you die. He did not know what he was doing. He saw you dying, and he could not endure it, so some inner part of him held onto you with a strength that defied even that of death itself. His tormented little mind could not suffer the hardship, and so it broke apart, but in doing so, he sacrificed his own identity so that you could live. You, and Kether, and Kivara, and Eyron and Lyric and the others. . . ."

"But . . . what of the Inner Child? And the Shade?"

"The Inner Child is the one who fled in terror from the horror it had seen, and cocooned itself deep in the farthest recesses of your common mind. The Shade is the primal force of your survival, the fury that you felt at death, the last defiant rebel against inevitable fate."

"And Screech?" asked Sorak, returning to the fore. "What gave birth to Screech?"

"You did," said the Sage. "He is the part of you that

knew the path that you would walk even at the moment of your birth, the embodiment of your calling to choose the Path of Preserver, and your fate to embrace the Druid Way. He was born at the moment Alaron had ceased to be, when in his last extremity he drew strength out of the world itself, and manifested in your mind. Screech is that part of you that *is* Athas itself, and every living creature the planet has produced. *You* are the Crown of Elves, Sorak, born of a chieftain's seventh son. The prophecy did not say that it would be an *elven* chieftain. Your father fell, when he came to the rescue of your mother, and then he rose again, when she tended to his wounds and saved him, and out of that a new life was created—your life."

"And the great, good ruler?" Sorak asked.

"Not a ruler, but one who hopes to guide," the Sage replied. "The avangion, a being still in the process of its slow birth, through me. And now that you have come, and learned the truth about yourself and me, another cycle in the process has become complete. Or, perhaps I should say, may soon become complete, depending on what you decide."

"What *I* decide?" said Sorak. "But . . . why should that decision rest with me?"

"Because it must be your choice," the Sage replied. "Your willing choice. You are the Crown of Elves, and it is you who must empower the next stage of my metamorphosis, without which I cannot proceed. But it is a decision you must *choose* to make, of your own free will."

"Why . . . of course, Grandfather," said Sorak. "Tell me what I have to do."

"Do not agree so quickly," said the Sage. "The sacrifice that you must make is great."

"Tell me," Sorak said.

"You must empower me with the tribe," the Sage replied.

"The tribe?"

"It is the only way," the Sage said. "They shall not die, but they shall live on in me. Not in the same way they have lived in you. Our spirits shall unite and be as one, and that one shall be the natal avangion. Merely the beginning of a long process yet to come, but a necessary step."

"Then . . . it was fated that all this should happen?" Sorak asked.

"Fate is merely a series of possibilities," the Sage replied, "governed by volition. Yet, for most of your life, you have lived as what you are, a tribe of one. Before you agree, you must consider this: could you bear to live without them?"

"But . . . I would still be Sorak?"

"Yes. But only Sorak. You would no longer have the others. You would face that which almost destroyed you once before. You would be alone."

Sorak glanced toward where Ryana slept, peacefully, with Kara sitting by her side, watching over her. "No," he said. "I would not be alone. I am not afraid."

"And what of the tribe?" the Sage asked.

"We understand," the Guardian replied. "We would miss Sorak, but at least a part of us shall always be a part of him. And I would like to see him heal, as I would like to join my father, whom I never truly knew."

"Then, come to me," the Sage said, holding out his hands. "Let Galdra be the bridge between us. Draw your sword."

Sorak stood and drew Galdra from its scabbard.

"Hold it out straight, toward me," the Sage said.

Sorak did as he was told.

The old wizard put his hands upon the blade, grasping it tightly.

"Hold on firmly," he said.

Sorak tightened his grip with both hands on the hilt.

"And now?" he said.

"And now, there shall be an ending," said the Sage. "And a new beginning."

And with that, he impaled himself upon the blade.

"*No!*" shouted Sorak.

But it was done, and as the blade sank into the flesh of the old wizard, Sorak felt a powerful, tingling sensation and a rush of heat, and then his head began to spin. Galdra's blade glowed with a blue light, and Sorak felt the tribe begin to drain away from him. He screamed as he sensed something being ripped loose inside his mind, and an ethereal, amorphous shape seemed to pass along the blade, from him into the Sage. It happened once again, and then again, each time coming faster and faster as the luminescent spirits of the entities that were the tribe passed along the blade, from him and into the old wizard.

And then it was done, and both Sorak and the Sage collapsed, the contact broken as the blade pulled free of the old wizard.

Kara got up and came to crouch beside Sorak, feeling for his pulse. Satisfied, she sighed and checked the Sage, who lay there groaning and breathing laboriously, blood flowing freely from his wound. She took the Breastplate of Argentum, as he had directed her while Sorak took his inner journey, and she fastened it around him. And as she watched, the talisman glowed brightly, and then he disappeared from view.

She waited, tensely, as the moments passed like hours, and then he reappeared, slowly fading into view. The wound made by the enchanted blade had closed, and there was now no sign of blood. The Breastplate of Argentum had disappeared, as well. She opened his robe and saw that it had melded into him, becoming part of his flesh, its silver links of faintly glowing chain mail now become silvery feathers on his chest, like the breast of a bird.

And then the Sage opened his eyes. They were completely blue, no whites, no pupils, just radiant blue orbs that seemed to glow. A long and heavy sigh escaped his lips.

"We are all together now," he said. And then he smiled, faintly. "It has begun."

TWELVE

"So my quest is finished," Sorak said as he awoke and saw Kara looking down at him.

"Life is a quest," Kara replied. "A quest for answers and for meaning. And yours is far from over."

"The only answer I have ever sought was who my parents were and what became of them," said Sorak. "And the only meaning in my life that I have ever found was in my search for the Sage."

"You have found the answer that you sought, and you have found the Sage, as well. That is more than most people could hope to do in their entire lifetimes. But that is still merely a beginning. There is more meaning in your life than you may realize. It is found in your dedication to the Way of the Druid and the Path of the Preserver. And you can also find meaning in the bond that exists between you and Ryana, which your search has only strengthened. You can find it in yourself, as well, as you explore the new meaning of who you are, and who you may yet become."

Sorak moistened his lips. "They are gone now," he said, thinking of the tribe. "It feels so strange. It feels . . . lonely. Is this what it means to feel as others do, this loneliness?" He shook his head. "I never knew."

He sighed. "They were afraid that if I found the Sage and asked his help, then he would somehow make them go away. And yet, throughout my quest, they helped me, despite knowing that it might mean their deaths."

"Not their death, but their release, and yours," said Kara. "And in that, you can find even more meaning."

"So what happens now?"

The pyreen smiled. "Life happens. The Path of the Preserver is a long one, and often difficult, but the Way shall guide you. The sorcerer-kings grow stronger, and with each passing day, the planet is despoiled and the threat of dragons grows greater. All of us must face our dragons, in due time. But for now, let time stand still. The gateway is now closed. Those stairs now lead down not to Bodach, but to a garden where Ryana waits, to learn what you have discovered. She has pestered me with countless questions, wanting to know what had happened while she slept, but it is not for me to tell her. Go to her."

Sorak swallowed hard and held his breath as he stared at the pyreen. "What of the Sage?"

"He rests now," Kara said. "He shall rest for a long time. He has completed a difficult stage in the metamorphosis, and it shall take him much longer to recover than it has taken you. He will sleep for days, perhaps even weeks, and he must not be disturbed. He asked me to wish you well, and to say good-bye. For now."

"I just hope they are happy now," Sorak said, thinking of the tribe. "I miss them. I feel a curious . . . emptiness."

"Yes," said Kara, "it is a feeling known by all, males and females alike. I am sure Ryana can tell you all about it. Go to her, Nomad. She has waited long enough."

He descended the stone stairs, past tower rooms that looked completely new, not even remotely like the ruin with the rotted floors that he had seen when first he climbed the steps up to the top. When he reached the ground floor, he saw a heavy wooden door where before there had been only a crumbling stone archway. He opened it and stepped out into a lovely garden filled with fragrant flowers and green plants with large fronds waving gently in the summer breeze. There was grass beneath his feet, lush and thick, green grass such as he had never seen before, and the song of birds filled the air.

At the far end of the garden stood a stone wall over which he could see a rolling plain stretching out before him. And, from behind him, the wind blew an unfamiliar odor, sharp, bracing, and refreshing. As he turned around and gazed out past the tower, he realized it was the odor of the sea. Its blue-green vastness stretched out before him, not a sea of silt, but a sea of water, more water than he could ever have imagined.

There was no sign at all of Bodach. They were in a time so ancient, the city had not yet even been built. There was just the tower, with nothing else around it. Nothing but the sea on one side, and a world that he had only imagined in his childhood dreams. A green world. A world untouched and unspoiled by defiler magic. It was so beautiful, it took his breath away.

"It *is* lovely, is it not?" Ryana said.

He turned and saw her standing a short distance away, holding a red flower in her hand. She held it out to him.

"It is called a rose," she said. "I never imagined that anything could smell as sweet."

She held it out to him, and he sniffed it, savoring its delicate perfume.

"It is wonderful," he said. "I never imagined that it could be anything like this."

"We cannot stay, you know," Ryana said. "Kara says we must go back. We do not belong here, in this time."

"I know," said Sorak.

"If only we could stay," she said wistfully. "When I see that this is how the world once was and think of what it has become, it makes me want to weep."

"Perhaps, one day, we can come back," he said. "And now that we know what the world can be, we shall know why we walk the Path of the Preserver. It shall have new meaning for us."

"Yes," she said. "The desert can be beautiful, even in its desolation, but there is room on Athas both for the desert *and* for this." She hesitated. "How do you feel now?"

"Strange," said Sorak. "Very strange. There is an emptiness inside me that I have never known before."

"They are all gone then?"

"Yes. All gone. I shall miss them terribly. I did not realize what it felt like, to be . . . normal. I feel like a mere shadow of my former self. Or selves," he added wryly. "Yes, I shall miss them. But I shall have to learn to live without them."

"You still have me," she said, gazing at him, then looking down at the ground. "That is, if you still want me."

"I have always wanted you, Ryana," he said. "You know that."

"Yes, I know. And I knew what stood between us. So . . . what stands between us now?"

"Nothing," he said as he took her in his arms and

held her close, kissing her neck softly. "And now nothing ever will."

* * * * *

"It is time," said Kara, as they stood in the top chamber of the tower. "The gateway is about to open."

"Can we not say our farewells to the Sage?" asked Ryana.

Kara shook her head. "We are between the worlds now. If you go down those stairs now, it will take you back to Bodach. You cannot reach the Sage's chambers, where he sleeps. And even if you could, you could not wake him. Someday, there will be another time. But for now, we must return back to the time from which we came."

"Very well, then," Sorak said. "We are ready."

Kara glanced out the window as the dark sun slowly dipped below the horizon and the last rays of its light faded from view. "The gateway is now open," she said.

They started down the stairs. As they descended, the stone walls seemed to age, and a thick layer of dust appeared upon the steps. They passed the lower levels, which no longer had floors, and the fresh smell of the sea was gone now, replaced by the harsh odor of the silt that blew in through the narrow apertures. They were back in their own time once again, and it suddenly seemed even more desolate than they had remembered.

"It will be night outside," Ryana said. "What of the undead?"

"We shall wait within the tower until sunrise," Kara said. "They will not come in, and we will be safe enough. Then, in the morning, we will leave the way we came. And if you wish, there will be time enough to take some of the treasure back with you."

Sorak glanced at Ryana and smiled. "I already have all the treasure I need."

"And I, as well," she replied with a smile, pausing at the bottom of the stairs and turning toward him. "But it could not do any harm to fill our packs."

And then she cried out as a bloody hand reached out from around the corner at the bottom of the stairwell and seized her by the hair, yanking her back sharply. An instant later, there was the sound of a blow falling, and then silence.

"*Ryana!*" Sorak drew his sword and ran down the last few steps with Kara right behind him.

He froze as he saw Valsavis, holding Ryana with a knife against her throat. He had knocked her senseless, making sure she could not attempt to use her villichi powers against him. He held her up with his arm around her chest and pressed the knife against her throat, point first, so that just one quick thrust would end it.

"One move, one blink of an eye," he said in a ragged voice, "and I shall kill her."

He looked as if he had been through a war. He was bleeding from several dozen places, and his left hand was gone, leaving nothing but a grisly stump at the wrist. His long, gray hair was matted down with blood, which also streaked his face, and his clothing had been torn to shreds.

"You left a fine trail of corpses for me to follow," he said hoarsely. "Unfortunately, some of the corpses followed me, as well. It took a bit of doing, elfling, but it seems I have managed to catch up with you once more."

"You are a most persistent man, Valsavis," Sorak said. "But you are too late. I have already fulfilled the object of my quest."

Valsavis stared at him for a moment, and then he started laughing. Sorak and Kara both gaped at him with astonishment while Ryana hung limply in his powerful grasp.

"You know," Valsavis said, "this is the first time in my life I have ever truly found something to be funny. So, you have crowned your wizard king, have you? And what a splendid palace he resides in! Hail the mighty druid king, hiding in a ruin, like a cowering rodent among the rotting corpses of Bodach. I had assumed this place held more than met the eye when I saw that the undead would not come in here. What a wail they set up outside when I came in. It seems they wanted me to come outside and play. It was a shame to disappoint them, but I had already killed some of them two or three times, and there's a limit to my patience. So, you have found what you were searching for. And to think, I could have fulfilled the object of my quest, as well . . . if only I had possessed the strength to climb those damned stairs." He started chuckling once again.

"Let her go, Valsavis," Sorak said. "There is nothing to be gained from this."

"There is *always* something to be gained," Valsavis replied. "It all depends on what you want, and what you will settle for. I was half dead when I came in here. But never have I fought so fiercely. You should have seen me, elfling. I was a bloody marvel. I waited here all night, and then throughout the day. I did not know what posed the greater danger, those corpses coming in here or you coming back down and finding me asleep. Still, I napped a little here and there, when

I passed out from the pain." He chuckled again. "You know, it truly is amusing. Nibenay would give anything to see this, but right now, some walking corpse is chewing on his yellow eyeball, along with my left hand. Of course, the Shadow King has doubtless withdrawn the enchantment from the ring and cannot feel it. Pity. I would so like to share some of my discomfort with him."

"Valsavis . . ." said Sorak. "It is finished. Let her go."

Valsavis snorted. "You realize that I came here to kill you," he said.

"Well, your success seems somewhat doubtful at the moment," Sorak said. "You can scarcely stand. Give it up, Valsavis. The Shadow King cares nothing for you. He has only used you, and look what it has brought you."

"It could have brought me everything," Valsavis said. "It still can. Nibenay would give much to know where he can find your master. He did not tell me who it was. He pretended not to know, but I am not a fool. There can only be one preserver wizard whom a sorcerer-king would fear. You see, elfling, even if Nibenay did not discover the location of the Sage through me, *I* still succeeded. I am *here*. And neither you, the priestess, nor the pyreen, nor even an army of undead could stop me."

"Indeed," said Kara. "Your tenacity is without peer. I must congratulate you."

"I failed only in one thing," Valsavis said, glancing at Ryana. And then he grinned with bloody teeth. "If I'd only had more time, priestess. Too bad. We would have made quite a pair, you and I. It really is . . . too bad."

"If you harm her, Valsavis," Sorak said through

gritted teeth, "then I swear you shall not leave this place alive."

"Do you, indeed?" Valsavis said. "And what about you, shapechanger? I will have you swear, as well. Swear by your vows as a preserver that if I release the priestess, you shall do nothing to interfere. Swear, or I will drive this point right through her lovely throat!"

"I swear by my vows as a preserver that I shall not interfere in any way, *if* you release Ryana unharmed," said Kara.

"You have my word," Valsavis said. "But first, the elfling must give up his magic sword."

"It would not do you any good, Valsavis," Sorak said. "You serve a defiler. Galdra's enchantment would not work for you."

"Give it to the pyreen, then," Valsavis said. "We will fight like men, with daggers and without enchantment, so we can see each other's eyes."

Without hesitating, Sorak removed his sword belt and scabbard, then handed them to Kara. Valsavis released Ryana, and she collapsed to the floor. He put his knife between his teeth, drew his own sword and tossed it aside, then grasped his dagger once again with his one remaining hand.

As Sorak drew his own knife, he realized that, for the first time, he would not have the tribe behind him. The Shade would not be there to storm forth like a juggernaut from his subconscious. The Guardian's gifts were no longer his to call on. The Ranger, Eyron, Kether . . . all were gone. He was deprived of Galdra, and Kara had sworn not to interfere.

He faced Valsavis alone.

But at the same time, the mercenary was seriously injured. He had even lacked the strength to climb the stairs. True, he had rested some, but he had also lost a lot of blood. How could he hope to prevail in such a weakened condition?

"I have no wish to kill you, Valsavis," Sorak said, shaking his head.

"You must," Valsavis replied emphatically. "You have no choice. I have found the sanctuary of the Sage. If I fail to return, then Nibenay shall just assume that I was killed by the undead and joined their ranks, and that you have gone on with your quest. But if I live, then I shall take what I have learned and sell it to him. And he shall pay whatever price I ask. One way or the other, Sorak, one of us shall not leave here alive."

"It does not have to be that way," said Sorak as they slowly started circling. "You have seen the treasure room. There is more wealth there than you could ever hope to spend. Surely, there would be enough to buy your silence."

"Perhaps, if my silence could be bought," Valsavis said. "But there would never be enough to buy my pride. I have never yet failed to complete a contract. It is the principle of the thing, you know."

"I understand," said Sorak.

"I thought you would."

They circled each other warily, crouched over slightly, watching for an opening. Each held his blade sideways, close to his body to avoid the possibility of having it kicked away or trapped by a quick grasp at the wrist. Valsavis lifted his arm out in front of him slightly to block, as did Sorak. They each held the other's gaze, watching the eyes carefully, for by watching the eyes, the entire body could also be seen, and the eyes were often the first to telegraph intent.

Sorak feinted slightly with his shoulder, and Valsavis started to lunge, but quickly recognized the feint and caught himself. They continued circling, cautiously, moving their blades, neither one offering the other an easy opportunity. It resembled a curious sort of dance, each of them moving, watching, feinting, reacting, and recovering, neither making the slightest mistake. And the longer it continued, the more the tension and stress increased, the greater grew the likelihood that one of them would make a slip.

The odds should have been in his favor, Sorak thought, for Valsavis was badly wounded, but he had at least a day to recover his strength while he waited for them at the bottom of the tower, and his long experience and iron determination had taught him to ignore pain and exhaustion.

Yet, at the same time, for Sorak, the experience was completely new. He could not depend, as he had learned by force of habit, on the alertness of the Watcher, nor could he summon forth the Guardian to probe his opponent's mind. And even if he could, Valsavis had already proved himself immune to telepathic probes. Sorak also knew the sharp instincts of the Ranger were now lost to him, and Eyron's abilities at calculation and strategy were gone, as well. He could rely on just one thing—the training he had received at the villichi convent.

"*Do not try to anticipate*," Sister Tamura had told them over and over during weapons training. "*Do not think about the outcome of the fight. Do not allow your emotions to rise to the surface, because they will defeat you every time. Find a place of stillness in yourself, and place your awareness completely in the present.*"

In the present, Sorak reminded himself as he felt his concentration start to slip, and in that moment, Valsavis lunged. Sorak barely brought up his blade in time to parry, and the mercenary reacted swiftly, lifting his knife in a vicious, slashing stroke. Sorak countered it, and what had been a tense, slow, and silent dance suddenly exploded into a frenzied flurry of flashing, clinking blades as they moved together, then sprung apart, neither scoring a cut.

Valsavis was breathing heavily, but he had drawn upon his inner reserves and was moving lightly on the balls of his feet, weaving his knife around in quick, complicated patterns as Sorak continued to move his own blade in response, each of them standing a bit closer now, waiting for the one faulty or slightly delayed countermove that would leave an opening.

Suddenly, Valsavis came slashing in and Sorak took the stroke on his own blade, and once again, their knives flashed in a rapid blur and a staccato symphony of metal upon metal. Sorak winced as one of the cuts struck home, opening a gash in his right forearm.

He sprang back quickly, before Valsavis could move in to pursue the advantage. Once again, they began to circle, their knife blades describing rapid, flowing arabesques in front of them. Gith's blood, he's quick, thought Sorak. He had never seen anyone so fast. After all he had been through, where was he getting the energy? He had barely been able to stand moments before. What was holding him up?

"You fight well, elfling," said Valsavis, weaving his blade through the air. "It has been a long time since I have had an opponent worthy of my skill."

"Pity you put your skill to such base uses," Sorak said.

"Well, one goes where the work is," Valsavis said and immediately moved in, slashing at his face.

Reacting purely by instinct, Sorak jerked his head

back, giving a sharp hiss of pain as the knife opened a cut on his cheek, just below his eye, and at the same time, he brought up his own knife and slashed Valsavis across his forearm.

Instead of moving back, Valsavis took the cut and aimed another slash at Sorak's face, in the opposite direction, and the blades clinked together two, three, four, five, six times before Sorak and Valsavis moved apart again, both bleeding from fresh wounds.

On the floor, behind them, Ryana stirred slightly and groaned.

Without taking his eyes off Sorak, Valsavis leapt backward, pivoted quickly, and kicked her in the head. She collapsed again with a grunt as Valsavis turned to face Sorak, who was moving in.

Don't get angry, Sorak told himself, keeping his gaze locked with his opponent's. Don't get angry, that's what he wants. Concentrate, stay in the present. . . .

"If you kill me, she will come after you," he told Valsavis as their blades danced.

"I wouldn't mind," Valsavis said.

"Kara has sworn not to interfere in this, but her oath does not bind her after the fight is over."

"That was thoughtless of me, wasn't it?" Valsavis said, feinting toward him.

Sorak ignored the feint and tried one of his own. Valsavis didn't fall for it.

"Even if you kill me, you will never reach the Shadow King with what you know."

"But if I kill you, I shall only have two to worry about, not three." He saw an opening and darted in.

Sorak tried to block, but was too late. He cried out as the knife opened a deep gash in his upper arm. Valsavis kept coming. As he stepped in and Sorak took the slash on his blade, Valsavis brought his knee up and drove it into Sorak's groin. Sorak grunted, and his eyes bulged with the shocking pain. His knees started to give. Valsavis struck him a sharp blow alongside his head with the elbow of his handless arm.

As Sorak started to go down, he slashed at Valsavis and drove his left thumb hard into the mercenary's solar plexus, collapsing his diaphragm.

The wind whooshed out of Valsavis, and he staggered back, gasping for breath. Before he could move out of reach, Sorak, striking out from a kneeling position, opened a deep gash in his thigh. For several moments, the fight came to a standstill as they scrambled apart.

Doubled over, Sorak fought to block the waves of dizzying pain. Valsavis, also crumpled, tried to get his wind back.

Groaning, Sorak put his head down, and the knife slipped from his fingers. Valsavis immediately lunged toward him, exactly as he had expected. With a smooth motion, Sorak drew a dagger from the sheath tucked into his high-topped moccasin and threw it. The blade struck Valsavis in the shoulder. He grunted with pain and instinctively brought his hand up, dropping his knife.

As Sorak tried to get back up, the huge mercenary kicked out at him and caught him in the head. Sorak fell to one side, then rolled as Valsavis kicked at him again. He twisted and lashed out with his leg, sweeping the warrior off his feet.

Valsavis went down hard, falling backward, but immediately brought his legs back and kicked up to his feet once more. The move threw him within reach of Kara, and before the startled pyreen could react, he quickly grasped Galdra by the hilt and pulled it free of the scabbard she was holding.

"*No!*" she cried out.

But he turned to bring it down on Sorak. It flashed with a blinding, eldritch light and shattered into fragments.

"*Aaah! My eyes!*" Valsavis cried out. He reached up and pulled the knife from his shoulder and started slashing out all around him, still blinded by the brilliant flash.

Sorak backed away from him, and then his foot struck something behind him and he tripped and fell over Ryana's prostrate body.

Immediately, Valsavis lunged toward the sound, but he tripped over Ryana as well and went down on top of Sorak.

For a moment, Kara watched anxiously as they struggled on the ground. Then there was a soft, thumping sound; a knife plunged into flesh and someone gave out a wheezing gasp.

And silence.

Kara stood, immobile, her breath caught in her throat. Finally, Valsavis moved. Her heart sank for a moment, but then she saw him roll over onto his back and Sorak slowly emerge from beneath the body. Kara expelled her breath in a long sigh of relief and rushed to his side.

Valsavis was still alive, but the knife protruding from his chest gave clear evidence that he would not be for long. Already, his eyes were starting to unfocus. His breaths came in ragged wheezes, and blood frothed on his lips.

"Well fought . . . elfling," he said, struggling to get the words out. "I . . . wouldn't have . . . wanted . . . to live out . . . my life . . . as a . . . cripple . . . anyway. Sorry about . . . your sword."

"It's just as well," said Sorak, leaning on Kara for support as he gazed down at him. "I never wanted to be king."

"You would . . . honor me . . . if you . . . took mine."

"As you wish."

"Did you . . . ever . . . learn . . . your truename?"

"It's Alaron," said Sorak.

"Alaron," Valsavis repeated, his eyes starting to glaze. "Don't let . . . the corpses . . . chew . . . my bones. . . ."

"I won't."

"Thank you . . . unnh! Damn. . . ." His breath escaped him in a long and rattling sigh, and then he breathed no more.

"Ohhh, my head . . ." Ryana said, regaining consciousness.

Sorak turned and crouched beside her. "Are you all right?"

She looked at his bloody face, scared by a deep slash, and her eyes grew wide. "What happened?"

"Valsavis."

He helped her sit up, and she saw him, lying stretched out on his back.

"Is he . . . ?"

"Dead," said Sorak.

"I'm sorry I missed it," she said.

Kara turned and went over to where the pieces of the elven sword lay scattered on the floor. She bent down and picked up the largest remaining fragment. It was the silver wire-wrapped hilt, with about a foot of broken blade remaining.

Ryana saw it, and her eyes widened once again. She gasped and turned to look at Sorak questioningly.

"The legend was true," he said. "Valsavis tried to

strike me down with it, but Galdra would not serve a
defiler."

"For generations, it was kept safe," said Kara.
"And now . . ." She merely shook her head sadly as
she held the broken blade.

"It served its purpose," Sorak said. "Besides, I have
another now." He picked up the sword that had
belonged to Valsavis. "A handsome and well-
balanced blade," he said. "Fine steel, very rare. I will
try to put it to better use than he did."

"Take this, just the same," said Kara, handing him
the broken sword. "Keep it as a symbol of what you
have achieved, and what we struggle for."

Sorak took it from her, holding Valsavis's handsome sword in one hand and the broken blade in the
other. He gazed at it thoughtfully. When it had been
whole, there had been a legend engraved on it in
elvish. "Strong in spirit, true in temper, forged in
faith." Now, only part of that legend remained.

"Strong in spirit," he read aloud. He nodded. "A
sentiment more true now than it ever was before. I
have found my own unique spirit, at long last."

"Then it will always have deep meaning for you,"
Kara said. "Carry it with you, Alaron."

He glanced up at her, then smiled and said, "My
name is Sorak."